Deadly Focus
Montana Peril, Book 3

Cover design by Lynnette Bonner of Indie Cover Design
www.indiecoverdesign.com

Printed in the USA

DEADLY FOCUS

MONTANA PERIL ~ BOOK 3

by Lesley Ann McDaniel

CRESCENT COVE series
Christian Romance

Testing the Waters
Book 1

Oceans Apart
Book 2

Sink or Swim
Book 3

MADISON FALLS series
Christian Romantic Suspense

Saving Grace
Book 1

Jill Came Tumbling After
Book 2

Find out more at **lesleyannmcdaniel.com**

Chapter 1

"You let me know when you and Janet nail down the reception menu." With her arms full of empty wooden produce crates, Valerie Hayes shouldered open the old screen door of the Rockford Diner, and stepped out into the alley. "I want to be sure we have everything you need."

"You know me, I can adapt to whatever you bring." Close on her heels with her own load of crates, Millie—the owner of the diner—let the door bang shut behind her.

"You do have a talent," Valerie said as they added the crates to those already stacked in the back of her old forest-green farm truck.

"And you have a talent for growing the best produce in the state."

Valerie chuckled at that. "It's like Dad says. 'Good soil and a lot of prayer.'"

"And the Hayes family skill." Millie pulled her sweater closed and shivered against a late-afternoon breeze. "It's nice to have something to look forward to, now that summer is officially over."

Valerie shut the tailgate and gave it a shake to make sure it was secure. "Been a while since we've had a wedding in this town."

"Not since Joe and Carrie." Millie winced as soon as the words left her mouth.

"It's okay, Mill." Valerie gave her a

reassuring smile as she joined her at the side of the truck. "I'm way over being upset about Joe. And Carrie's one of my best friends now, so it all worked out."

"I'm so glad." Millie brushed a strand of her slightly graying hair off her forehead with the back of her hand. "I just don't want you to think it's not going to happen for you too."

"Yeah, well." Valerie removed her wool gloves from the pocket of her barn coat, grateful for their warm fleece lining now that the fall weather had taken a turn. "Unless Mr. Right drops from the sky, it's not looking likely. This is a small town."

"It might be a small town, but it's a big world." Millie's warm, motherly tone was as comforting as the food the locals loved her for. "Wouldn't hurt you to get out and explore it."

"Thanks for your concern, but I'm fine." Tugging on her gloves, she looked up at the darkening October sky.

The truth was, Valerie had given up on the notion of finding her own Prince Charming, or of ever exploring the world. Taking care of her dad and the farm seemed to be about all she could handle. And at thirty years old, she knew that if God had other plans for her, surely He would have made them clear by now.

Shivering, Millie eyed the sky with concern. "You better hustle to get back to the farm before this thunderstorm hits. It'll be dark soon too. I don't like you being on the road all alone, especially not on that stretch where there's no cell service."

Valerie pulled her in for a quick hug. "I'll be fine, *Mom*."

"You like to tease me, but your mom was one of my best friends. She'd want me to look out for you."

"You're right. But I'm not alone. I have Rex."

As if on cue, Rex—her handsome good boy of a German shepherd—barked from inside the cab of her truck.

"Oh." Millie raised an eyebrow. "And is Rex a trained auto mechanic now?"

Valerie gave her a look. "No, but he's the best guard dog a girl could ask for."

"Good to know that if your ancient truck breaks down, you'll be safe while you wait in the torrential downpour for someone to come to your rescue."

"We're fine. I just had my 'ancient truck' serviced." She patted the fading *Hayes Family Farm* logo on the passenger door. "Hal promises it should be good to go for a while."

"And how long has Hal been promising that?"

She paused. "For a while."

"Uh-huh."

Chuckling at Millie's smirk, Valerie was about to cross around to the driver's side of her truck when something caught her eye. There was an old, red cargo van parked a ways down the alley, facing the other direction. Funny, she hadn't noticed it till now. An inexplicable chill ran down her spine.

"Hey, Mill." She frowned. "Have you ever seen that van before?"

Millie turned to look. "No. But it's behind the sheriff's office, so maybe they're having someone transported."

"They have someone in their cell?"

"Not that I've heard. Course, Jeremy doesn't always let word get out."

"Hm."

Jeremy was the sheriff and one of Valerie's closest friends. She'd run into him earlier that day, making her delivery to McNarry's Market. He'd just finished questioning a couple of high school boys about why they were out buying candy bars instead of sitting in math class. He hadn't mentioned anything to her about having an occupant in his cell, but Millie was right. They didn't always want that to get out.

"Well, you be safe, now." Millie reached out to rub Valerie's shoulder. "Gotta get ready for the dinner rush." Pulling her sweater closed at the neck, she blew her a kiss and ducked back into the warm kitchen.

Laughing to herself about how Millie thought of the dozen or so people who would stop in the diner over the next few hours as a *rush*, Valerie crossed to the driver's side. She was about to yank the door handle when the sound of an engine roaring to life brought her gaze back to the van. A gloved hand popped out of the driver's side window and shifted the side mirror, almost as if the person were using it to look at *her*.

Shaking off the irrational thought, she hurriedly climbed into her truck and started it.

"Let's go home, boy." She gave Rex a scritch behind his ear. "Must be this gloomy weather that's creeping me out."

Chapter 2

Not ten minutes later, Valerie was on the road, with Rockford several miles behind her and the farm several miles ahead. She'd managed to relax a little and enjoy the beauty of the drive—even with the low-hanging, dark clouds. It was always a good opportunity to clear her head.

She glanced over at Rex, who sat fully alert in the passenger seat, panting and watching the passing scenery.

Running a hand down his neck, she thought about Millie's concern. How was it that she could appreciate it, and also feel a little insulted by it?

"We do okay, don't we, boy?"

Rex gave her hand a lick, which she took as agreement. She'd learned a long time ago that she needed to be self-sufficient, because with so much of the responsibility of running the farm landing squarely on her shoulders, she only had herself to rely on.

As she turned off the highway onto the side road that wound through foothills and farmland, the song on the radio turned fuzzy. That always happened right about here, and while she generally switched it off and enjoyed the silence, today the waning afternoon light made her crave connection to the outside world. She twisted the dial till she heard a clear-as-a-bell voice she recognized as a popular pastor.

"...and remember, brothers and sisters, that as children of God, even in the darkest of times, we are never truly alone. Proverbs eighteen ten tells us, 'The name of the Lord is a strong tower. The righteous run to it and are safe.'"

Valerie smiled at the clear reminder. Proverbs 18 was one of her favorites. "I hear You, God. You are my strong tower."

"He is my refuge," the pastor continued, "and my fortress. My God, in Him I will trust."

She glanced again at her furry copilot. "That's so comforting, isn't it, Rex?"

He responded with a hearty *Woof*.

Chuckling, she reached over to scratch behind his ear. As she did so, she caught a movement in her rearview mirror. Behind her a ways, a vehicle had just rounded the bend and was coming up faster than it should, especially considering that this was a narrow road and nightfall was approaching.

Not to mention that it had started raining.

Considering that there was nothing up this way but a handful of farms, it pretty much had to be someone she knew. Unless it was a bunch of dumb high schoolers out for a joy ride, but that would be weird on a Tuesday.

She flicked off the radio, rounded another curve, and glanced in the mirror. Nothing. Then suddenly, the vehicle appeared. She gasped. *A van?* It looked like the same one she'd seen in the alley.

Flicking her gaze between the road ahead and the mirror, she tried to make out the features of the driver, but it was impossible to see. He—or she?—was too far back.

Doing her best to stay calm, she eased up on the gas. If the guy was in such a hurry, he could pass her. But he didn't. He just hung back, keeping a steady distance behind her. Too close for comfort, but not close enough for her to get a look at his face.

Realizing that her hands were shaking, she considered what was ahead. No way was she about to lead this guy to her own front door. But heading down a side road with no easy turnaround when he might follow her seemed even worse.

She rounded another bend. There! The road just past the Gallaghers' big red barn. A quick check of the mirror told her that the van hadn't come around the curve yet. If she timed it right, she could slip out of sight.

After passing the barn, she took a sharp right, then slowed and turned again into the dirt area behind it. She stopped, confident that her truck was hidden from view. Pausing, she listened. The faint sound of the van's rattly engine grew a little louder, then the van seemed to slow. Her heart raced, while her eyes darted from one corner of the barn to the other.

The rain had gotten bad enough to cause concern. What would she do if the van appeared and her truck got stuck in this mud? Darn the community for not wanting cell towers out here. No towers, and no service, making her a sitting duck.

Then the rattling sound got quieter, like the driver had continued down the road. If he really was tailing her, he probably assumed she'd gunned it and he'd have to do the same to catch her.

Slowly, she edged her truck around the corner of the barn, then kept going till she could see the road beyond. No sign of the van.

She exhaled, and looked at Rex, whose big brown eyes seemed to question her sanity.

"Don't worry, baby." Giving the back of his neck a rub, she chuckled in relief. "Your mom reads too many suspense novels."

Feeling a little ridiculous, she pulled

back onto the road. Now that she really thought about it, what was so unusual about another vehicle being on the road behind her? It must have been the residual eerie feeling she'd gotten seeing that van in the alley. That and the fact that she hardly ever saw another vehicle out this way, and when she did it was generally someone she recognized.

That thought brought with it a fresh sense of unease. Where was that van headed, especially in this weather? She shook it off. Maybe someone at one of the farms beyond theirs was getting a delivery of some sort. It was none of her concern.

But then, what kind of delivery would have necessitated parking in the alley behind the sheriff's office? If Millie was right and they were releasing someone, why would that *someone* be getting transported way out here?

No sooner had that unsettling thought crossed her mind than her truck started to sputter. Her eyes lowered to the dashboard as it went dark, and the truck lost power.

"No...no!" Her heart racing anew, Valerie pulled to the side of the road just as her truck came to a dead stop.

She twisted the key in the ignition. Nothing. Her truck had gone lifeless.

Leaning back, she tipped her face upward. "Lord, are You trying to prove Millie right?"

This didn't come as a complete surprise. The truck was older than her and had been chugging along on a wing and a prayer since before she'd even learned to drive. She had known for some time that she'd either need to put money into this truck or invest in a new one.

But at the same time, she'd just had it serviced. It wasn't like Hal not to notify her of impending doom. And with money being so tight, there was no room in the budget for a new vehicle.

She looked out at the darkening sky, and the worsening storm. This was no time to sit there feeling sorry for herself.

After tugging on her thick wool hat, she grabbed the waist pack she used as a purse, and hooked it under her coat, then retrieved the umbrella she always kept under the seat. At least that might keep her dry even if her coat wouldn't. She opened her door and swung her legs out, then patted her thigh to signal Rex.

"Come on, Toto." As he enthusiastically dove across her seat and landed next to her, she opened the umbrella. "We need to get home before Auntie Em starts to worry."

As they set off on foot, she amused herself with the image of her dad wearing an Aunt Em apron and standing at the door calling her name. It was going to take forever to walk the rest of the way home, which was also partially uphill. She might get cell service once she got closer, but in this weather, she shouldn't count on it.

A big gust of wind hit her face, pushing her back a step and threatened to turn her umbrella inside out.

Great. Pulling her hat over her ears to stave off the cold, she chastised herself for not telling Millie she'd call when she got home. She'd been so close to making that promise, strictly to make Millie feel better. But now it fully dawned on her how much better it would make *her* feel to know that Millie was waiting on her call. When it didn't come, Millie might call Dad, which would alert him to jump into his truck and come looking for her. He'd do that on his own eventually, but it could be a while before he realized he should worry.

She had only made it a few yards from the truck when a movement up ahead stopped her in her tracks. A flash of light.

The van.

It was coming back.

Next to her, Rex let out a whimper,

confirming her own sense of unease. Should they duck out of sight? Too late. By now the driver had surely seen her.

She tried to tell herself she was being ridiculous. Whoever it was had probably made their delivery, or whatever they were doing. Either that, or they realized they were on the wrong road. Squinting, she tried again to see the driver, but it was useless. Her dark feeling deepened.

Then, still about fifty yards away, the van pulled over and stopped. Why would he stop so far away, if he wanted to help her?

What was she supposed to do? Here she was with no cell service and no vehicle. Why had she always scoffed at the idea of carrying a gun?

Rex let out a low growl, reminding her that she still had him. *Thank God.*

"You're right, Toto." She gave his head a reassuring pat. "Something tells me this is no Professor Marvel."

The van door opened. She held her breath.

Then, over the roar of the wind, another sound came into her awareness. Was that another vehicle coming from behind her? She cautioned a glance over her shoulder just as an RV ambled around the bend. That was the second strange vehicle to make its way up this road. What on earth?

Not sure how visible they were under these conditions, Valerie shooed Rex closer to the ditch while the RV slowly made its way past them. Then it, too, pulled over and stopped, not quite parallel to the van, whose driver hadn't emerged, but hadn't shut their door either.

Valerie took a few careful steps to her left so she had a better view. The driver's door of the RV opened. What was happening? Did these people know each other?

The van door slammed shut as the

driver launched into a U-turn and squealed away. *That was weird.* Why would it go back the way it came?

Not knowing if she should be relieved that the van was gone, or concerned that the RV *wasn't*, Valerie remembered the message she had just heard on the radio. *God is my refuge and my fortress.* She shot up a quick prayer, asking for a hedge of protection.

A man jumped down from the driver's side of the RV. He took a moment to watch the van disappear around the curve up ahead, then turned back to face Valerie. He looked to be about her age. She couldn't see well enough to be sure, but he didn't seem familiar to her.

"Hey!" He waved his arm as if she might not have noticed him. "You look like you could use some help."

Feeling Rex's comforting presence by her side, she took a few steps closer. What was she supposed to do? Accept help from a stranger or take a chance on the mystery van making another appearance?

As the man moved slowly toward her, he held up his hands, the way people did when they wanted to show they were unarmed. Rex barked, not in a threatening way, but the way he did when he was happy to see someone. She glanced down at him and noticed a suggestion of a tail wag. *Seriously?*

"I can give you a ride."

She looked up to see that he had stopped again, still maintaining what he probably hoped was a nonthreatening distance. "Or I can make a call, if you'd rather."

"There's no cell service along here." She felt really silly shouting, but the rain made normal volume impractical. She quickly explained about her truck, and that she only needed to go a few miles.

He took a few more steps, and Valerie swallowed hard. It wasn't helping her confusion that this guy looked like a cross between Austin Butler and Chris Hemsworth.

He was still a good twenty feet away, but he smiled at Rex and held out a hand. "Hey, doggo."

Rex responded with a bona fide wag. That did it. She needed to get home, and she had no good options. But one thing she could count on was her dog being a good judge of people.

Chapter 3

When Derek Bradford had decided he needed to shake things up in his life, picking up a drenched stranger and her equally soggy dog in the middle of nowhere had not been what he'd pictured. But here he was, with a very nervous looking passenger and her German shepherd, who'd made himself at home between the front seats of his RV.

They'd been on the road for less than a

minute, and already he was grateful that she'd accepted his offer. Not only was the rain now coming down in buckets, but there had been a couple of dramatic lightning flashes that were a little too close for comfort. With darkness closing in on this winding road, a woman and her dog would have been next to invisible to any passing motorists.

She had said she only needed to go a couple of miles. The least he could do was to try to lighten the mood for the short drive.

"Looks like it's your lucky day."

From the corner of his eye, he saw her cast him a confused look.

He nodded toward the windshield as he cranked the wipers up to their highest speed. "Thunder and lightning held off till you were under cover."

"O-oh..." Her nervous titter was probably more to be polite than because his attempt at lightheartedness actually deserved a laugh. She let out a jittery breath and studied the outside like she was looking for something.

Then he remembered that van. It hadn't fully registered at the time because he was so focused on how he could convince this woman she could trust *him*. But there was a story there. Was she in some kind of danger beyond being stuck in the rain?

"So..." He started, not quite knowing what he wanted to ask. "That guy in the van—"

"It was a man?"

Not the response he'd expected. "What?"

"You said *guy*. Did you see the driver?"

"Oh...no. I guess I assumed. So...you don't know him? Or, I guess maybe *her?*"

"No. But it was...strange." She continued looking out into the darkness, like she was watching for something. Or someone. "My turnoff is just a little further."

He nodded, still feeling responsible for putting her at ease. "I'm Derek, by the way."

She paused long enough for him to assume she wouldn't respond in kind, and who could blame her?

He quickly let her off the hook. "And who's this?" He dipped his head toward the dog, who was apparently the only one here who didn't feel awkward.

"This is Rex."

Rex gave a friendly bark, likely in response to hearing his name.

"You're a good boy, Rex." Much to Derek's relief, Rex didn't seem to see him as a threat. Could be that had been the deciding factor in her accepting the ride.

"Hey, what were you doing on this road?" Her tone had turned harsh and a little accusatory. She winced. "Sorry if that sounded rude. It's just that, nobody really comes out this way unless they live here, or they have business with one of the farms."

"I think I took a wrong turn. I was on my way to the campground at Blueridge Summit." He tapped the Montana guidebook in the cubby below the dash.

His mysterious, and still unnamed, passenger picked up the book and paged through it. She let out a chortle. "You might want to get an updated guidebook."

"Oh no. Don't tell me they don't stay open in the winter anymore?"

"They're not just closed in the winter. That campground has been abandoned for a decade. And you're right. You did take a wrong turn."

"Abandoned, huh?" He rubbed the back of his neck. "That's what I get for relying on my collection."

"Collection?"

"Yeah, I'm kind of a travel book junkie. I like to pick them up at used bookstores."

He felt her studying him for a moment,

then she jerked a little and returned the book to its cubby.

"The turn is just ahead on the left." She leaned forward, like she couldn't quite see past the onslaught of rain.

At her instruction, he carefully turned onto a dirt road. His headlights swept across a sign which read *Hayes Family Farm*, but beyond that, all he saw was a curtain of rain.

She stroked Rex's head, as though he was the one who needed reassurance. "Power must've gone out."

"You don't have a generator?"

"We do, but..." She let her thought trail off, leaving him to wonder what, specifically, had her concerned.

"You're not all on your own out here, are you?" Instantly recognizing that his question might not have sounded the way he intended, he added, "Just because...I want to be sure you're safe."

"I'm fine." The way she bit off the

words confirmed that he had overstepped. "My dad is here."

"Look, I didn't mean—"

"See the house?" She pointed to a structure up ahead, to the right of what looked like a barn. "You can pull up in front of it."

As he swung a wide curve to align her door with the walkway, a flashlight beam illuminated the front porch of the house. The figure of a man appeared.

"Thanks for everything." Like a prisoner who'd just been granted her release, she flung her door open and reached for the umbrella she'd left at her feet.

Rex stood, tail wagging, as his mistress held the umbrella out far enough to open it. By the time she had stepped down, the man Derek assumed to be her father had rushed out to greet her, protected by his own umbrella. While she encouraged Rex to follow her out, she and the man had a brief exchange that was drowned out by the storm. Then she stepped to the side and her dad leaned over the passenger seat with his right hand extended.

"Thank you for bringing her home."

"Of course." Derek accepted the man's firm shake. "I'm just glad I came along when I did."

"God looks out for people, son."

He said that with a certainty that might have convinced Derek if life hadn't already shown him otherwise. But he wasn't about to argue, so he said, "Yes, sir."

"You got much further to go?"

"Actually, my plan fell through. I think I'll just head back into town."

"It's no use trying to find your way in this." He tipped his chin toward the sky. "You can wait it out here, if you like."

His daughter's head snapped in her dad's direction and she put a hand on his arm.

He patted her hand and continued speaking to Derek. “You can park over there next to the barn. Then come on over to the house. Dinner’s almost ready.”

Seeing his daughter stiffen at that, Derek shook his head. “I don’t want to impose. I’ve got plenty of—”

“We won’t take no for an answer. The very least Valerie and I owe you is a hot meal.”

He stepped back and shut the door, leaving Derek with no more opportunity to decline.

Valerie. Her name was Valerie. And she was lovely.

But by the way she appeared to be giving her dad an earful as they hurried toward the house, she was none too pleased with the invitation.

Chapter 4

"Dad, I know you want to be polite." Valerie trotted to keep up with her dad as they dashed toward the house. "But this guy's a stranger."

"If it weren't for this *stranger's* help..." He paused while they caught up to Rex, who waited patiently for someone to open the door. "...you'd be out in the rain and I'd be setting out to search for you right about now."

"You were going to do that?" She shook out her umbrella as her dad opened the door, then followed Rex inside. "You've never done that before."

"You've never been this late before." He pulled her into a hug, then set her back, holding her by the shoulders. "You think I don't worry?"

"I don't want you to worry." Although, under the circumstances, his worry had been justified.

Shivering, she pulled off her hat and coat as she looked into the living room and the dining room beyond. Funny how cozy a few candles and a roaring fire in the fireplace made their home, especially on such a dreary night.

Kicking off her wet boots, she sniffed the air. *Chicken?* Suddenly, she realized how hungry her little adventure had made her. "Dad, you offered him a hot meal. Did you plug the stove into the generator?"

"Plugged in the fridge and the freezer."

Dad took her coat from her and hung it next to his on the hall tree by the front door. "I put the chicken in the Dutch oven on top of the wood stove."

"How very homesteaderly of you." Appreciating the warmth of the fire crackling in the living room, she joined Rex at the fireplace. "And don't change the subject."

"Which subject?"

The sound of someone jogging up the front steps was followed by a polite tapping on the door.

Valerie sighed. "*That* subject."

Dad gave her a look as he moved to answer the door. "You should appreciate the opportunity to talk to someone your own age."

Turning to face the fire, she rolled her eyes. Why was everyone so set on fixing her up with any man who fell from the sky? Besides, they didn't even know if this guy was single.

Disregarding the sound of the door creaking open and her dad ushering in their dinner guest, Valerie considered that her trepidation might just be residual confusion from the van incident. Would she ever know what that was all about?

"Thank you again for your kind offer, Mr...Hayes?" Derek had a nice voice—smooth and comforting. "I assumed from the name on the sign."

"Surprised you could read it. We normally have a light out there."

"I had my high beams on. My name's Derek, by the way. Derek Bradford."

Finally warm, and feeling more up for being hospitable, Valerie turned in time to see her dad hanging up Derek's jacket, and Derek turning to face her. She gulped. Seeing him now with the light from the fire dancing across his chiseled features, her knees went a little weak. Chris Hemsworth had nothing on him.

She forced herself to look away, suddenly ultra-aware of what a sight she must be.

“I’ll just...” Dad started toward the dining room. “...get dinner on the table.”

“It smells delicious.” Derek pushed up the sleeves of his fitted long-sleeved T.

“Need any help, Dad?” Valerie caught herself combing her fingers through her ponytail, and clasped one hand with the other. Why was she nervous?

“No, no.” Turning back, he gave her a wink.

She glanced down at Rex, who stood and looked up at her expectantly.

“Oh...I have to feed Rex.”

“I got it.” Dad turned from where he was about to open the door to the kitchen. “Come on, boy.”

He patted his thigh and Rex enthusiastically obeyed, leaving her alone to serve as hostess. When Derek remained in the entryway, it dawned on her that she was being anything but hospitable.

"Come on in and get warm."

A look of relief washed over him as he stepped into the living room. The cozy, potentially romantic setting was not lost on her.

There was an awkward silence for several moments as he held out his hands to warm them. "So, you've lived on the farm your whole life?"

She glanced at him suspiciously. Why was he asking that? Then she realized he was referencing the display of framed family photos gracing the mantel. The fact that most of the photos they had of her as a child had been taken on the farm, gave testimony to the smallness of her life.

"Yep. This has always been home."

He nodded. "So, no siblings, then? Just you?"

"Just me..." What was he getting at? "I should see if my dad—"

The door from the kitchen swung open, and Dad reappeared, carrying a platter of roasted chicken. “Get it while it’s hot.”

Thankful that Dad had, hopefully, put a stop to this line of questioning, Valerie gestured toward the dining room.

Several minutes later, the three of them were seated at the table, and Rex had stretched out in front of the fireplace for his post-dinner nap. Normally, Valerie would enjoy a rainy evening and a candlelight dinner, but she still felt shaky. How could she relax playing hostess to someone they didn’t know from Adam?

Although, she did have to admit that nothing about Derek suggested that he was anything other than what he appeared to be. Then again, how many suspense novels had she read where the stalker or serial killer presented as a charming, average guy?

She shook off that thought. Maybe she

should switch to reading romances.

"So, Derek—" Dad ladled gravy onto the heap of mashed potatoes on his plate. "—you have a family?"

Valerie swallowed a gasp. *Way to put the guy on the spot, Dad.*

"Nope. Just me." He smiled, like the question hadn't seemed like the beginning of an interrogation or a job interview. "My parents and my younger brother live in Minneapolis."

"Huh." Dad nodded, seeming pleased with how his little cross-examination was going so far. "That where you're from?"

"Originally. Now I live in DC."

Valerie lifted her gaze to him.

Dad raised an eyebrow. "You're not a politician, are you?"

Derek chuckled. "No, sir. But I have been known to follow them around town. I'm a photographer."

Her forkful of steamed carrots hovered halfway between her plate and her mouth. *A photographer?* Interesting.

Dad gave a thoughtful nod. “You’re a long way from home.”

“Not that far, really. I mean, compared to other projects I’ve worked on.”

“You travel for work?” Valerie’s attempt at nonchalance came off as unconvincing.

“Used to. I’m a freelancer so I take assignments. Now that I’m based out of DC, I get plenty of assignments near home.”

“So you’re on vacation?” She bit into the buttery carrots.

He tipped his head from side to side. “More of a personal project, actually.”

After slipping a bite of potato into his mouth, Dad pointed his fork at Derek. “Sounds like you lead an exciting life.”

“I have no complaints. I’m sure farming has its share of excitement too.”

Valerie sputtered. “Hear that, Dad? Our lives are *exciting*.”

The glint in her dad’s eye reflected both his good humor and the candles glimmering on the table. “I think getting up before dawn to fill the water tanks and inspect the fences qualifies as exciting.”

Valerie made a show of turning her eyes upward. “Please, Dad. You’re going to overwhelm him with the glamour of life on the Hayes Family Farm.”

Derek smiled. “Have you always been a farmer, Mr. Hayes?”

“My whole life. Grew up on a small farm on the other side of Dupont.”

“Oh, so this farm wasn’t in your family?”

Dad had just put a bite of chicken in his mouth, so he responded with a shake of his head.

“My parents bought this place when they were newlyweds.” Valerie knew her dad didn’t like the questions that often accompanied this topic. She had gotten pretty good at dodging the details that didn't need sharing. "They worked hard to build the business."

"Well, I'm sure it's rewarding," Derek said. "Hard work always is."

Dad jolted, and scraped his chair back a little too abruptly. "Almost forgot the biscuits. 'Scuse me."

As the kitchen door swung on its two-way hinges from Dad's hasty retreat, Derek leaned toward her. "I hope I didn't say something I shouldn't have."

She shook her head. "It's just hard for him to talk about the past. And when I try to focus on the positive things, he gets embarrassed. He's a very humble man."

He nodded politely, as if her vague answer explained it all. It didn't, but Valerie hoped it would be enough for a stranger just passing through. Their life was small and unexciting. The details couldn't possibly matter to this man who clearly had more compelling things to think about.

Chapter 5

After what had turned out to be a surprisingly pleasant meal, Derek had offered to pay them back for their kindness by taking a look at Valerie's truck in the morning. Dad had accepted before Valerie could object.

So...maybe she hadn't tried all that hard. She kind of had to admit that Dad was right. It was nice to have someone her age to talk to. And he'd be on his way soon enough.

Derek had retired to his RV, and since Dad had insisted on doing the cleanup, Valerie and Rex had gone upstairs. She was drained, but it was going to take a little while for her to wind down.

Since the hot shower she craved was out of the question, thanks to the power outage, she told herself that a cold sponge bath was good for her circulation. Maybe not so good for her anxiety, but slipping into her favorite flannel jammies helped make up for that.

Entering her bedroom, she cast the beam of her small flashlight to Rex's bed, at the foot of her own, where Rex turned in a circle, then plunked down with a contented grunt. Valerie chuckled. At least he was unfazed by the events of the day. His ability to totally relax comforted her. If he sensed any threat, he wouldn't be so quick to let down his guard.

The hour was still early—even by farm-girl standards—but the lack of light made it seem later. Normally, she wound down by curling up in bed with a book, but she remembered where she'd left off the previous night. The heroine had just escaped certain death and gone on the run, not knowing who, if anyone, she could trust. Not exactly a prospect she wanted to dwell on after her own adventure that afternoon.

Chewing her lower lip, she crossed to her closet to pull out something to wear tomorrow.

Most days, she'd grab a pair of jeans and whatever flannel shirt her hand touched first, and call it good. In fact, she hadn't put special thought into what she was going to wear for a normal workday since before Carrie came to town. That was when Valerie had realized that no amount of cute, well-put-together outfits was going to turn Joe's head in her direction.

An ache settled in her chest at that thought. It wasn't that she felt heartbroken over Joe. It was the loss of the dream that weighed heavy. Joe wasn't the man for her—she'd accepted that. Accepting that love was going to elude her altogether...that was a tougher pill to swallow.

Standing inside the long closet that was just deep enough to qualify as a walk-in, she ran the beam of light over her options. She had cute clothes, but normally there was no reason for her to care about how she looked. When her day involved traipsing through muddy fields and hoisting boxes of soil-encrusted produce, fashion wasn't much of a priority. So why was she thinking about it now?

"No reason." She answered out loud because the voice doing the asking was loud in her head and needed to be shushed.

Just as she reached for her fitted burgundy blouse with the flouncy collar, her light caught something on the floor in the far corner. It was a box that had been sitting there unopened for such a long time it had practically become invisible to her. She pondered, then stepped back out and shut the door behind her. Some things were best left in the past.

After laying out her blouse on the back of the stuffed chair near the window, she went to the dresser for undies and socks. She added the skinny jeans she normally reserved for the rare occasion when she met Carrie and Janet in town for dinner. They were comfy, and she liked the way they looked with the blouse.

Standing back, she studied the ensemble she'd put together. Cute. And if it made her happy to plan to look nice, that was reason enough to do it. It had nothing at all to do with the fact that she'd be seeing Derek again in the morning. But if his presence served as a reminder that she felt better when she put in a little effort, no one could fault her for that.

Turning off the flashlight, she crossed to the window and parted the curtains. The rain had let up some, but there were no lights on as far as the eye could see. Not that they had close neighbors, but she missed the security light above the barn door, which normally illuminated the front yard and part of the road. Maybe they should consider updating to some kind of solar powered lights to avoid nights like this.

As her eyes adjusted, she made out the shape of the RV parked next to the barn. There was a dim glow of what must be some kind of camping lantern, or maybe a small lamp if he had his own power source. Leaning her shoulder against the cold window, she pondered. What must Derek's life be like? This man who loved travel enough to own a collection of guidebooks and a really nice RV. A wave of envy ran through her that she couldn't deny.

Of course, she still had a measure of hesitation about the guy. Sure, he had gotten her safely home, but how did they know he was who he said he was? It wouldn't be a bad idea for her to do an internet search and see if anything came up.

She crossed to her bed and snagged her phone from where she'd tossed it on the bedside table, then started typing as she crossed back to the window. *Derek...Bradford.* That was what he'd said...

When nothing happened, she sighed and lowered her phone. No internet, which was no surprise in this weather. She could try again in the morning.

Of course, by then it wouldn't much matter. He was going to help Dad look at her truck, then he'd be on his way, probably by the time she got back from her morning deliveries. More likely than not, she'd never see him again after that.

She glanced out again at the warm glow in his window. Then something snagged her eye near the corner of the barn. Her heart caught in her throat. Something had moved. Keeping still, she stared, but nothing out of the ordinary happened. Either she had imagined it, or it was just a tree blowing in the wind.

Except that...there were no trees next to that corner of the barn.

Chapter 6

Valerie woke up before dawn to find the clock next to her bed flashing the happy message that the power was back on. She quickly dressed and put on a little mascara—something she normally didn't take the time to do. But today was another delivery day, and she had to put on a good face for the public. She clucked at her image in the bathroom mirror. *Right. That's the only reason.*

She went downstairs to find a plate of bacon and eggs staying warm in the oven, lunch already simmering in the slow cooker, and a note from her dad letting her know that he and Derek had gone to rescue her truck.

After eating breakfast and spending an hour trimming back raspberry bushes and watching the sun rise, she caught sight of Dad's blue pickup truck backing up to the garage so they could unload her truck from the trailer. The sight of her poor old truck came as a relief. Whatever its problem was, at least it had survived the night all alone on the side of the road.

She finished the row of bushes she was working on, then loaded the dead branches on the small trailer, which was hooked to the back of the tractor. She whistled for Rex to join her in the cab of the tractor, then headed toward the buildings.

A few minutes later, she parked the

tractor. As she and Rex walked to the garage, she caught sight of her reflection in the window of Dad's blue pickup, which he'd left in the driveway. A couple of tendrils of her crazy, wavy hair had escaped her messy bun, giving her face a softer look that she liked. She shrugged her brows and looked down at Rex, who wagged his tail and eyed her adoringly. She could always count on him to make her feel loved.

As the two of them entered the garage, Derek and Dad glanced up from where they leaned in under the raised hood of her truck. She tried not to read anything into the half smile Derek gave her.

"There she is." Dad picked up an old rag and wiped his hands on it. "I need to go check on Jordan and Moe. Make sure they got that old tractor moving okay."

"They're fine." Valerie swatted the air. "They headed up to the orchard an hour ago."

Nodding, Dad tossed down the rag and started for the door, rubbing the back of his neck. “Okay, so JJ and Dax—”

“Are boxing up orders in the barn.” Valerie felt her jaw tighten. She knew exactly what Dad was up to. Hopefully, his attempt at matchmaking wasn’t so obvious to Derek.

Was she really that pathetic?

“Well then, I’ll just go help them so you can get on the road.” He patted her arm as he passed her on his way to making his exit.

Sighing, she gave him a side-eyed look and joined Derek. “So, you have a lot of experience fixing old trucks?”

He chuckled. “Not a lot. But my first car was a seventy-five Ford Bronco, so I spent my share of time under the hood.”

“Mmm. A Bronco’s different than a pickup.”

“They have their differences.” He gave her that half smile again. “They also have their similarities."

True enough. She leaned in to have a look. "What's the prognosis?"

"Not sure yet. I'm hoping it'll be obvious, but I might need a few minutes."

She nodded. "I'll leave you to it, then. Look...I know you're probably anxious to get going, but you can stay for lunch if you like. Dad's got enough soup in the crockpot to feed our crew twice over, so you're welcome to stay."

"I appreciate that. But, full disclosure, your dad already issued the invitation."

"Of course he did."

"Also..." He winced. "He invited me to stay on after lunch."

She frowned. "How much after?"

He hesitated. "All winter."

Her mouth dropped open. "B-but...don't you have other plans?"

"My plan was to find a homebase for the winter and branch out from there to photograph the landscape."

Valerie felt her cheeks start to burn. How could her dad ask someone to stay on their property for the winter without talking to her about it first? She was an equal partner in this business, and it was her home too. Her thoughts raced. This was *so* not okay.

"Sorry, I need to..." Taking a couple of steps backward, she bumped into the oil drum that Dad's tool box was sitting on, nearly sending it toppling. She caught herself, and cleared her throat. "It's a busy day. I need to get back to work."

Clucking her tongue at Rex, she started for the door. When he didn't immediately follow, she looked back to see him lingering near Derek.

Terrific. It was reassuring that Derek had passed the Rex test, but she didn't want her guard dog to let his guard down.

She gave a quick whistle, reminding him where his priorities lay, and the two of them left the garage and made a beeline to the barn.

Dad was making himself useful, helping JJ and Dax put today's delivery orders into crates. While this job needed to get done, she couldn't put off having it out with him.

JJ and Dax were trusted employees, but they didn't need to hear her and Dad's personal business, so she stopped a few feet inside the barn and waved him over.

"Dad."

He looked up, innocent as a newborn foal. "'Scuse me, boys." He crossed to her. "You get the problem sorted out?"

"I think we have another problem to sort out."

"Oh? What's that?"

"Don't pretend you don't know." She resisted the urge to raise her voice. "You asked him to stay on for the winter? Without talking to me about it?"

"Guess we're talking about it *now*. It will be good to have someone else on the farm over the winter. Derek said he'd be willing to help with the work in exchange for us letting him park his rig here."

"We already have Jordan and Moe." She plunked her hands on her hips.

"Only till Christmas. We agreed we can't afford anyone beyond that this year. Derek would work for free. Seems like a good trade-off."

"Hang on." She folded her arms and eyed him narrowly. "Was this his idea?"

"Nope. My idea. Pretty good one too, don't you think?"

Oh, no. She wasn't conceding that easily. "What does he know about farm work? He's a photographer."

"Says he's done manual labor. I got a good feeling about him. 'Sides, we'll get to know him. And it's not like he'll be staying in the house. I don't see a problem."

Valerie grappled to pinpoint what was bugging her. "Won't it cost extra to have him here? What about electricity?"

"Said he has *solar*." He put an exaggerated emphasis on the word. "And he'll pay for whatever else he needs. Might be nice for you to have someone around other than me."

"You say that like you think I don't have any friends."

"I'm not saying you don't *have* friends. It's just that you only see them when they're on your delivery route."

She started to protest, then realized that was actually pretty true. "I don't have time to be a social butterfly, Dad. I have to work."

"Just pointing out facts, that's all."

She grunted. "Well, the fact is that we already made a winter plan for the farm *together*, and I don't think this is a good id—"

The rustling of footsteps brought her head around to where Derek stood in the open doorway. Her heart dropped to her stomach. Obviously, he had heard enough to know that they were talking about him.

"There's...uh..." He cast his eyes downward, then looked up again and pointed his thumb in the direction of the garage. "There's something I think you should see."

Something about his tone twisted her stomach in a knot. *What now?*

Chapter 7

As Derek walked back to the garage with Valerie and Mr. Hayes, he pondered whether he should address the elephant in the barnyard. Obviously, they knew he had overheard enough to detect that Valerie didn't want him to stay. But he didn't want to embarrass them.

The worst part of it though, was that he had hoped she'd be receptive to the idea. She'd been justifiably standoffish when they'd first met, but he'd been under the impression that she'd warmed up to him by the end of dinner last night. Their farm was peaceful, beautiful, and close enough to town. Sure, he could find another location. But Valerie was what made this place special. She was definitely someone he wanted to get to know better, but clearly, she didn't feel the same.

Before Derek could speak, Mr. Hayes clapped his hands and rubbed them together. "So, you figure out the problem, son?"

"I'm afraid so." He gave Valerie an apologetic look. Not that this was his fault, but he hated being the one to give the bad news. "All the oil has drained from your engine."

"What?" She stopped, staring at him. "How?"

He lifted an arm, inviting her to precede him into the garage. "Let me show you."

They approached the truck like it was a patient on life support. He picked up the oil pan plug from where he'd left it on the oil drum. "Seems like the plug wasn't properly tightened when you had your oil changed."

"But I just had it serviced." She leaned over the engine, understandably unconvinced. "Hal wouldn't have done that."

"Hal's your mechanic?"

"Has been for years." Mr. Hayes studied the plug. "He's way too careful to let that happen." He looked away like a thought had occurred. "Wonder if he had Gil work on it."

Derek frowned. "Who's Gil?"

"Hal's employee." Valerie groaned. "Hal keeps him on because he's good with cars and Hal has a soft heart. A lot of us don't particularly trust him, so Hal doesn't have him work on our cars. But I can't see him being that careless either."

Derek rubbed his jaw. "Would Gil have any reason to do this on purpose?"

"I don't think so." Her incredulous look was endearing. "He hasn't had a beef with me personally."

Setting down the plug, Mr. Hayes grunted. "Wouldn't put it past the guy to try to manufacture more business."

She pursed her lips. "That wouldn't be very smart."

"This is Gil we're talking about, honey. *Smart* isn't his strong suit."

She tipped her head back in acknowledgement. "So, is my engine ruined?"

"I'm no expert." Derek stepped back, wishing he had better news. "But it looks that way."

Valerie sighed. "We need to call Hal and see what he thinks."

Her dad nodded. "I'll make the call, then we'll have to tow 'er in."

As Mr. Hayes left the garage, Valerie

massaged her temples. "This is terrible timing. I need my truck. This week, especially. With the fall market coming up. And Janet's wedding." She took a deep breath. "Dad has work to do and I have deliveries to get done this morning."

"Not in this truck." Derek paused. "Can you use your dad's?"

"Not if he's using it to tow my truck into town."

He wiped his hands on a rag. "I can do it. Tow your truck, I mean."

"Oh...no. You don't have to—"

"You've been so hospitable to me. It's the least I can do. Although, I understand if you're not comfortable having me do it." He paused. "I also get why you're not comfortable having me here all winter. I can be on my way today."

She grimaced. "It's nothing personal. It's just that..."

The way she left her sentence hanging there unfinished led him to think it actually *was* personal, but he had to be okay with that.

"It's a crazy world," he offered. "You just never know."

She nodded. "Exactly."

"Well..." He paused, trying not to notice the way her burgundy blouse brought out the red in her hair. "I'll go bring my RV around so we can get the trailer hooked up. Then I'll let your dad know we've had a change of plans."

As he turned and headed for the door, he fully hoped but barely expected her to call him back. When she didn't, his hope faded. It was just as well, he supposed. Honestly, the last thing he needed was to let himself long for something that wasn't meant to be.

Later that morning, Valerie and Rex eased

up the road in her dad's truck to the Shadow Ridge Ranch, the home of her friends—Carrie and Joe—and Joe's grandma, Mrs. Brannon. Valerie's heart warmed at the sight of Carrie standing from one of the rocking chairs on the sprawling front porch, where she'd no doubt been waiting for Valerie.

Dad had made a good point. It was a highlight of her delivery days to catch up with her friends, even if it was just for a few minutes.

She pulled the truck up to the steps leading from the side of the porch and got out as Carrie stepped down to meet her.

"Why do you have your dad's truck today?" Carrie opened the passenger door to let Rex get out and stretch his legs.

Valerie grabbed one of the boxes with *Shadow Ridge* scrawled across the top and handed it to Carrie. "Let's just say, yesterday was an interesting day."

She hoisted the other box containing

the rest of their order and launched into the details, beginning with the van in the alley. By the time they made it to the back door, through the mudroom, and into the kitchen, Valerie had gotten to the part of the story where Derek discovered the loose oil plug.

"Wait a minute. Go back..." Carrie set her box down on the counter and plunked a hand on her hip. "You're telling me your truck broke down and you got a ride from a stranger." She eyed her narrowly. "That sounds awfully familiar."

Valerie had to laugh. "Don't think I wasn't thinking about how you met Joe."

"And look where that landed me." She swept a hand around their homey and expansive kitchen, the heart of their beautiful home.

"Just because I met Derek in a thunderstorm doesn't mean I should expect lightning to strike twice."

"Hmmm." Carrie's playful expression

turned thoughtful. "You don't think this guy had anything to do with your truck dying, do you?"

"I really don't see how. I mean, it's a mystery, but I think he just came along at the right time."

"Did you look him up online? If he's really a photographer, maybe he has a website. Do you know his last name?"

"Bradford." She bit her lower lip. "Do you think that's an invasion of his privacy?"

"It's the world we live in." Carrie waved her over to her laptop on the kitchen table. "I think it's okay to check on people."

Valerie sat next to Carrie as she opened her computer and shifted it so it was in front of Valerie. "It doesn't much matter anyway. He's leaving after lunch."

"Oh." Carrie stuck her lip out in a near-pout. "But...don't you want to know?"

Valerie pondered. She did, actually.

She typed his name into the search bar.

Carrie squinted at the results. "He's a balding attorney?"

"No..." She typed *photographer* next to his name, and a website came up. She clicked.

"That's him?" Carrie shifted the computer so she could see the picture of him better. "You didn't mention the heartthrob factor."

Chuckling, Valerie slid the computer back. "Do you get to talk that way, as a married woman?"

"No, but I do get to talk that way as a caring best friend. I'm only looking out for your best interests. He's very heart-throbby."

"He's also very talented." Valerie scrolled through some of the examples of his work. "Look at these shots." Not wanting to waste time, she clicked on the *About Derek* heading. "Grew up in Minneapolis. Traveled the world as a freelance photographer. Now resides in Washington, DC. Yeah, that's what he told us."

"He's been all over. What's he doing in Montana?"

"Photographing the landscape for a personal project. That's all I know. Rex has taken to him." She shut the laptop, not wanting to fall down this tempting rabbit hole. "Dad too. In fact..." She hesitated, not sure if she should share this. "Dad offered to let him stay on our property for the winter in exchange for doing some work around the place."

Carrie's eyes widened. "What? You said he was leaving."

"He's leaving because I put the kibosh on that idea."

Carrie stared at her. "Valerie Nicole Hayes. Do you mean to tell me that a good-looking, well-traveled, gainfully employed man, who already has the approval of your dad and your dog, has literally landed on your farm and you are making him leave? What is your problem?"

Valerie put her elbows on the table and buried her face in her hands. "We don't know him." She pulled her hands away. "We can't just go inviting a stranger—"

"Everyone's a stranger at first. If it hadn't been for the kindness of strangers taking me in when I had car trouble, I wouldn't be here right now. Who knows what would've happened to me?"

"That's different." Valerie smiled. "You're *you*."

Carrie chuckled. "Thanks, but Joe and his grandma weren't so sure about me. It wasn't exactly a straightforward situation, if you recall."

"True. You were a little mysterious."

"I'm so grateful they gave me the benefit of the doubt. Maybe you should do that for this handsome stranger too. Especially since he's willing to help out."

"It's just that...my dad only asked him to stay on because he's trying to play matchmaker. It's embarrassing."

"Are you sure that's the only reason?"

Valerie frowned at her.

"Look." Carrie turned in her chair to face Valerie directly. "I know money's tight, and you made the decision not to hire on help for the winter. If this guy is any help at all, it would make things easier on you." When Valerie opened her mouth to protest, Carrie quickly added, "And on your dad. Did you ever stop to think that maybe he sees this as a fair exchange to get some extra help? He's not getting any younger, you know."

Valerie's stomach buckled. Was she really so self-centered that she hadn't seen past the implication that she was incomplete without a man, and also that she was incapable of finding one on her own?

Maybe Carrie was right. How could she be so selfish to turn away free labor when the farm was hurting and so was Dad?

Chapter 8

After completing their morning deliveries, Valerie and Rex returned to the farm to find Derek in the barn helping Dad box up her afternoon orders.

"There she is." Dad looked over at her with a cheerfulness in his eyes that made her heart feel lighter. "We're finishing the last orders, sweetie." He wiped his hands down the front of his jacket. "Say, did Derek tell you about the project he's working on?"

A flame of guilt flared in her chest. Dad seemed so happy talking to Derek. How could she have been so selfish not to see that the social interaction was good for him too? Rolling in her lips, she shook her head.

"It's a coffee table book about Montana seasons. That's why he's here now. Fixing to get some nice autumn shots."

Admittedly, that piqued Valerie's interest, but all she managed to say was "Huh."

"Now that you're back, I'll go tell JJ and Dax to start loading these orders in the truck." Dad headed for the door. "Then I'll get some sandwiches made to go with the soup."

As Dad made his exit, Valerie checked the order sheet on the table in front of Derek and went to the sweet potato bin to grab a couple.

"Your dad does most of the cooking?"

"The lion's share." She fit the potatoes in the box and checked them off the list. "He won't admit it, but his back gives him trouble, so I try to get him to do tasks that don't require much lifting. Cooking, keeping the books for the business."

"He seems to like cooking." Derek picked up a head of kale and carefully placed it in a plastic bag. "If last night's dinner was any indication, he's good at it too."

"He's gotten better." She took the bagged kale from him and placed it on top of the sweet potatoes. "If I wanted to keep him from doing the heavy lifting, I had to convince him I loved his cooking. It was touch and go for a while there."

He chuckled at that. Then his look turned serious. "Your dad said I could get some shots of the apple orchard this afternoon. He invited me to stay for dinner. I'll get going after that."

She hesitated. That *was* what she had

told him she wanted. "Did you have another place in mind? To camp, I mean?"

"I was thinking I'd check out that abandoned campground. Might be kind of kitschy."

"Or creepy." She shivered. "And you'd have quite a challenge finding it in the dark."

"You have a point." He added some white potatoes to the box. "There's an appetite for photos of abandoned places, but I don't think that's my niche."

"Besides, it's so far out. If you're planning on staying in the area all winter, you should camp someplace closer to town. Trust me, with nothing to get around in but that big ol' RV, you'll want to be close to civilization in the dead of winter."

"You have any suggestions?"

Valerie drew in a breath. How could she tell him she'd changed her mind without sounding like she was flirting with him?

Then again, what would be wrong with that? They were both single. Wasn't it possible that part of the appeal for him of staying here might be that he was interested in her? Did she even dare hope?

She exhaled, biting her lip. Why was she so bad at this?

"I really like this area," Derek went on. "But I could keep heading south. Closer to Yellowstone, maybe."

"Oh...yeah." To her surprise, her heart sank. "Yellowstone's beautiful."

That answered that. If he could so easily decide to move on, then clearly she didn't figure into the equation. It had been silly of her to even consider the possibility. If he didn't *want* to stay here, she couldn't exactly force him.

"It gets dark so early." She cleared her throat. "If you're staying for dinner..." She absently checked the list to be sure the order was complete. "...you might as well wait till morning to hit the road."

He looked at her with narrow eyes, one corner of his mouth crooking upward. "You're sure?"

She was about to say more when her phone rang, startling her. She retrieved it from her back pocket. "It's Hal."

She answered, very aware that Derek was alert for her response to whatever the news was.

Hal confirmed that Derek's assessment had been correct. "I can order an engine to replace yours." He cleared his throat. "Since it looks like negligence on the part of my shop—"

"Hal—"

"Hear me out. I know I was careful. I always am. But I can cover the cost of a used engine, or share the cost of a new one. It's up to you."

She groaned. Hal ran a successful business, but that didn't mean he was living on Easy Street. Everyone in this community had their struggles. Besides, she was far from convinced that it was the shop's fault.

"It's an ancient truck," she said. "Go ahead and find a used engine and we'll talk about it."

She glanced over at Derek, whose eyes conveyed his sympathy.

Deep brown eyes...but now was not the time to dwell on that.

While she couldn't in good conscience let Hal eat this cost, it was an expense she hadn't anticipated. With the increase in their property taxes, there was no room in the budget for an engine. But she needed her truck.

"How long will this take?"

"Depends on where I find the engine. Best case, a week."

While she pondered that, Hal added, "Do you have time to come back into town today? There's...something else. Something I want to *show* you."

Her stomach buckled at the tone of his voice. She tried to imagine something *good* that he might want to show her, but nothing came to mind. She looked over at Derek, who eyed her curiously.

“Yeah.” She swallowed. “I’ll stop by after my deliveries.”

Chapter 9

As Valerie and Rex followed Hal from the waiting room of his garage, she couldn't help but notice Gil glancing up at her from where he leaned under the hood of Forrest Hartley's old Dodge. He scowled slightly—although it was a little hard to distinguish that from his normal resting expression of overall disdain for humanity—and nodded a vague greeting.

"I gotta tell ya." Hal rubbed the back of

his neck as he led the way to the bay in the back, where her truck rested on an overhead lift. “It’s a mystery to me how that plug got loosened.”

“Dad and I don’t blame you, Hal.” The more she’d run over it in her mind as she’d done her afternoon deliveries, the more convinced she’d become that this had nothing to do with Hal. Not that she had any other theories.

“I appreciate that. I was wondering myself until I found...here, let me just show you.” Standing at the rear of the truck, he pointed upward. “Take a look at this.”

She looked up at a black rectangular item stuck haphazardly to the underside of the bumper. “What is it?”

“I’m no expert, but I’ve watched enough crime shows to venture a guess. I’d say it’s a tracking device.”

Alarm shot through her. “But why...?”

“No clue.” He shook his head. “You

seen anyone you don't know near your truck?"

Rarely did she see anyone around town who she didn't know. But yesterday.... Did the person in the van have something to do with this?

Then a second person came to mind. She didn't want to think about it, but there was no denying that all of this had started right around when Derek had shown up.

A wave of relief that she hadn't told him she'd changed her mind about his staying for the winter rushed through her. Could she trust him? Did this tracking device have something to do with him arriving when he had, just in time to save her? But the question came back to...why?

Realizing that Hal was looking at her, waiting for an answer, she simply said, "Not really."

After a brief discussion, they agreed to leave the device in place until Jeremy had a chance to take a look at it. Hal gave her an estimate for her replacement engine, and Valerie decided to walk around the block to Jeremy's office. With a week and a half until his wedding, she hadn't planned to bother him about the events of the previous day. But if someone had gone to the trouble of putting a tracking device on her truck...that changed everything.

Just as she and Rex rounded the corner onto Rockford Street, the main street of town, she saw a young woman pushing an older woman in a wheelchair across the street toward the diner. Of course the older woman had to be Maggie Kaufman. She was the only person in town who used a wheelchair. But who was she with?

Judging from the woman's neat ponytail, teal pants, and white work shoes, along with a short, tan puffy coat, Valerie guessed that she must be a caregiver.

Maggie hired someone?

Valerie waited till they got to her side

of the street and the woman turned the chair, then she gave Maggie a little wave. Maggie returned the wave as the young woman opened the door to the diner and they disappeared inside. It did Valerie's heart good to see Maggie getting out of her house. Dad would be pleased too. She made a mental note to mention it to him.

A minute later, when Valerie walked into the sheriff's office, his assistant Ashley looked up from the front desk and broke into a grin.

"Hey. Two of my favorite people." She opened a desk drawer and produced a dog biscuit, which she held out to Rex.

Rex sat, then looked up at Valerie.

"Good boy."

At that, he took off like a shot to claim his treat.

Valerie laughed as she unbuttoned her coat and joined her happy boy in front of the desk. "Is Jeremy busy?"

"Yes." Ashley grimaced at his closed

office door. “But he should be done soon.” She leaned forward conspiratorially. “He’s talking to Crystal.”

“Her yard again?” Loosening her scarf, Valerie lowered herself into the chair next to the desk.

She nodded. “The complaints keep rolling in.”

Valerie winced. “Poor Jeremy.”

Ashley rolled her eyes as the door opened and Crystal’s raspy voice peeled out into the front office.

“I could sue you, you know. For using your authority to intimidate me. You think you can move into the neighborhood and tell everyone else what to do.”

“This has been going on for a while now, Crystal.” Jeremy spoke in his characteristically calm voice. “It’s got nothing to do with Janet and me moving in across the street.”

Crystal stomped out, flinging her purse strap over her shoulder and looking like she deserved whatever talking-to she'd just received, but would never admit it. "It's harassment."

"Now, you know I'm on your side here." Jeremy ambled out after her. "We're going to be neighbors, and I think we can keep things civil." Seeing Valerie, he gave her a nod. "You just let me know if you need help getting that cleanup done."

"I don't need *help*." Crystal brushed a tuft of her wild, brassy-blond hair off her face, then tugged at the zipper of her brown motorcycle jacket. "And my yard is fine."

Jeremy rubbed the back of his neck. "Rockford town ordinance seven oh four and the list of formal complaints seem to say otherwise."

Tossing her head, Crystal whirled around, her eyes connecting with Valerie's. She made a point of firing her a glare which, if looks could kill, would have landed Valerie in the ER. She made a dramatic exit out onto the sidewalk, then reached back to give the door an unnecessarily forceful tug.

"What did you do to get on *her* bad side?" Ashley said.

"Nothing." Valerie shrugged. "Just stumbled into her line of fire, I guess."

Jeremy sighed, then, turning to Valerie, shifted gears. "What brings you around this afternoon? Just saying hello?"

"I wish." Standing, Valerie gave him a tight smile. It wouldn't be unusual for her to stop in just to say hi, considering that she and Jeremy had run with the same friend crowd practically their whole lives. "This is more, official business. You got a minute?"

His brow creasing, he nodded, and stepped aside for her and her canine shadow to precede him into his office.

Slipping out of her coat, she took one of the two seats facing the desk while

Jeremy crossed around to his own chair. As Rex settled comfortably in front of the wall heater, Valerie launched into a quick account of the oil plug and her ruined engine, then showed him the photo she'd snapped with her phone of the tracking device.

Working his jaw, Jeremy used his thumb and forefinger to enlarge the image. "Seems a little too coincidental not to be connected. Any idea who might have it in for you?"

"Do you have to put it that way?" She shuddered. "The obvious answer is Gil, just because my truck was in the shop. But Hal doesn't think he'd do anything like that, and I can't think of any reason why he would."

"Yeah." Setting the phone on his desk, he flipped open a notepad. "Much as I don't care for the guy, he hasn't caused any trouble in a while."

"There was something else strange

that happened yesterday. Right before my truck died."

Valerie gave him a brief rundown of her encounters with the van in the alley and again on her way home. "It was right behind your office." She nodded to the window behind him, which overlooked the very spot where the vehicle had been parked. "Must've been about four. Do you know anything about it?"

Jutting out his lower lip, he shook his head. His look of concern did nothing to quell her sense of unease.

"You get a look at the driver?"

She shook her head. "It was a man...or I think it was. To tell you the truth, all I really saw was a gloved hand adjusting the side mirror."

"Then you're sure it was the same van following you?"

"Yes. But I don't know for sure that he was *following* me..." She bit her lip. "Except that after I lost him, he came back. Right after my truck died. I was on foot by then, and he stopped like maybe he wanted to help."

His eyes shot from the pad where he'd been jotting notes to her. "Must've been scary."

"A little. But I had Rex with me." She glanced over at her boy, who had relaxed into a heavy sleep on the rug. She went on to tell Jeremy about the RV, and the driver of the van making a U-turn. "I took a chance and accepted a ride home from the guy in the RV." She swallowed, knowing how risky that sounded. "It seemed like the safer option."

"Yeah..." Jeremy leaned forward, his demeanor turning even more serious. "So this guy got you safely home. Do you know anything about him?"

"Actually, he's..." Valerie swallowed again. "He's still at the farm. He's been helping box up orders and Dad invited him to stay for dinner."

As she quickly filled in the gaps, she tried to overlook the way Jeremy's face paled. He'd become less trusting and more cautious since Janet's little boy, Caleb, had been kidnapped last year. Valerie tried, and pretty much failed, to convince herself that was why he wasn't just brushing this off as a weird experience that they didn't need to worry about.

He asked for Derek's full name and muttered something about having Ashley run a check on him. "And send me that photo." Nodding at the phone still sitting between them, Jeremy started tapping on his computer keyboard. "I'll include it in the case file."

Her stomach dropped. "You think it's that serious?"

"Val, someone put a tracking device on your truck. We need to figure out who. And why." After asking her a few more questions, he added, "I'll ask around and see if anyone's seen this van, or any other unusual activity around town."

She picked up her phone and began the process of sending the photo. "Sorry to bring trouble the week before your wedding."

"Hey, you're not the one bringing it." The caring look he gave her marginally eased the fire smoldering in her stomach.

"If you don't mind..." He tapped once more at the keys and glanced at the clock on the wall. "I'll be swinging by your place to meet this Derek guy for myself."

She nodded, not sure if she felt relieved to have Jeremy's input or nervous that he thought she needed it.

Chapter 10

Taking the turn onto their private road, Valerie sighed. The sight of the sun setting behind those mountains never got old.

A quick glance in the rearview mirror told her that Jeremy, who had told her he'd be leaving shortly after she did, had caught up to her. She chuckled. One of the perks of being the sheriff was that he could go over the speed limit without having to keep an eye out for the sheriff.

The barn came into view and she felt some of the tension leave her shoulders. The RV was still there.

Rex let out a happy little grumble.

"I'm glad he's still here too." Valerie patted his head. "Jeremy came all this way to talk to him."

Rex barked.

"What?" She tossed him a look. "You think that's *not* the reason I'm glad he's still here?"

Cocking his head, he answered with a whine.

She chuckled. "I'll thank you to keep your observations to yourself."

She pulled her dad's truck into his usual spot in the garage, then leaned over to open Rex's door for him before getting out herself. She and Rex exited the garage just as Jeremy pulled his patrol car into the driveway and got out.

"I'm telling you, Val..." He shook his head as they started toward the house.

"The thought of you out on that road all alone at this time of day—"

"I wasn't *alone* alone. I had Rex."

"Rex is great. But he doesn't make up for no cell service. I've got half a mind to talk to the town council again."

"Good luck with that." As they started up the front steps, she whistled for Rex to join them. "You know half of the council members are convinced those things are part of Satan's end times plan."

"They might not be wrong. There's a lot of evil in this world." Reaching the porch, he stomped the mud off his shoes onto the welcome mat. "But if the evil towers would help protect our people from the evil *men*—"

"I'd like to be there when you make that argument." Smirking, she opened the front door to the faint sound of cheerful conversation coming from the kitchen, backed by Frank Sinatra's light baritone. The delicious aroma of sausage and oregano made her mouth water. "Mmmm. Dad's making lasagna. I can tell." Watching Jeremy wait for Rex to barrel up the front steps, she unbuttoned her coat. "You want to stay? He always makes a big panful."

"As great as that sounds, Janet's expecting me." He removed his own jacket and hung it next to Valerie's. "We're meeting with our wedding photographer tonight."

"Exciting." She shoved away that annoying green-eyed monster that always tried to rear its ugly head whenever the wedding was mentioned. As sorry as she felt for herself, she was thrilled that Jeremy had found Janet. They were about as perfect for each other as a couple could get.

Tipping her head in a follow-me gesture, she headed for the kitchen. She pushed open the door to the sight of Derek tossing a salad and Dad brushing a loaf of

French bread with butter.

Dad looked up at their entrance, his expression cheerful. “There she is. Jeremy. Don’t tell me our girl requested a police escort?”

“Not exactly, sir.” Jeremy entered the kitchen, followed by an enthusiastic Rex, just like he’d done a million times over the years. “But I am here in an official capacity.”

“Official, huh?” Dad frowned. “The case of the loose oil plug?”

Jeremy gave a half smile, but said nothing, giving Valerie the impression that he didn’t want to let on about the tracking device until he’d had a chance to question Derek.

“Stay for dinner, son?” Dad picked up a knife and began chopping at a pile of garlic on the cutting board, adding to the already intoxicating aroma which permeated the room.

“’Fraid I’ll have to take a raincheck.”

"He and Janet are meeting with their wedding photographer tonight, Dad."

When Derek perked up at that information, she jolted, remembering her role as hostess. "Jeremy, this is Derek." As Jeremy extended his hand, Derek wiped his on a towel.

"If you've got a minute"—Jeremy gave Derek's hand a firm shake—"I wanted to ask you what you observed about the truck."

"Sure. No problem."

Jeremy tipped his head toward the door to the dining room and led the way. As soon as the two men had left the room, Valerie crossed to the sink to wash her hands. "You two seem to be hitting it off."

Shaking his head, Dad laughed. "He's a nice young man. He's got some stories to tell, too, what with all his travels."

"I'll bet." A dull ache hit her squarely in the chest. "Traveling makes a person more interesting. Or so I hear."

"This will make a good story too. How he got himself caught up in a small-town criminal investigation." Chuckling again, he spread the garlic over the bread. "Guess we're blessed our sheriff has so little to do that a loose oil plug warrants an official investigation."

"I'm afraid it's more than just the oil plug, Dad."

Dad's hand froze on the handle to the oven door. "Oh?"

She grabbed a clean dog bowl from the shelf over the sink, prompting Rex, who had sat down next to the table, to spring to his feet, tail swishing in anticipation.

As Valerie filled the dish and served Rex's dinner, she filled her dad in on Hal's discovery. "That's why I went to see Jeremy. Hal and I agreed it was necessary."

"Jeremy doesn't think Derek had something to do with this *device*, does he?" Dad placed the loaf of garlic bread in the oven.

"It was pretty convenient that he just happened to show up on our road when I needed help, don't you think?"

"Sweetheart. You read too many of those mystery novels. Why would he want to plant a tracking device in your truck?"

"I don't know. Why would *anyone?*"

Leaning against the counter, Dad considered. "Doesn't add up. If he put it there, wouldn't he have removed it when he had a chance? Before we took the truck to the garage?"

Raising her thumb to her lips, Valerie thought about that. "You're right. But who else could have done it?"

Her dad just shrugged. "Guess we have to trust that Jeremy will get to the bottom of it."

"Yeah." Valerie recalled the other thing she wanted to tell her dad. "Hey, you'll never guess who I saw in town. Maggie."

Dad's eyebrows rose. "Oh? Where?"

"Going into the diner. She was with somebody. A young woman. Did she hire someone?"

His gaze fell, then he gave a noncommittal shrug. "Must've."

Valerie folded her arms, surprised at his underwhelming response to this bit of news. Knowing how much Dad cared about Maggie's well-being, she'd expected more enthusiasm.

Before she could press him on his response, the door swung open and Derek reentered. His eyes met Valerie's and for a moment she wondered if he thought she suspected him of having something to do with the tracking device. She looked away, then forced an upbeat expression.

"That was quick." She watched as Rex, who had devoured his dinner as usual, made the rounds from Dad to her, then surprisingly, to Derek.

Derek knelt to rub Rex behind the ears. "I just told him what I knew. Wasn't much." Standing, he shrugged. "He wanted to know why I was on your road when I was, of course. So I explained about the wrong turn. He agreed with you about my need for an updated guidebook."

Valerie smiled at that. "I hope you didn't feel like a suspect."

"He's just doing his job." He rubbed the back of his neck. "A tracking device. That ups the ante."

"Yeah. It pretty much eliminates the option of just letting it go."

"Jeremy seems really sharp. I'm sure he'll get this sorted out." He pointed his thumb in the direction of the dining room. "He wants to talk to you, by the way."

"Oh, right." Patting her leg in an indication that Rex should pull himself away from Derek, she headed out of the kitchen.

Jeremy stood by the front door with his jacket on, jotting some notes in his ever-present notepad. He looked up as she joined him, then closed the pad and shoved it in his pocket.

"Well?" Clasping her elbows, she kept her voice low. "Is he cleared as a suspect?"

"His answers lined up with everything he told you. And Ashley just texted that her check on him came back with no red flags. I really don't think your guest had anything to do with the suspicious activity."

Valerie let out a breath. "Well...good."

"You want my opinion?" Jeremy gave her a crooked smile. "I think it was God's providence that put him out on that road just at the right time."

Her cheeks warmed at that thought. She'd felt God's protective presence more than once in her life. The thought of Him sending Derek felt a little daunting but not at all unbelievable.

Jeremy reached for the doorknob. "I'll check out his story, just to be on the safe side, but I'm more concerned about that van. If I'm right about God sending Derek to protect you, stands to reason there was a threat."

Valerie gulped.

"I don't mean to scare you, Val. Just watch your back and try not to go anywhere alone if you can help it." He pulled the door open, letting in a burst of cold air. "I'll ask around and see if anyone knows anything about that van." He stepped out onto the porch.

Valerie leaned on the door jam. "We better figure this out before you leave on your honeymoon next week."

"I'm sure we will. But even if we don't, I'm putting Bobby in charge while I'm away. Of course, Kyle will be his backup. In the meantime," he said, turning to face her again, "I don't hate the idea of having someone else staying on the property with you."

"You think my dad was right to invite Derek to stay?"

"I think you can trust your dad's judgement." With a wave, he set off down the front steps.

Valerie shut the door and leaned her forehead against it. At the sound of the kitchen door whooshing open, she turned to see Derek entering with a stack of plates and silverware. He gave her a contrite look and set the stack on the dining table. With a sigh, she said a quick prayer, then went to help him set the table.

"So..." His voice shook a little as he glanced her way. "Am I cleared?"

"You can rest easy. In fact..." She rolled in her lips. Started to speak but stopped. Then started again. "He thinks that you staying here isn't such a bad idea."

"Yeah?" Hope filled his eyes. "And what do *you* think?"

She swallowed hard. "I think Dad could use the help and..." She looked away. "And it's good for him to have someone besides me to talk to. He won't admit it, but I know he gets lonely."

Derek gave her a nod and a nice smile. Her chest warmed.

A girl could get used to that smile.

Chapter 11

Raising his camera viewfinder to his eye, Derek let out a breath. He adjusted the focus and clicked off several shots, hoping his images would capture the beauty of the morning mist rising from the fields, with those magnificent mountains beyond. He'd made a point of getting out here before first light to be sure he didn't miss this opportunity. Now that he knew he'd be staying a while, he'd started to plan the shots he wanted to capture in the area.

Hearing voices in the distance, he looked back toward the farm buildings. Mr. Hayes was over near the barn with Jordan and Moe, two of the young guys Derek had met the day before. The three of them were hooking a trailer to a tractor and exchanging friendly banter. Wanting to capture the feeling of the moment, Derek took a few shots of them, then started walking back.

Seeing him approach, Mr. Hayes gave him a nod. "Morning, son."

"Morning." He nodded at the younger men. "You heading back to the orchard today, guys?"

"Same as yesterday." Jordan secured the hook of the trailer. "Apples, apples—"

"And more apples." Moe came up behind Jordan and tugged on the flaps of his wool cap, then ducked out of the way, laughing as his friend swatted at him.

"Gotta get the rest of the fruit off those

trees before it freezes." Mr. Hayes rubbed his gloved hands together. "Today's Thursday. It's going to get down to twenty-five over the weekend."

"Brr." Derek shivered. The thought made this forty-five-degree morning feel downright tropical.

"We better light a fire under ourselves today." Jordan began attaching a second trailer to the one they already had hooked to the tractor.

"To keep warm..." Moe jumped in to help him. "Or to make us work faster?"

"Both, genius." Jordan gave him a good-natured roll of his eyes.

Derek found their enthusiasm for their job inspiring. "Can I help?"

"You know, son..." Mr. Hayes put his hand on Derek's shoulder and guided him away from the barn, toward the open area in front of the house. "We have things under control here, but Valerie could use some help."

At his nod, Derek followed his gaze out to a field dotted with bright-orange. Their other two hired workers picked pumpkins and carried them to the edge of the rows, where Valerie transferred them from the ground to a trailer attached to another tractor.

Mr. Hayes looked admiringly at his daughter. "She tells me she likes hoisting those pumpkins, but I'm wise to her. She thinks I'm better off picking a tiny apple off a tree than a giant pumpkin off the ground." He winked.

Derek smiled. "Sounds like she's looking out for you."

"She's a good daughter." Mr. Hayes's face turned serious. "This business with the truck has me more concerned than I want her to know. I'd appreciate you helping me keep an eye on her."

"I-I'll do the best I can. But I'm sure there's nothing to worry about. The sheriff will get this figured out."

"Hope so. But I don't want her going places on her own. Best as we can avoid it, anyway."

Derek nodded. "I understand."

"Meantime..." He looked back out toward the field. "Pumpkins are one of our most popular crops. If you want to earn your keep, that'd be the place to start."

Mr. Hayes patted Derek on the shoulder and turned to go back to helping the guys with the apples. Derek returned his focus to Valerie. So, he had his assignment. Pumpkins and protecting.

He stood there for a moment, stricken by her natural beauty. She probably had no idea how glamorous she looked in jeans, her loose-fitting chore coat, and mud-covered boots. Knowing that she was unaware of his presence, he raised his camera and took some shots of her. She might not like it, but if she could see herself through his lens, maybe she'd appreciate that he had caught her looking so natural. And lovely, in a way that he wouldn't be able to express in words.

Good thing he had his camera to do the talking for him.

Just as Valerie hoisted one of the heavier pumpkins of the morning into the trailer, she noticed Rex, who had been lounging on the cold ground next to the tractor, spring to his feet with his tail wagging. She looked up to see Derek making his way toward them, his camera bag slung over his shoulder.

Using the back of her hand, she wiped away the perspiration that had somehow appeared on her brow, in spite of the chilly fall air. Why was her heart suddenly outpacing the tempo of Rex's tail?

"Hey, boy." After greeting the dog, Derek gave Valerie a small smile as he set his bag on the seat of the tractor. "Your dad said you could use some help."

Valerie chuffed. *Oh, did he now?* "We don't expect you to work here full time, you know."

"Your dad and I figured out an arrangement." He crossed to the row where she had left off and lifted one of the pumpkins. "He says you're pressed to keep up with everything until the winter crops are planted."

"That's true." She went over to the tractor and grabbed a pair of men's work gloves, which she handed to Derek. "But that's the way it is pretty much every fall. We always manage."

She returned to her task of transferring the pumpkins from the ground into the trailers. She appreciated Derek's willingness to help, but he didn't need to know that they had to get their usual amount of work done in spite of having to cut back on labor, thanks to the higher property taxes the state thought they could afford.

As he worked, Derek looked out to where JJ and Dax diligently picked the pumpkins, then carried them to the edge of the trail. "Do you have any other help?"

"Our regular summer crew finished up a few weeks ago. JJ and Dax will stay on till the pumpkins are harvested. Jordan and Moe will help finish up our fall harvest, then they start cutting the Christmas trees while Dad and I plant the winter crops."

"Sounds really organized."

"As organized as it can be, considering all the unpredictable factors. We have our system."

"Your dad says you have your hands full getting ready for the fall market in a couple of weeks."

She smiled. "My dad says a *lot* of things, doesn't he?"

He returned her smile. "We had a lot of

time to talk."

"We count on the fall market to get us through the winter. If we don't make our projected profit, we'll be scraping by till spring." And taking out a loan to pay that tax bill—something that would set them behind for the foreseeable future. "That's why we need to get everything harvested so we can sell it all. With the temperature dropping this weekend, we can't waste time."

"Well, I'm happy to help." He set another pumpkin in the trailer. "I'm also hoping to take advantage of the fall colors while the weather holds."

"Like I said, you're part-time labor. It's going to start freezing overnight, but we're in for some sunny days." She had to admit, as great as it was to be finishing this chore in half the time she'd allotted, having someone to talk to lightened the load even more than the extra pair of hands. "Do you know where you want to go?"

"I read about a road that leads to the top of Shadow Summit."

"You'd get a colorful view from up there." She agreed. "I wouldn't want to make that drive in an RV, though. It's pretty narrow and twisty."

He winced. "Didn't really think about that. Back home, I'm used to walking or grabbing a Lime bike or scooter to get around the city."

She laughed, eying him curiously. "A lime...what?"

He chuckled. "Lime bike. You download the app, and when you need a ride, you just find a bike location on your phone. It's kind of like taking an Uber."

She laughed again. "You city people speak a different language."

"Sorry. Yeah, I guess we do. An Uber is like a taxi." He smiled. "Anyway, sounds like I might need to rent a car if I want to go exploring."

"Considering that the nearest car

rental place is in Luxton, you'll have an hour's drive there. You're not in Kansas...or DC...anymore."

"Thank goodness. I'm enjoying the break."

As he continued to work, she realized they'd gotten so much done while they talked that they'd actually passed the trailer. "I'm just gonna move the tractor down the trail a ways." She climbed into the cab, expecting Rex to join her, as he always did. But he seemed content sniffing along one of the pumpkin patch rows.

She twisted the key, bringing the engine to life, and watched Derek's broad shoulders as he moved to the next row. Dad had been right about him. He looked completely comfortable with farm work. But to see this as a "break" from his normal, exciting life? One filled with travel and city living? Photographing what she could only imagine must be famous people and significant events?

Yeah, he was either being polite, or there was more to him than met the eye.

Driving slowly past him, she sighed. At least what met the eye was a welcome sight to this boring farm girl.

Before Valerie knew it, she and Derek had caught up to the row where JJ and Dax were picking. Since it was getting close to noon, the four of them finished filling the trailers and Valerie sent the two workers to take the morning's harvest to the barn while she, Rex, and Derek walked back to the house.

A few minutes later, they approached the back of the house, where Jordan and Moe stood at the handwashing station, doing more splashing each other than actual hand washing.

Valerie snorted. “I swear those two are like a couple of kids.”

Derek, who had retrieved his camera before they’d started walking, paused to reel off a few shots of the spirited pair.

“Huh.” She huffed out a laugh. “I thought you wanted shots of the landscape.”

“Oh, I do. I’m just so used to photographing people. Every shot tells a story.”

“Their story is a goofball comedy.” When Derek paused again, she added, “Why don’t you get washed up. I’m going to go in and see if Dad needs any help.”

Rex followed Valerie up the back steps and into the enclosed back porch, which they used as a dining room for the farm hands, then into the kitchen. Dad stood at the counter putting together a whole loaf-of-bread’s worth of egg salad sandwiches.

“Need any help, Dad?” She headed to the sink to wash her hands.

"You wanna grab that bag of carrots in the fridge?"

"Sure. Hey, we made it almost to the end of the patch." She dried her hands and crossed to the fridge. "The guys should be able to finish up this afternoon while I deliver that order out to the Fraziers."

"So, you're ahead of schedule. Looks like I was right about Derek."

"He's a good worker." She gave him a bemused smile. "It didn't hurt to have an extra pair of hands."

"Good. Because that extra pair of hands is going with you to the Fraziers'."

"Dad—"

"What? You said yourself he's a good worker."

"Yes, but we can't expect him to give us all of his time. And besides..." She knew exactly what her dad was doing. "I don't need a babysitter."

"Humor me. Until we figure out why someone put that thing on your truck, I don't want you driving around by yourself."

She wanted to argue, but he had a point. She did feel vulnerable, even having Rex with her. And Derek wasn't exactly a chore to be around. "Fine." She poured the baby carrots into a bowl. "But *only* because it'll make you feel better."

"Uh-huh." As he carried the platter of sandwiches toward the back door, he gave her a wink.

When she looked down at Rex, she could have sworn he winked too.

"Et tu, Brute?" Sighing, she picked up the bowl, along with a bag of potato chips. "He's nice, I agree. But let's not get ahead of ourselves."

Chapter 12

Derek sat in the passenger seat of Mr. Hayes's truck while Valerie drove and Rex happily paced from one side of the narrow backseat to the other. The leg room back there would be a challenge for Derek, but it seemed to suit Rex to a T.

For the fifteen or so minutes they'd been driving the load of pumpkins from the Hayeses' farm, Valerie had thrown out ideas for places that were easily accessible for photo shoots. On a clear day like today, everything Derek saw had potential. He'd felt more creative inspiration in the last few days than he had in years.

At a sign that read *Fraziers' Famous Corn Maze*, Valerie pulled off the road. She had told him they were delivering a load of pumpkins to a farm for resale, but the sight in front of them wasn't at all what Derek had expected. Next to a gleaming white two-story farmhouse, a dirt field was practically filled with cars and school buses. Several kids ran and played in a grassy area lined with picnic tables. Behind them, a couple of square buildings looked like a carnival arcade, and a single-file line of adults, kids, and even some dogs, moved slowly past a pair of ticket-takers into a gate-like opening in a wall of corn stalks.

He let out a low whistle. "You didn't tell me we were coming to the Disneyland of rural Montana."

"The Fraziers do the corn maze every year." Valerie smiled as she maneuvered around a group of kids being led in a line from one of the buses toward a big, red barn, which had a sign over the door reading *Tickets and Fun Found Here*. "It's a popular field-trip location for schools from miles around."

Valerie wended her way through the parking area to the back of the barn, where three men sat in front of a couple of large aluminum tubs, peeling the husks off corncobs. At the sight of the truck, the older man waved and all three stood.

"That's Mr. Frazier and two of his sons, Aaron and Chad." Valerie shut off the engine. "Come on. I'll introduce you."

Before they'd even made it out of the cab of the truck, Aaron and Chad had started unloading the pumpkins into wheelbarrows.

"Well, if you ain't a sight for sore eyes." Mr. Frazier grabbed the brim of his well-worn trucker hat and adjusted it. "We was just sittin' here sayin' we was about to run outta pumpkins. They've been movin' extra good this year."

"That's encouraging." Valerie released Rex from the backseat, then held out a presentational hand toward Derek as he rounded the front of the truck. "Mr. Frazier, this is Derek. He's helping out around our place for the winter."

Mr. Frazier gave Derek's hand a firm, work-roughened shake, then Derek grabbed another wheelbarrow. While he assisted Aaron and Chad, he noted that Mr. Frazier removed what looked like a check from his pocket and handed it to Valerie.

Valerie looked at it and frowned. "Oh...this is more than you owe."

She tried to return it to him, but he gently pushed her hand back.

"Consider it a tip. We're havin' a good season so far, and we want to bless you and your dad. You put that toward your tax bill."

"Thank you." She gave him a quick hug. "From both of us."

"Now, you know we're all like family 'round here. You'd do the same for us. The state ain't taken' your farm if we all have anythin' to say about it."

That caught Derek's attention. The Hayeses were in danger of losing their farm?

Not wanting to let on that he'd overheard this information, he pushed his wheelbarrow into the barn. One of the two young men introduced himself as Aaron and told him to unload the pumpkins into the large bin outside the gift shop—a small building that appeared to do double duty as a storage shed.

After making a second run, Derek returned the wheelbarrow to the barn, which echoed with the happy voices of people waiting in line to buy their tickets.

He was about to head to the truck when he saw Valerie and Rex coming his way.

Clasping her elbows against the chilly air, Valerie smiled. "You have gone above and beyond helping me out today. I'm actually ahead of schedule."

"My pleasure."

A group of teens walked by, all glued to their phones.

Derek chortled. Kids were the same all over. "I take it they have cell service out here?"

"Hit and miss. There's a tower up the road a ways, past the Frazier farm, for those rich people who came in and bought up property so they could *get away from it all*. I guess cell service isn't one of the things they need to get away from."

At the sound of children laughing, they turned to watch a group of kids wearing bright-orange vests over their coats skipping toward the snack stand. The comforting nostalgic feeling of this place made Derek want to linger.

"You know..." An idea brewed. Sure, it was a longshot, but what did he have to lose? "That corn is calling my name." He offered her his arm like an escort at a debutante ball. "May I buy the lady an ear?"

Releasing her elbows, she held up her palms and started to shake her head. "No...I—"

"Come on. Humor the city boy."

When he raised a brow, along with his offered arm, she let out a breath and dropped her hands.

"Now that you mention it..." She sniffed the air and looped her arm through his. "That smell is irresistible."

His chest warmed, even as his stomach growled.

A few minutes later, they collected their buttery, seasoned cobs, along with a couple of hot apple ciders, from the counter at the snack stand.

"Your order will be right up." The young blond working there—Annica Frazier, according to her name tag—looked like she might be a year or two out of high school. At the sound of a cheerful ringtone—was that the *Batman* theme?—she removed a cell phone from her pocket. "Frazier Farms...uh-huh. Okay. Hang tight... Hey, Jimmy." She tapped the phone and called out to one of the boys cooking corn. "Some kids are stuck at the tower."

"On it." Jimmy removed his apron and headed out a door in the back of the snack stand.

Valerie laughed. "That happen often?"

Annica shrugged one shoulder. "Often enough."

"Why did they call your cell phone?"

"Because our business phone is in the house." She rolled her eyes. "I gave up on Dad getting around to putting an extension out here. I just forward the Bat

Phone to my cell." She nodded at a food tray that one of the boys had set on the counter. "There you go. See you tomorrow night, Val."

As they walked away, scanning the tables for a couple of available seats, Derek asked, "What's tomorrow night?"

"Janet's bachelorette party."

"Janet." They set their snacks down on an empty table. "That's the sheriff's fiancée?"

"You've been paying attention."

"I pick up on things."

He sat, and was about to dig in when he recalled that Valerie and her dad made a habit of saying grace before meals. Seeing that she had closed her eyes, he did the same.

After a few words of thanks from Valerie, Derek took a bite of the corn and immediately wished he'd gotten two for himself. It was honestly nothing like the pre-husked ears that came on a plastic-wrapped Styrofoam tray that he sometimes got at his local Aldi. A guy could get used to this.

"Mmmm." Valerie gave a slow blink, apparently sharing the same appreciation. "This was a good idea, City Boy."

"Agreed."

Taking another bite, Valerie looked around like she was observing the activity now that she'd slowed down enough to notice. She swallowed. "My parents brought me here every year when I was a kid. The way I looked forward to it, it might as *well* have been a trip to Disneyland."

He traced her gaze to where a bunch of happy kids tossed rings onto plastic corncobs and shot cartoon ducks.

"I haven't been to a shooting gallery in years." He smiled. "Care to go test your aim?"

"Uh-uh. For me, it's more of a spectator thing." She shuddered. "I don't like guns."

"They're pretend guns."

"Yeah, but they *look* real." She cupped her hands around her cider. "Poor fake ducks." Taking a sip of the hot drink, her gaze grew wistful. "When I was a teenager, the big thing was to go through the maze at night."

"At night? You mean, you snuck in?"

"No!" She chuckled. "I can't imagine my friends, especially Jeremy, doing something like that. No, it's open late on Friday nights." Holding her cob with both hands, she twisted in her seat, then used her elbow to point at a large sign near the entrance to the barn.

"Friday Night Dark Harvest." He shuddered. "Sounds creepy."

"It's fun to be scared when you know you're not really in danger."

The way her gaze fell let on what she was probably thinking. Real danger, even the threat of it, wasn't any fun at all.

But Derek didn't want her to dwell on that now. "How long has it been since you've gone through the maze?"

Her expression lifted. "Oh, gosh. Not since high school." She took a bite of corn. "We're all busy. Most of my friends are starting their own families. Unless I'm making a delivery, I don't even think about coming out here."

He tipped his head sideways. "We're here *now*." Having made quick work of his corn, Derek rolled up the paper tray and tossed it into a nearby trash can. "What do you say?"

"Now?" Her brow creased. "I have work to do."

"But you said yourself, you're ahead of schedule. You can take a few minutes to have some fun."

She wiped her mouth with a napkin. "You're becoming a bad influence on me, you know that?"

"An influence, maybe." He held up his

palms like two plates on a scale. "But is that influence bad..." He lowered one hand and raised the other. "...or good?" He reversed his hands.

Laughing, she shook her head. "I guess that remains to be seen."

Biting her lip, she looked down at Rex, who gazed up at her as if he understood the meaning of the word *fun*, and was all for it. Derek mimicked Rex's puppy dog eyes.

Breaking into a smile, she threw her hands up. "I can't argue with both of you. Let's do it."

As they gathered their trash and stood, Derek felt a lightness in his chest. The thought that she might be warming up to him didn't feel half bad.

Chapter 13

Darting through the maze with Derek and Rex, Valerie felt like one of the kids. How could she have forgotten how much fun this place was? Next to her, Rex did a happy little hop, something Valerie hadn't seen him do since he was a puppy. *Guess this is good for him too.*

"Oh, man." Derek raised his hands in surrender as they rounded a corner and came up against a dead end.

As they turned around and headed back the way they'd come, Valerie pointed to a hand-painted sign that read *Tower*. "We're almost at the middle. There's a tower there, so you can get your bearings." As they rounded another corner, her gaze skimmed the top edge of the stalks. "There."

She pointed to what they could see of the red roof of the two-story structure that resembled a fire lookout tower. One more turn and they came out at the open area surrounding the structure's spindly base.

"We going up?" Derek asked.

"Got to." She shrugged. "All part of the fun." She looked down at Rex, whose ears had drooped. "Sit, Rex. Stay." She turned to Derek. "The stairs are too steep for him, and he hates the metal mesh."

"After you." Derek waited for a couple of enthusiastic middle schoolers to finish bounding down the steps, then held out his hand.

Together, they climbed the stairs that were so steep they almost qualified as a ladder.

As they emerged onto the platform, Derek scanned the three-hundred-sixty-degree view. "Now that is worth all the trouble it took to get here." He took his camera from his shoulder bag, which he'd retrieved from the truck after they ate, and started clicking.

She watched him with admiration. "You always experience life through the lens?"

He gave her a playful side-eye. "Just doin' my job, ma'am."

"Oh, I wasn't criticizing. I like how you see things."

Facing her, he held up the camera, giving her a *may I?* look.

Flinging one hand behind her head, she did an exaggerated fashion-model pose, then laughed and leaned on the waist-high wooden railing next to him.

When it gave slightly, she remembered that it was even older than she was, and shifted her weight off of it.

"Look at that mountain range." He took aim at the nearby mountain that looked like it had been dipped in icing.

"That's Sugar Peak. A very distinctive landmark."

"Sugar Peak, huh?" He snapped a shot. "Sweet."

She blew out a laugh.

Lowering the camera, he looked past her at the old-fashioned red phone, which had been attached to the pedestal up here for as long as she could recall.

"That the famous Bat Phone?"

"Sure is. If you're really lost and you need help getting out of the maze, you pick up the receiver and it automatically connects you to the Fraziers' business phone."

"What an a-maze-ing idea." With a smirk, Derek headed for the stairs.

Chuckling, Valerie followed. "How long have you been waiting to say that?"

Tossing a smile over his shoulder, he started down. "You don't think I can be spontaneously hilarious?"

She answered with an exaggerated roll of her eyes. "I think your humor is a little on the corny side."

"Aw..." Derek looked back at her again. "I'll try to do butter."

She gave him a well-deserved playful swat on his shoulder, which he responded to with a melodramatic "Ow!"

Once they had reunited with an overjoyed Rex, they took the path opposite the one they'd emerged from. It spilled into an open area with three other paths leading out from it like the spokes of a wheel.

Valerie examined their options. "Which way?"

Derek watched as a group of middle schoolers came from the path to the left and continued straight, while a couple of young moms carrying toddlers went to the right.

"Well, Dorothy and Toto..." Derek crossed his arms in front of his chest, extending his index fingers. "People do go both ways."

"You couldn't resist that one, could you?"

"Didn't even try." When the middle schoolers reappeared and darted down the path to the right, Derek tipped his head in that direction. "Come on."

Valerie followed his lead, while Rex ran ahead a few paces, then turned as if to say *What's taking you so long?*

Derek caught up to Rex, who happily trotted alongside him. The pang of betrayal that Valerie had felt when Rex had first taken to Derek had softened into a feeling of security. Rex was a man's man of a dog, who made no secret of his feelings for Dad, Jeremy, Joe, and

Valerie's other male friends. It was reassuring that Derek had won his approval too.

When a line of kids wearing neon-green vests embroidered with the words *Dayton Springs Montessori School* wound around Valerie like a snake, she paused to let them pass. Tilting her head back, she appreciated the crystal-blue sky. What a perfect day to take a field trip. Or to play hooky from work for a little while.

She'd been worried about making enough money to pay their tax bill and get through the winter, but today, she was overcome with a calm reassurance that everything would be okay. The farm was solidly on track to get the harvesting done before the first frost of the season. They had more than enough inventory to fill their upcoming orders and stock their stand at this year's fall market. Taking a little time away from work seemed to be resetting her perspective. Maybe Derek wasn't such a bad influence after all.

The happy chatter of the school kids faded, and Valerie lowered her gaze. Ahead of her, a hand-painted sign that said *This Way*, with an arrow pointing in either direction, stood on a post where the path ended in a T. She had no idea which way Derek and Rex had gone.

Suddenly, her face went cold. No one was visible up ahead, and the dirt and dried plant debris on the path gave no clues. Her heart kicked it up a notch. Why hadn't she paid better attention?

A rustling sound brought her swiftly around just as a section of stalks a few yards back on the right side of the path swayed and something black disappeared into the field.

She jerked back. *What on earth...?*

Keeping her eyes on the still-shifting corn stalks, she took a few steps backward, then whipped around and launched forward. At the intersection, she hesitated. To the left, she saw no one on the path. But if it had been a person she'd seen, they could cut through the field on that side. She pivoted to the right, just as a pair of strong hands grabbed her shoulders.

"Hey..." Derek loosened his grip. "You okay?"

Closing her eyes, she deflated. It was Derek. She was safe.

Feeling Rex's warm tongue on her hand, she looked down and patted his head. "I'm fine...I just..." She turned back to where she had seen the stalks move. "I thought I saw someone in the corn..."

Eying her narrowly, he let go of her arms. "You want to show me where?"

Nodding, she walked back to where she'd seen the movement, but there was nothing to indicate that anyone had been there. No broken stalks. Not even a footprint.

Had she imagined it? Or had it been a

crow, coupled with her overactive imagination?

She shook her head. "I think I got a little spooked is all." No longer in the mood for frivolity, she forced a smile. "You figure out how to get us out of here?"

Still studying her, he pointed to where he and Rex had emerged at the T. "I heard some kids shouting about what a *cinch* it was just past that turn. I think the way out is pretty straightforward."

"Great." Whistling for Rex to follow, she set out, grateful for her bodyguards, both human and canine.

Chapter 14

While Mr. Hayes dug through his collection of board games in a dining room sideboard, Derek stoked the fire in the living room.

"Haven't played Scrabble in a month a' Sundays." Mr. Hayes freed a box from the stack and set it on the dining table. "I probably should warn you, though. I play to win."

"Wouldn't want it any other way."

Derek chuckled.

After a full Friday spent helping Valerie with the pumpkin harvest, then taking a break to get some amazing nature shots, Derek looked forward to a guys' night with Valerie's dad. Scrabble and nachos sounded just about right.

As he stood back to admire the crackling fire, a creaking sound caught his ear and he turned to see Valerie coming down the stairs with Rex on her heels.

Holy cow.

Every molecule of saliva evaporated from his mouth. If he had appreciated her country-girl beauty, and he most certainly had, the sight of her dressed to go out kicked it up to a whole other level.

She wore a tentative smile and a flowy lavender dress that somehow managed to be both modest and alluring. The sheer sleeves ended at her elbows, and the full skirt hit just barely below her knees, revealing...*wow*...a pair of shapely calves, made all the more intriguing by the just-high-enough heels of her cream pumps.

Realizing that she'd caught him staring, he looked away, rubbing the back of his neck and gazing absently into what he assumed to be an office just past the stairway. Before he could try to find his voice to tell her how incredible she looked, Mr. Hayes walked into the living room. It was a good thing too, because Derek probably would have tripped over his tongue fumbling for the right words.

"Sweetheart." Mr. Hayes's voice, on the other hand, sounded fatherly and warm. "You are a vision."

"Thanks, Dad." Entering the living room, she ran a hand over her hair, which she wore down with the front strands loosely caught up in clips on the sides of her head. "It's great to remind myself I'm a woman every once in a while."

Looking away for fear of his cheeks turning to two red beacons, Derek tried not to think about how hard it would be to forget that fact. She was a woman, all right. A very special woman.

"You sure you don't want one of us to drive you?" Mr. Hayes raised a graying brow. "I hate to think of you being out there on the road—"

"Carrie and I will be just fine. We'll be in her car, and I doubt anyone's tracking *her*. Besides, I want you two to relax and enjoy tormenting each other over word scores, and eating too many jalapenos."

"Speaking of that..." Mr. Hayes clapped his hands together. "Time for me to get dinner going."

As he retreated into the kitchen, Derek looked at Valerie. By the way her eyes twinkled as she rolled them upward, he was pretty sure she suspected her dad's intentions every bit as much as he did. Not that he minded, of course.

Facing him, Valerie opened her mouth to speak, but stopped at the sound of a car outside. "My ride's here." She started for the entryway.

"Have fun." He followed after her. "Wait. Bachelorette parties aren't anything like—"

"Uh-uh-uh." She held up her hand like a stop sign. "What happens in Luxton stays in Luxton." Grabbing a cream-colored wool coat off the hall tree, she broke into a chuckle. "Which is about as wild as it sounds. We're having dinner, then…" Putting on her coat, she made a show of looking toward the kitchen, where her dad had retreated. "Ice cream cake." She winked. "Don't tell my dad."

With a smile, she flipped her gorgeous length of hair out from under the collar of her coat and opened the door. She gave him one more smile before turning to wave at a car parked at the end of the walkway. Derek stepped out onto the porch and watched until she was safely in the car and it pulled away.

Hearing a whimper, he looked down to see that Rex had joined him. He bent to pet him.

"She'll be back, boy. Now, come on." He stood and went back inside, then waited for Rex to follow. "It's guys' night, and you, my friend, are one of the guys."

"See, this is why I like to allow extra time." Carrie pushed open the door to the gas station convenience store, awakening its welcome-in jingle. "I didn't realize my tank was so low."

"It's no problem." Valerie entered after her, appreciating the warmth of the store on this cold evening. "I'd rather stop now than on our way home."

"Me too." Carrie started for the checkout counter, where a couple of twenty-something employees stood chatting with each other, then pivoted. “Hey, I’m grabbing a water. You want one?”

“Sure.”

They walked past the rack of chips and cookies, and the prepared-foods counter where hotdogs glistened on a carousel and nacho cheese sauce dripped from the spout of a pump. The smell of pizza and hotdogs made Valerie’s stomach growl, adding to her excitement about the dinner they were heading to. Benedict’s Italian Bistro was so much better than anything this place had to offer.

“When am I going to meet this Romeo of yours?” Carrie tugged open one of the glass doors of the refrigerator case and grabbed two water bottles.

“He’s not my *Romeo*, and you could have come to the door when you picked me up.” Taking one of the bottles, Valerie noticed a man in the far back corner checking out the beer selection.

"I didn't have a chance." Carrie allowed the door to close with a *thwunk*. "You came flying out of the house like it was on fire."

"I did not." Looking around the well-stocked store, a thought struck her. "You know, since we're here, I should pick up a couple of things. With just the one vehicle, we might not make it to the market for a few days."

Carrie popped her phone out of the pocket of her purse. "It's only five thirty. We've got time."

From the corner of her eye, Valerie saw the beer guy turn his head in their direction then allow his gaze to linger. She'd only glanced at him briefly, and he hadn't looked familiar, but she could be wrong. If he was one of the farm's customers or someone she just hadn't seen in a while, she didn't want to be rude.

When she met his gaze, his lips raised in a subtle smirk. His eyes traveled to her feet and back to her face, then he slowly returned his attention to the beer.

Valerie shuddered. His dark, unkempt hair and unshaven face hid what were probably handsome features. Greek, or Italian, maybe. But no, he didn't look familiar, and the way he had leered at her gave her the creeps.

"What do you need to grab?"

Realizing she'd been distracted by the scruffy beer guy, Valerie turned her focus back to Carrie. "Oh...uh...bread, for sure. Maybe a box of cereal." She started down the closest aisle, even though it was lined with cookies and chips—nothing she needed. Suddenly, she felt anxious to get out of there.

At the end of that row, they rounded the corner and Valerie looked down the next aisle. Bread and cereal. *Thank goodness*. She grabbed a couple of loaves of sandwich bread, not even caring what the brand was.

"Your dad likes Corn Flakes, right?" Carrie had made her way down the row and was scanning the offerings.

"Um...yeah, that's great." Valerie's gaze darted from one end of the aisle to the other, but she saw no one. She could hear voices coming from the front of the store, and the door jingled. With any luck, that had been the sound of the beer guy making his purchase and leaving.

Carrie joined her, hugging a family-size box of Corn Flakes. "What else?"

"Umm..." There were more things that she needed, but it was no use trying to remember what they were. Her mind had gone blank in the cortisol rush of real-or-imagined stranger danger. "Actually, this should do it."

"'Kay." Shifting the box to one arm so she could access her purse, Carrie started for the front of the store. "Next time Grandma and I head into town, you can give me your shopping list. You've got all those men to feed."

"You're the best." Valerie hoped her voice sounded normal, because her body wouldn't stop quivering.

To her relief, the creepy stranger was nowhere in sight as they approached the checkout. One of the employees was grabbing some cigarettes from the rack behind the counter for an older man in a camo coat and a trucker hat, while the second employee mopped up a spill under the soda machine. She and Carrie stepped up behind the cigarette man as he told the clerk which gas pump he'd used.

Valerie's stomach rumbled. "I'm so hungry."

"I haven't been to Benedict's in ages." Carrie bounced on the toes of her cute Frye ankle boots. "What are you going to order?"

Aware that someone had stepped into line behind them, Valerie cautioned a peripheral glance. Her breath caught. It was the creepy beer guy, holding a case of Budweiser and standing a little too close.

"I..." She faced forward, not wanting him to know he was making her uneasy. "I haven't decided. How about you?"

"I think the pumpkin ravioli. I'm so glad they've started their fall menu."

"Yeah, that sounds good."

Valerie exhaled as the man in front of them finished paying and stepped away. They moved up to the counter and Carrie gave the young man her pump number then swiped her card. At least they'd be able to make it out to Carrie's car while Creepy Guy paid for his beer.

"I can help you over here." Moving into place behind the second register, the other employee waved Creepy Guy over.

Shoot. Valerie swiped her card as the first employee began ringing up her purchases. She snuck a glance at the man next to them, who had taken out a crumpled wad of bills and dropped them on the counter.

When her card terminal flashed *Approved*, she scooped up her items.

"Would you like a bag?" Her clerk didn't seem to notice she'd already started for the door.

"No, thanks."

She and Carrie stepped out into the dark parking lot and headed toward Carrie's car, which was parked on the other side of the far gas pump. Carrie continued chatting about appetizer options, clearly oblivious to Valerie's trepidation. As they walked, the sound of the bell over the door behind them struck fear in Valerie's heart. She picked up her pace as best she could in those stupid shoes. Why did women ever think heels were a good idea?

At the car, she clasped the door handle as Carrie crossed around to the driver's side. Heart racing, Valerie resisted the urge to look over her shoulder. She wanted to know where Creepy Guy was, but she didn't want him to see her looking. The last thing she needed was for him to consider any form of eye contact as an invitation.

Finally, Carrie opened her door and Valerie heard the click of her own lock disengaging. She yanked open the door and dove in, then locked it the second it was shut.

"You okay?" Carrie's brow creased as she fastened her seatbelt.

"Yeah, I'm just..." She watched as the creepy guy set his case of beer on top of a decades-old sedan so he could open the door. "That guy was weirding me out is all."

"*That* guy?" Carrie leaned forward as she started her car. "I didn't even notice him."

Valerie shook it off. "I'm just jittery. And hungry." She twisted around to set her items on the backseat. "Let's go party."

Chapter 15

"Whoa..." Derek studied the tiles in front of him, then looked at the board in gleeful disbelief. "Thanks to your S-I-N—"

Mr. Hayes snorted, nearly spilling his ginger ale. "On the board, son. Just to be clear."

Derek grinned. "Yes. On the board." He positioned a tile with the letter I on it, then one with an S.

Frowning, Mr. Hayes angled his head

to watch. "Well, I'll be."

Derek placed the last letter, completing his word. "Read it and weep." Sitting back, he heaved a sigh. "Guess I should've warned you...I play to win."

"Well, indeed you do." Mr. Hayes calculated the score. "Your *sinister*—"

"On the board." Derek winked. "Just to be clear."

"Yes." With a glint in his eye, Mr. Hayes finished tallying. "On the board. Your *sinister* won you the day."

Derek took a tortilla chip from his plate and scooped up the last remnants of ground beef and cheese, then popped it into his mouth. "Want a rematch?"

Yawning, Mr. Hayes checked his watch. "Think I'll take a raincheck. News starts in ten minutes. I like to keep apprised of the local goings-on."

"Fair enough." Derek began clearing the board. "Hope the women are having a nice time."

"I have no doubt that they are. Valerie has some good friends. Course, I'd like her to get together with them more often. She spends most of her waking hours 'round us menfolk."

"Women need other women, that's for sure." Derek paused. "If you don't mind my asking, what happened to her mother?"

The way Mr. Hayes's face paled made Derek wish he could retract the question.

"I'm sorry," he said. "It's really none of my—"

"No, no. It's fine. It's just that, when people say time heals all wounds, they don't mention that some scars never stop aching."

Derek felt the dull throbbing in his own chest that had become less frequent but no less intense. He knew what Mr. Hayes meant. As much as he hated the ache, it brought him an odd comfort. The trade-off for no longer feeling the pain of loss would be to forfeit the happy memories. And he never wanted to do that. Whatever Mr. Hayes's story was, Derek would bet the man felt the same.

He waited a moment, seeing that Mr. Hayes seemed to be gathering his thoughts.

"It was cancer," he finally said. "Same as so many folks. Valerie was thirteen, so it was hard on her."

"Hard on both of you."

The glisten in Mr. Hayes's eyes offered a harsh contrast to his weak smile. He nodded slowly. "We made it through. I try not to think about how different our lives would be if..." As his voice trailed off, his gaze grew distant. Then, he snapped back, blinking. "I should get these dishes done before the news comes on."

Derek pushed back his chair. "Let me help you—"

"Wouldn't hear of it." Mr. Hayes stacked the plates and stood. "Why don't you go give that fire a nudge and turn on the TV. Channel seven. I'll make us some hot cocoa."

Derek didn't argue. He had a feeling the man wanted a minute to himself to maybe let a few tears fall.

He'd been there enough times himself to know how that felt.

Valerie adjusted her little plastic tiara as she stepped out the front door of Benedict's, along with the other tiara-wearing bridesmaids, a few friends, and the radiant bride-to-be.

Janet, whose chin-length veil was attached to her head with a larger, sparklier tiara, threw her arms open and pulled Valerie and Carrie into a hug. "That was the best bachelorette party I've ever had!"

Valerie laughed. As co–maids of honor, she and Carrie had been tasked with planning the party Janet had wanted the first time she got married—to a man who'd turned out to be a greedy narcissist who faked his own death, then kidnapped their son and was now in prison. Even though Janet had told her sister, Sharon, she wanted a low-key, dignified evening with a few close friends, Sharon had thrown the party she herself had wanted. According to Janet, Sharon's motto in those days was "Drink now, ask questions later," which would explain why Janet's early escape from that party had gone unnoticed by Sharon and her pals.

Tonight had been much different.

"Too bad there was no ice cream cake left for Caleb." Carrie stepped back from the hug.

"He's three." Janet swatted the air in front of herself. "A cake made out of Tahitian vanilla bean ice cream and imported chocolate would be wasted on him. I've got some Choco-Tacos in the freezer, so no worries."

Since everyone else had parked in the lot next to the building, Valerie and Carrie said goodnight and headed for the primo spot Carrie had scored on the street right in front of the restaurant.

"Thanks again for driving, Care."

"My pleasure. I just hope you get your truck back soon. *And* that Jeremy figures out who put the tracker on it." She shivered as she removed her keys from her purse and unlocked her car door. "Reminds me too much of that thing I went through with Lucas. It was awful knowing that someone was out to get me."

Valerie felt a chill run through her at the comparison. Carrie's little brother had gotten her involved in a scary business deal a few years ago, and his old boss had gone after Carrie.

Shivering at that memory, she stepped

off the curb and around the front of the car. "I don't think anyone's out to get me."

Behind her, an engine roared to life. Then an ear-shattering squeal cut through the peaceful night. She turned to see a car with no headlights coming straight for her. As she stumbled around the front of Carrie's hood, the dark car swerved and took off down the street. It whipped around the corner and the roar grew fainter.

Carrie looked to where the car had disappeared, then back at Valerie. Her brow rose. "You were saying?"

After a restless night, Valerie awoke earlier than she wanted to. On a normal Saturday, she would sleep in for an extra half hour, but today, there was no point in trying. She was still too pent up after the excitement of the previous night.

She swung out of bed and stretched, prompting Rex to spring to his feet and stand there wagging his tail.

"Hey, my good boy. You ready for breakfast?"

A rhetorical question, if ever there was one.

Valerie stood and crossed to the window, hoping not to see frost on the ground. She pulled back the curtain and peered out. It was still dark, but the ground appeared to be blessedly free of frost.

She was about to step away when the door to the RV opened. She jumped back, then leaned against the wall, peering through the opening at one side of the window.

Derek stepped outside, bundled up in a thick coat and a wool hat, and carrying his camera. He pointed it upward, leading Valerie to look up too. The sky twinkled with stars against the black backdrop. Beautiful.

Suddenly wide awake, she hurried to dress and make herself look presentable, then crept down the stairs, not wanting to wake Dad. She opened the front door to let Rex out, as was their usual routine. Seeing that Derek had progressed from the RV to the yard, she grabbed her coat and stepped out onto the porch. From the top of the steps, she watched as Rex made a direct line to Derek, drawing his attention from his lens.

"Hey, boy." Derek greeted Rex, then turned toward the house. Seeing her, he perked up and headed her way. "You're up early."

"I was about to say the same. You want some breakfast?"

"Sounds great."

He started up the steps. Valerie whistled to Rex, who had run out into the front field, as he did every morning. He came running to the house and up the steps, then barreled in ahead of them.

Derek waited for Valerie to enter, then he followed and shut the door.

"How was the party?"

"Great." She hung up her coat and headed for the kitchen. "Janet was happy, so I call that a win."

"Not too wild, then?"

"Not at all. Well..." Once in the kitchen, she went to the coffeepot, which was already full, since she made a habit of setting the timer at night for the next day. "Not until after."

"What happened after?"

Sighing, she grabbed a couple of mugs out of the cupboard. "I stepped off the curb in front of the restaurant, and this car came out of nowhere and almost hit me." She lifted one shoulder as she filled the first mug, well aware that she was trying to downplay the incident. "Probably just some stupid kids out for a Friday night joyride."

"You're kidding me." He crossed around to stand next to her. "Is that what the police said?"

"We didn't report it." She handed him the mug.

"Valerie—"

"Neither of us got a good look at the car." Suddenly feeling irrationally defensive, she filled the second mug. "Luxton is where the teens congregate on the weekends. The police there deal with incidents like that all the time. There wouldn't be much point."

"But...what if it had something to do with—"

"It didn't." She set the coffeepot down a little too forcefully. "How could it?"

He ran a hand over his face. "You need a bodyguard."

"I don't need a bodyguard. I have Rex."

At the sound of his name, Rex cocked his head and swished his tail. Sipping her coffee, Valerie crossed the room to grab his dish.

"Rex isn't always with you. Obviously." Derek sounded genuinely concerned. "Do you have a gun?"

She scoffed at the notion.

"We do."

Valerie jolted, not realizing that her dad had appeared in the doorway. "What do you mean? We have a *gun* in our house?"

"Not just *a* gun." He entered the room and grabbed his favorite mug from the cupboard. "I have mine, and your mom had hers."

Valerie's mind raced. Mom had been gone for seventeen years. There had been guns in this house *for years* without her knowing? "Why didn't you tell me?"

"Because I know how you feel about guns." He poured his coffee and ambled over to the pantry. "I figured the day would come when I'd tell you."

"Dad!"

"What? I was right, wasn't I? Today is the day. Oatmeal sound good?"

Derek nodded.

"So..." Sorting through her jumbled thoughts, Valerie filled Rex's dish. "I'm supposed to just start carrying a gun around with me? I don't even know how to shoot."

Derek shrugged. "I can teach you."

She stared at him for a moment. "City Boy knows how to shoot a gun?"

"You think cities are gun-free zones?" Grabbing a pan from the rack over the stove, Dad chuckled. "You need to start watching the news."

Wanting to argue, but not really knowing why, she nodded at Derek's camera. "I'd rather learn how to shoot *that*."

Derek looked at his camera, then at her. "I'll make you a deal. I'll teach you how to shoot the camera if you also learn how to shoot the gun."

Valerie grunted. She set Rex's dish on the floor then folded her arms and leaned against the counter. "Look, you two. I think you're making something out of nothing. Just because someone wanted to track my truck doesn't mean..."

Both men looked at her with raised brows. She recalled her question to herself when her truck had broken down. Why *had* she never thought that carrying a gun was a good idea?

Sighing, she looked at Derek. "You busy today?"

Chapter 16

After breakfast and morning chores, Derek and Valerie trudged out to a field that was a safe distance from the house. As they approached a fence that looked perfect for setting up the targets, he scanned the area to make sure there'd be no danger of hitting anything they shouldn't.

He squinted at a large, gray house off in the distance. "That your closest neighbor?"

She looked at him, then toward the house. "That's still our property. It's the original farmhouse, but no one lives there."

"It's just sitting there empty?"

"Part of the roof gave out in a rainstorm. There wasn't money to fix it, and since my parents lived in the house they built, we just didn't do anything about it."

"Why did they build a new house? That one looks like it's got a lot of character."

"It does." She sighed. "Long story."

She looked away, implying that it wasn't a story she wanted to tell, so he wouldn't push.

At the edge of the field, he reached into the bag of damaged pumpkins he'd retrieved from the compost pile, and took out one that had been gnawed-on by some critter. He positioned it on a fencepost, then stepped back to make sure the height was good. It was a far cry from the professional range in DC where he'd learned to shoot, but it would definitely do the trick.

"I still don't get it." Valerie removed another pumpkin from the bag and followed his lead. "Why did my mom feel like she needed a gun?"

"Don't know." He looked around as they walked several paces away from their targets. "Living way out here. No close neighbors. Did you ever have times when it was just you and your mom at home? When your dad was gone or out in a field somewhere?"

"Of course. All the time." Her eyebrows shot up. "Oh...my mom wanted to know that she could protect *me*."

Derek shrugged. "I'm guessing that was a big part of it. I'm also guessing that your dad needed to be sure your mom was safe."

"So it was all about taking care of each

other."

"Now you're catching on." He caught her eye. "People get protective of their loved ones."

When she looked away, he hoped she hadn't taken that wrong. He cared about her safety—absolutely. But he hadn't meant to imply any right to declare anything like *love* just yet. He was here temporarily, and he had no intention of making things complicated.

He reached for the backpack Valerie had looped over her arm, and took out the small gun that had belonged to Mrs. Hayes. After showing her how to load it, he handed it to her, then retrieved and loaded his own gun.

Gripping the pistol with both hands, she rolled her shoulders. "They make it seem so easy on those cop shows."

"Actors have to look confident. Same's true for you. If someone's threatening you, you want them to believe you're willing to shoot them."

"So, I can just pretend I'm in a movie." She struck a cop pose. "Like I'm one of *Charlie's Angels*."

"I've never seen it, but sure." Using his own gun, he demonstrated how to grip it. "Now I want you to practice aiming at that pumpkin. See this." He pointed at the top of his gun. "Keep both eyes open, and line up the front and back sights."

He demonstrated, taking aim at one of the sorry-looking pumpkins, while she did the same with the second one.

"When you're ready, and you've aimed..." Derek pulled the trigger. A satisfying spray of orange shot out from his vibrant victim.

"Whoa." Valerie gave him a sideways look. "I don't know if I should be impressed or intimidated."

"I had good training." He nodded toward the fence. "Your turn. Just remember the steps."

"I know." She lifted the gun. "Ready, aim, splat." She adjusted her stance. "What did that poor pumpkin do to deserve this?"

He shifted so he could check her aim. "Pretend you're taking its picture."

"I'd rather do that than spatter its guts."

"The skill set is very similar."

She bit her lip. "Ready...aim..." Pulling the trigger, she jolted back.

A chunk of the pumpkin went flying.

She sputtered out a laugh. "I hit it. On the first try."

"Nice work, Quick Draw McGraw." He put his hand on her shoulder. "All you need is a little practice and you'll be putting Charlie's Angels to shame."

Smiling, she turned to face him. Suddenly, his supportive gesture felt a little too intimate and he removed his hand.

She cleared her throat. "At least we're

putting the rejected squash to good use."

He was about to respond when they were interrupted by a buzzing sound. "You get service out here?"

"It's hit and miss." Valerie handed him her gun and retrieved her phone from her back pocket. She looked at the screen. "It's Janet."

As she tapped on it to answer, Derek set the guns down and walked over to reset their targets. He glanced over at Valerie, whose serious expression made his pulse jump. A moment later, she crossed to him as she pocketed her phone.

"I have a maid-of-honor emergency, and I'm hoping you can help." Reaching him, she put her hands together in a prayer gesture. "Do you happen to have any experience with doing wedding photography?"

Valerie turned Dad's truck down the quiet residential street that would soon be home for Janet, Jeremy, and Caleb. Since the contractor's truck took up the space in front of their house, Valerie eased to the curb next to the junky house across the street.

"Uhhh..." Derek hunched down to get a good look out the driver's side window. "You weren't kidding when you said their place still needs work."

"Oh, gosh." Valerie sputtered out a laugh. "That's Crystal's house. And believe it or not, this is an improvement. People have been complaining, and Jeremy had to lower the boom."

"So this looks...nice?"

"By comparison. But it won't last. We've tried for years." Turning off the engine, she looked over at the freshly painted cornflower-blue, two-story bungalow. "*That's* Janet and Jeremy's place."

Derek let out a breath. "That's a *relief*."

While Derek grabbed his iPad, Valerie freed Rex, and the three of them headed for the house. Every time Valerie came by, the place won her over even more. Like most of the older homes in town, it had seen good times and bad. Seeing the improvements her friends were making gave her hope for the future of the town.

As they climbed the front steps, the unmistakable whine of a table saw grew louder from inside. Valerie rang the bell, hoping that Janet would be able to hear it over the construction sounds.

A moment later, the door opened to a wild-haired Janet, dressed in jeans and a paint-spattered T-shirt. Seeing them, she let out a breath. "I'm so happy you're here."

She gave Valerie a hug, then ushered them in, along with Rex, who proceeded to check out everything in the living room like a detective investigating a murder scene.

"You must be Derek." Janet offered her hand. "Thanks for saving the day." Furrowing her brow, she turned to Valerie. "Hey, are you okay? Carrie told me what happened."

So many things had happened lately, Valerie wasn't sure what she meant.

At her confused look, Janet pursed her lips. "That car. We all saw it tearing down the street with its lights off, but we didn't know it almost hit you."

"O-oh." Valerie snuck a look at Derek, who seemed alarmed by Janet's account. "That was nothing. Probably just some kids."

"Even so..." Janet was distracted by the appearance of the contractor, who waved her into the kitchen. "It could have been tragic. Excuse me a sec."

Janet disappeared into the kitchen and Derek set his iPad down on a card table in the center of the living room.

"Did you hear that?" He jabbed a thumb in the direction of Janet's exit. "She said it could have been *tragic*."

"But it wasn't. If it'll make you feel better, I'll mention it to Jeremy."

"I just want you to be safe."

"Now that I have my mom's gun...or *will* have it, once I feel confident enough to keep it on me—"

"Sorry about that." Janet reentered, wiping her hands with a paper towel. She gestured toward the folding chairs next to the table. "Thanks so much for doing this, Derek."

"I want you to see my work before you commit." He waited for the ladies to sit, then took the third chair. "You should only hire me if you like what you see."

"Considering that the only professional photographer who lives within fifty miles of Rockford is on a plane with his wife headed for Colorado at the moment, I'm pretty sure I'm going to like what I see."

Valerie leaned her elbows on the table. "I hope their daughter is okay."

"It's just a broken leg. But her parents want to be there to help with her three kids, so we'll figure this out." She brushed a strand of honey-blond hair from her face. "The next time I plan a wedding at the same time I'm getting ready to move into a house that's behind on renovations, remind me of this day."

"It's all going to be okay." Valerie patted her hand. "A week from today, you'll be Mrs. Jeremy Hingston, and none of these details will matter."

Janet clutched Valerie's hand, her face pinched with gratitude.

Derek unfolded a little stand and set his iPad in the center of the table. "I think Valerie told you that I'm a photojournalist, but I worked my way through college doing candid photo shoots and wedding photography."

Valerie leaned forward to watch his slideshow. How incredible was it that this man happened to be here right when they needed him?

What was it that Jeremy had said about God's providence?

A half hour later, a much more relaxed Janet saw Valerie and Derek out. "You have no idea what a relief it is to not have to scout out another photographer."

"Happy I can help."

Relieved that this problem had been so simple to solve, Valerie gave Janet a hug. "See you in the morning."

As they turned and started down the porch steps, Derek eyed her curiously. "What's going on in the morning?"

"Church. Worship starts at nine, so we leave at about eight thirty." Valerie paused, then added, "You're welcome to come along. Just be prepared to stay after service to help put together gift bags for the wedding guests. That's tomorrow's project."

When he didn't answer, she glanced his way. He was wincing, like her invitation had somehow caused him physical pain.

"Something wrong?" She checked for cars, then stepped into the street.

"No...no." Shaking his head a little too emphatically, he picked up the pace, suddenly in a hurry.

She dropped back a step and mouthed, "Okay."

Patting her thigh for Rex to follow, she crossed around the rear of the truck. She was about to open the door for Rex when Derek placed a hand on the side of the truck bed and looked like he wanted to say something. She stopped and waited.

"It's just that...tomorrow...Sunday...I

thought maybe I'd—"

A guttural sound erupted from behind Valerie. She whipped around to see Crystal's pit bull, Buster, come roaring across the junky yard and lunge at the chain-link gate, just a few feet from Valerie. It flew open and he came at her with murder in his wide red eyes.

Valerie stumbled back against the truck just as Rex lunged at Buster with a vicious warning growl. The two animals were instantly locked in battle with Rex clearly having the upper paw.

A bleary-eyed Crystal stumbled out her front door, tugging a bathrobe around herself. "Hey! Leave him alone!" Crystal's warning didn't seem to register with either dog.

Shaking, Valerie whistled. Rex immediately released the locked-jaw hold he had on his opponent. He obediently retreated to Valerie's side as Crystal grabbed the collar of a whimpering

Buster. She yanked him back into the yard and made a halfhearted attempt to secure the flimsy latch on the gate.

"He's bleeding," Crystal squawked. "Your dog attacked him."

"Your dog was the one who attacked." Derek had come around the front of the truck and was holding up a hand as if to warn both Crystal and her dog to stand down.

Valerie gave Rex a quick once-over. Confident that he didn't have any battle wounds, she opened the door to the back seat and he jumped in.

Keeping a grip on Buster's collar, Crystal waved a fist in the air. "I can't afford any more vet bills." She jabbed her index finger in Valerie's direction. "I'll sue you if I have to."

Valerie's body trembled, as much from the human attack as the canine one. "Crystal." She made an effort to keep her voice calm. "If you can't afford vet bills..."

She wanted to say, *you shouldn't own a dog*, but she knew that would only fan the fire. Instead, she said, "Maybe talk to Dr. Ames about her donation fund."

Crystal shot daggers at her. "I don't need no charity."

Make up your mind. Valerie took in a deep breath. *Either you can afford to treat your dog or you need help.*

As Crystal retreated into the house with a whimpering Buster, Derek adjusted the gate latch, then reached into the truck to give Rex a scratch on either side of his neck.

"Good boy, Rex." He tipped a nod at the gate. "We need to let Jeremy know what happened."

"There are kids in the neighborhood. I can't even think about what could happen if..." Valerie took in a deep breath and rubbed the sides of her arms.

Derek gave her a concerned look. "You okay?"

"Yeah. It's just that...I always knew Rex would protect me. But this is the first time he's ever really been put to the test."

Derek smiled. Then, to her surprise, he reached out and pulled her into a hug.

Instantly, her body relaxed. In this sea of confusing incidents, Derek felt like a safe harbor.

Too bad he'd be sailing away in a few short months.

Chapter 17

Valerie stood on the front porch, watching Rex disappear into the morning mist, which hovered over the field in front of their house. She shoved her hands into her coat pockets and shivered. It had finally frosted the night before, but they'd managed to prepare for it. Soon winter would set in, and the thought left her feeling chilled.

The door opened behind her and she

twisted a look over her shoulder. Dad stepped onto the porch, his hand still on the doorknob.

"You want to leave Rex out?"

"Sure. He can guard the house and keep the rabbits in check." Nobody could accuse her of not giving her dog a sweet life. He had the freedom of roaming the farm, and a nice dog door entry to the enclosed, heated back porch, where he had a soft bed and an all-you-can-eat, Kibble-and-water buffet.

"Should warm up this morning." Dad tugged the door shut, then made sure the lock had engaged. "Supposed to rain later, though."

Valerie smiled to herself. Dad and his farmer friends could have entire conversations made up of nothing but weather-speak.

While they made their way down the porch steps. Valerie let her gaze wander over to the RV, noting that the blinds were still closed. Derek hadn't come over for breakfast, but he had mentioned yesterday that he'd probably catch up on some sleep this morning. Still, she had hoped he might have changed his mind about going with them. After the incident with Buster yesterday, the subject of church hadn't come up again.

"You want me to go knock on his door?"

Startled that her thoughts had apparently been so transparent, she snapped her attention back to Dad. "N-no. He has things to do today."

"Mmm." Dad nodded, obviously wanting to say more, but resisting. He pointed toward the garage. "I'll bring the truck out while you give Rex his marching orders."

As Dad headed for the garage, Rex reappeared, wagging his tail and carrying a stick in his mouth. He trotted over to Valerie and dropped the stick at her feet, then looked up expectantly.

"Baby." She bent to retrieve the makeshift toy.

She was about to throw it when the sound of Dad opening the garage door distracted Rex. He took a couple of hopeful steps in that direction.

"You know you don't get to go to church, buddy. It's your job to hold down the fort. And if it rains before we get back, you get to track all the mud you want onto the back porch."

She bent to pet his head, then glanced at the RV one more time and sighed. So, Derek apparently didn't share her faith in God. Why hadn't it occurred to her before yesterday that she shouldn't even entertain a romantic thought about anyone before knowing the most important thing about him?

This should serve as a confirmation that her decision to remain single had been solid. And—she gave the stick a good toss into the yard—she needed to stick to it.

A distant noise alerted Derek that Valerie was in danger. Desperate to help her, he tried to scale some indiscernible obstacle that stood between them.

Slowly, it became clear that it was Rex's bark that had alerted him. The dog was restraining the danger, but he couldn't hold it off much longer. He needed Derek to step in...

Dragging his weighted eyelids open, Derek realized that the dream wasn't real, but Rex's persistent bark was. He rolled onto his side to look at the clock. Eleven minutes past nine? How had he slept so late?

He rubbed a hand across his face and sat up. Then a wave of guilt rolled over him. He should have gone with the Hayeses to church. Was that why he'd overslept—giving himself an excuse?

Deep down, he knew he wasn't ready to face God. Not after what had happened to Erin. Sure, he understood that God was everywhere, all the time, not just in church. It wasn't like Derek could hide—not really. But he could do a pretty good job of ducking and weaving.

Besides, he wanted to spend the day scouting photo locations. Even if that meant driving around in his house on wheels.

He stood and began the six-foot trek from his bed to the bathroom. Maybe he should consider buying a small car to tow. Or a motorcycle.

When he stepped out of the bathroom a minute later, it struck him that he'd never heard Rex bark for this long. For all Derek knew, that was what he did when Valerie left him home alone, but something sounded wrong. He went to the window over the kitchen sink and opened the shade. Peering out, he saw nothing but a haze hanging over the fields.

Just like the incomprehensible sense of dread that hung over his heart.

After the church service, Valerie stepped outside with Carrie and Janet to get the components for the gift bags. A strong breeze brushed her face and she looked up at the gray sky. Dad was right. It was going to rain later.

"The countdown's on, babe." Carrie threw an arm around Janet's shoulders as they walked. "Less than a week left of being a single Sally."

Valerie tried to ignore the tightness in her chest. She really was going to be the sole remaining single of their group. At least now she could say it was by her own choice.

A few stragglers were on their way out of church. On the other end of the small parking lot Valerie saw Maggie and her nurse, who had just positioned Maggie's chair next to a small, blue sedan.

"Hey, you guys." Valerie got the attention of the girls. "I'll meet you at the car. I just want to say hello to Maggie."

She peeled off and crossed to the sedan as the nurse bent to secure the locks on Maggie's chair.

Seeing Valerie, Maggie broke into a smile. "Valerie! Honey, I haven't seen you in ages."

"Sorry, I haven't been by with my dad." She bent to give the woman a hug. "You know how men are. He'll mention over dinner that he visited you that day."

"I know how busy you are. But now that I have Hannah, I'll be getting out more."

"Hi, Hannah." Valerie smiled at the fresh-faced woman of about thirty. "I'm so happy that Maggie has some help. How long have you been in town?"

"A couple of weeks. I was hired through an agency in Billings."

"Now I can come to church every week." Maggie fairly beamed. "Isn't that wonderful?"

"Yes, it is. Did you see my dad today? He's helping some of the men put together a wedding arch. My friend Janet is getting married next week."

"To the sheriff, I heard." Maggie held up her hands, jazz-style. "Isn't she a lucky gal?"

"She is. I'm helping her out too, so I should go. But I'll see you again soon. Nice to meet you, Hannah."

"Likewise."

Feeling buoyed, Valerie walked to where her friends were gathering shopping bags from the trunk of Janet's car. Since the two of them were loaded down, she grabbed the ones that remained.

"Looks like you cleaned out the Billings Hobby Lobby." Valerie quipped. "Did you leave anything for the other—"

A loud squeal turned their attention toward the street, where an old Ford pickup that had probably been white a few decades ago but was now a solid shade of *dirt* tore by at twice the speed limit.

Valerie rolled her eyes to the sky. *Crystal.*

Balancing her bags, Janet reached up and closed the trunk. "That woman has a problem.

"Hey," Carrie chimed in, "maybe she was the one who almost hit you. Same creative driving style."

"True," Valerie said, as the three started their trek back across the parking lot, "but it wasn't a truck."

Carrie twisted her mouth. "Doesn't

Crystal own two or three old junkers? It could have been one of those."

"Yeah." Janet grimaced. "But she has no reason to have it in for Valerie."

"She does now," Valerie muttered.

Carrie frowned. "What are you talking about?"

"Well, as of yesterday, she's probably blaming me for Buster getting taken away."

"What?" Carrie stopped in her tracks. "Why?"

Valerie paused, but encouraged Carrie to keep moving. "Buster tried to attack me."

"Wait..." Carrie said. "Friday you almost got hit by a car, and yesterday you almost got attacked by a dog? Does someone have a voodoo doll that looks like you?"

"Creepy." Janet shuddered. "We need to pray a hedge of protection over you."

"I'll take the prayer," Valerie said. "But

I think I was just in the wrong place at the wrong time. Anyway, when we told Jeremy, he said he's required to report it to animal control. Since there have been a number of complaints about Buster, they took him away."

Janet nodded. "Best thing that ever happened to poor Buster."

"That's terrible." Carrie slumped under the weight of her bags and the conversation. "They're not putting him down, are they?"

Valerie exchanged a look with Janet, which apparently wasn't lost on Carrie.

"Poor Buster." Carrie sounded like she might cry. "But that happened yesterday. So it doesn't explain the incident on Friday."

"Exactly." Valerie agreed. "It wasn't Crystal."

"Wouldn't surprise me, though," Janet said. "I've seen that woman pull out of her driveway like a bat outta hell."

As they started up the steps, Valerie said, “Sorry you have to live across the street from her.”

“Jeremy says we have to keep praying for our neighbors.” Janet sighed. “I’m praying she decides to move.”

Before stepping back inside, Valerie turned to scan the overcast sky. A storm was on its way. Something about that thought sent a chill down her spine. As happy as she was to be able to help Janet, a strange urge to get home made her hope the project wouldn’t take long.

Chapter 18

Valerie fidgeted in the passenger seat as Dad maneuvered his truck up their long drive. Putting the bags together had been fun, but she hadn't been able to shake the feeling that she needed to get home. She'd pretty much written it off to anxiety brought on by everything that had happened to her over the past several days, but now that they were almost there, she wanted to jump out of the truck and run the rest of the way.

As the buildings came into view, she sat forward. "That's strange."

"What is?" Her dad frowned.

"Oh...just that Derek's RV isn't there." Her face went cold. "You don't suppose he'd..."

No, he wouldn't take off without telling them. He'd been a little weird about her invitation to church, but then there had been that hug. And after they'd gone to update Jeremy about both the car and the dog, Derek had given her a photography lesson. He wouldn't just run off like a scared horse. She really needed to get a grip.

Without giving a response to her speculative half question, Dad curved around in front of the house.

Not seeing Rex, Valerie perked up. As a rule, even if he was asleep on the back porch, he'd hear the truck and come running. "I'll get out here." She undid her seatbelt. "I want to call Rex while you get parked."

After jumping out of the truck, she stood at the end of their walkway and whistled, then called his name. She scanned the fields, watching for movement. Nothing. Not so much as a sound.

After a minute of her whistling and calling, Dad came from the garage. "No sign of him?"

She shook her head. "No. You don't suppose Derek might have taken him on his photography outing, do you?"

"Seems unlikely. You get the young man's phone number?"

"Hey, you're the one who semi-hired him. Shouldn't that be your responsibility?"

"I think we both need to make a point of—"

The sound of an engine drew their attention to the road, where the RV ambled its way toward them.

"Well, it's good to see that one of our boys is accounted for." Dad squeezed her arm. "You see if Rex is with Derek, and I'll see if he's in the house."

Clutching her arms, she stood there waiting while Derek swung around and parked. She started toward the RV, hoping to see Rex jump out, but also hoping he wouldn't. She didn't want to have to give Derek a lecture about the evils of dognapping.

When the driver's door opened and Derek got out and started toward her, anxiety won out over relief.

"Hey." He gave her a hesitant smile. "How was church?"

"Good, but..." She sighed. "You don't have Rex with you?"

"N-no." His face turned serious. "To tell you the truth, I didn't see him at all this morning. I heard him, though."

"Heard him...?"

"Yeah. He was barking like crazy a little after nine. I thought maybe—"

"Sweetie?"

They turned toward the house, where Dad stood in the front doorway waving them over.

Valerie's heart jumped into her throat as she exchanged a look with Derek and bolted for the house. Without needing to be told where to go, she made a beeline for the back porch. There, her boy lay on his bed, his chin resting on his paws, eyes wide with self-pity.

"Aw...baby." She plunked down on the floor next to him, aware that Dad and Derek were hovering over them.

"You think he got into something he shouldn't a'?" Dad asked.

She stroked Rex's soft head, thinking back to the handful of times he'd been under the weather. "That or he's got some kind of bug. It happens."

That was true, but why now? Didn't

she have enough on her plate without having to worry over a sick pup?

Having been reassured by a phone call with Dr. Ames, the town veterinarian, Valerie had kept an eye on Rex all day. While he hadn't had much of an appetite, he'd lapped up plenty of water, and had even gone outside to wander around and munch on grass a few times.

Now, as she clobbered Derek at Uno, and Dad washed the dinner dishes, Rex napped on his favorite rug in front of the fire.

"Uno!" Valerie couldn't help gloating a little as she dropped her remaining card on the table.

"Oh...man." He set down his cards and shook his head. "Well, I can't say you didn't warn me you were good at this game."

"I learned to be competitive at an early age." She gathered the cards and began shuffling. "Another round?"

"I think I've had enough defeat for one evening." Derek looked over at Rex. "He seems normal, yeah?"

"I'm praying it's just one of those things." After the week she'd had, she really didn't need one more worry. "Dr. Ames said if it's just a bug he should be better by morning."

Dad entered from the kitchen carrying his evening mug of hot cocoa. "Kitchen's spic and span. Think I'll call it a night."

"I'm about to do that too." She slid the cards into the box. "Oh, Dad. I meant to ask if you saw Maggie in church today."

He glanced down, like her well-intentioned question had triggered the bad memories. That was why she generally avoided this subject, but if they never talked about it, how could they expect to move forward?

When he looked up, his smile seemed forced. “It was good to see her.”

“Mm. I think it’s great that she has help now. She deserves to get out more.”

Her dad just nodded. “Well. I’m heading to bed. Night.”

“Night.” Frowning, she watched him amble toward the stairs. She’d hoped for more of a positive reaction. But with everything he had on his mind, maybe he was just distracted.

“Who’s Maggie?”

Derek’s question jolted her from her thoughts. “She’s an old friend of my parents. She’s been in a wheelchair for years. She finally hired a nurse, so it looks like she’s getting out more.”

“So...why doesn’t your dad seem happy about it?”

“It’s not that he’s not happy.” She smiled sadly. Derek was perceptive, that was for sure. “It’s just...there’s so much to this story. Maggie's husband, Daniel, was Dad's best friend."

"Was?"

She nodded. "Since childhood. They owned this farm together. They were practically like family." She stood and returned the Uno deck to the drawer of the sideboard. "In fact..." She scanned the gallery wall in front of her, and pointed at one of her favorites. A group shot from one of many wondrous summer days spent at the lake. "That's her right there."

Derek stood and joined her. There was something so appealing about a man who showed genuine interest in things like this.

"Before the wheelchair."

"That's right. It would have been her last summer before."

"Great photo." He leaned closer to study the faces of the happy group standing on the shore of the lake next to a small boathouse. "That looks like a young

Mr. Hayes." He pointed at her dad, in his Bermuda shorts and short-sleeve shirt, holding up a string of sunfish.

"Sure is. He and Daniel—" She pointed out the nice-looking man in the goofy fishing hat who had his arm around Maggie. "—had just come in from the lake with dinner for all of us. Sunfish."

"Don't tell me that's you." His finger aimed at the smaller of two little girls in the image, and the only one who could possibly be her, considering that the older girl was an angelic-looking blonde.

"Guilty. Who else would have that wild hair."

"I think it's cute."

"Right. That's my mom next to me." A pang of something that felt like regret slipped over her almost unnoticed. Not wanting to stray from the story she'd started to tell, she went on before Derek could ask. "Anyway, Daniel's family owned the cabin. They used to invite us to go there with them."

He nodded, still studying the image. "Who's the little renegade?"

His finger hovered over the older boy standing behind her, looking at her pigtail like it was taking everything in him to resist pulling it.

"Zak. Daniel's nephew." She pursed her lips. "I remember doing my best to avoid him. He's next to his mom, so his dad must've taken the picture. He was probably standing on the front porch of the cabin." Stepping away, she fought a sense of melancholy. "I haven't seen any of these people in years. It's funny, the lake isn't far from here, but we never go there. We didn't go to the cabin again after Daniel died."

Derek turned to look at her. "When was that?"

"It was a long time ago. I was about five, so it would have been the winter after this picture was taken. One night, the

Kaufmans—Daniel and Maggie—were driving home in a snowstorm. They lived in the original farmhouse."

"The one we saw when we were out shooting."

"That's right. When they all bought the property, my parents built this place." She waved her hand at the surrounding walls. "Anyway, something happened and their truck went off the road. They were both in the hospital for weeks, and Mom and Dad ran the farm on their own. I remember that was a rough time."

"I bet."

"Unfortunately, Daniel didn't make it. And on top of not being able to walk, poor Maggie was left with huge hospital bills. Obviously, she wasn't able to keep their half of the business running."

"That's awful."

"My parents felt like they were responsible for her, since they were in business together. They paid her what they could afford for her half of the farm, and let her stay in the house on the other side of the property."

"She was like family."

"Yeah. Everybody always talks about how generous my parents were to let her stay on. That's why my dad gets embarrassed. He just saw it as doing the right thing."

"Of course." He rubbed the back of his neck. "So she lived all alone in that big house?"

"Crazy, right? I remember as a kid going over there sometimes with Mom or Dad to do things for her. I used to admire how she managed. She didn't use the top floor, of course, which I guess explains how it fell into disrepair."

"That's a shame."

"Then after my mom..." Swallowing, she looked down. Losing Mom was another story and not one she wanted to get into right now. "Anyway, everything got harder. Dad went over there less often. Then part of the roof came down in that storm..."

"Must have been scary for Maggie."

"It was kind of a blessing, though. I'm sure she felt isolated out there. She got a little place in town. I guess she gets enough from disability to pay the taxes and whatever else she needs. My dad still looks out for her. He's been a good friend."

"That's some story."

"Yeah." The clock chimed, startling her. By what was probably some Pavlovian response, she yawned.

"You need help getting Rex upstairs?"

"Let's find out." Starting for the foyer, she patted her leg. "Come on, baby."

Rex obediently hauled himself to his feet and followed. He wasn't moving at his usual brisk pace, but when they reached the bottom of the stairs, he headed up on his own.

She looked at Derek. "Guess we're

good."

Looking relieved, he grabbed his coat. After giving them both one more look, he said goodnight and left. Valerie followed Rex up the stairs. It had felt good to share that piece of their family story with Derek.

Now if only she could broach the subject with Dad in a way that wouldn't shut him down.

Chapter 19

Valerie forced her eyes open, gasping for breath. Her room was completely dark, but something had dragged her from sleep. What was it?

She rolled her head to one side. The softly glowing clock next to the bed told her that it was three thirty-three. Her head felt fuzzy. Rain pelted the window, but that couldn't be what had pulled her from sleep.

Then it came again. A soft, high-pitched whimper.

She bolted upright and practically flung herself out of bed and to the floor where Rex lay, panting and drooling.

"Baby..." Panicking, she stroked his side. He felt ice cold. His breathing was so shallow it was barely perceptible.

She stood but her legs were so shaky she had to hold onto the bed to get to the table where she'd left her phone. She fumbled to bring up the contacts, and finally found Dr. Ames's number.

Waiting for her to pick up, she went back to Rex. How was she going to get him to the car? Even with Dad's help...

But then she remembered. God's providence. She didn't have to do this alone.

Derek paced the length of the tiny waiting

room of the veterinarian's office, while Valerie sat in one of the molded plastic chairs with her head in her hands. Every now and then, he overheard a bit of her muttered prayer, which had been ongoing since Dr. Ames had told them to sit tight. It was good that it brought her comfort, although from Derek's experience, it wouldn't change the outcome.

He rubbed the back of his neck. How long did it take to pump a dog's stomach?

Needing to feel useful, he crossed to the hospitality stand next to the unmanned reception counter. He popped a coffee pod into the Keurig machine and positioned a cup in front of it. After filling that cup and a second one, he crossed back to the bank of chairs and sat next to Valerie.

She looked up, bleary-eyed. "Thanks." She took the offered cup and sipped from it, then cradled it in her hands like she found comfort in the familiar action.

"Tell me about Rex." Derek wasn't sure if it would help, but he remembered someone saying something similar to him about Erin in a waiting room not all that different from this one. He had a vague recollection that talking had made the pain a little less unbearable.

She smiled. "I got him when he was a baby. A couple of months old." She pointed to the wall opposite them, which was covered in photos of dogs and cats, along with an occasional rodent, lizard, or bird.

Tracing the wall with her finger, she stood up, and he followed.

"There he is." Her finger landed on an image of a plump-faced German shepherd puppy holding a stick in his mouth. "That was five years ago." She shook her head. "Feels like yesterday."

"You always have dogs?"

"My mom did. Lucy." Again, she searched the wall, then pointed to a yellow lab positioned a little higher up. "Mom really loved that dog." She meandered back to the chairs. "She died when I was thirteen." She sat. "My mom, I mean. Not the dog."

"Your dad told me." Derek lingered at the photo wall. Each shot captured a moment in the life of each beloved pet but told a whole story of love and companionship.

"Lucy and I bonded in our grief." She sputtered out a sad chuckle. "It might sound dumb, but knowing that Lucy missed her too really helped me."

Retaking his seat, he tried to think of something profound to say. When nothing came to mind, he said simply, "Dogs are pretty great."

"The best. After Lucy, I tried to convince my dad that he needed another dog. I worry about him being lonely."

"He wouldn't do it?"

"I think he'd had too much loss at that

point. Inviting someone in who wouldn't stick around forever didn't seem very appealing to him."

Sneaking a glance at her, he wondered if she was talking about herself too. He'd sensed a standoffishness about her, and that could explain why.

"A couple of years after Lucy," she continued, "I got Rex. I felt like I needed someone."

Derek was no psychologist, but he'd bet that Valerie had *stuck around* because she felt responsible for her dad. He'd venture a guess that she was sacrificing her own dreams to be there for her dad, which was noble, but maybe not the best thing for either of them.

Not wanting to pry, he took a side-door approach to his actual question. "So that's Rex's story. Now tell me about you."

"Me?" She looked at him with eyes that were warm and brown, and filled with emotion. "There's not much to tell."

“I’m sure that’s not true. What are your goals?”

“My *goals?*” From the way she said the word, it was as if he’d spoken Chinese. “Just keeping the farm afloat.”

“An admirable goal. What else?”

She sat up straighter, causing the chair to let out a *creak*. “In case you hadn’t noticed, that’s a pretty full-time job.”

“I know. But you’re allowed to have more than one goal.” To counter her evasiveness, he went with a different approach. “When you were a kid, how did you see your life?”

“You mean, what did I want to *be* when I grew up?” She let out a breath. “If you must know...I used to make things, like Christmas wreaths and little decorations. Sometimes I’d go with Dad when he did the deliveries and I’d sell my creations.” She shook her head. “Just a crazy thing I used to do.”

“There’s nothing crazy about that. I bet

you sold everything you made."

"Because people wanted to be nice to the cute little farm girl. But my dream was to start a country store on the property where we could sell our produce and locally made items." She lifted her cup to her lips. "And I wanted to travel."

That last bit came out muffled by the lid of her cup. Before he could ask her to repeat it, she opened her mouth to speak again.

"What about you? I know you're doing a book, but why here? In Middle-of-Nowhere, Montana?"

"Ahh, sneaky change of subject. But *if you must know...*" He made a sarcastic face as he mimicked her. "My family visited Montana when I was a kid, and I thought it was the best place on earth. Hiking. Horses. All the things that make up a city kid's version of paradise."

"But you've traveled all over since then. You still think *this* is paradise?"

"Pretty much, yeah."

"Huh." Sitting back, her brow furrowed in thought. "But you live an exciting life in the city. Why come here now?"

Her question hit like a gut punch. That wasn't something he wanted to talk about. Because face it, not wanting to deal with his reason for leaving had been the reason he'd left.

"You know how life is." It was his turn to be evasive. "Something happened and I decided I needed a change. At least for a while. When I thought about where I wanted to be, I remembered that *Montana* feeling."

"Something happened?" Turning in her chair, she met his gaze. "What was—?"

The door to the back opened and Dr. Ames came out, dressed in scrubs and looking weary.

Valerie couldn't get to her feet fast enough. "How is he...?" Her voice trembled.

The doctor's look of weariness turned to a light smile. "He's stable. I want him to stay overnight so I can keep an eye on him. It's going to be touch and go for about twenty-four hours."

Moving next to Valerie, Derek put his hand on her shoulder. This was good news, at least for now, but he couldn't shake the thought that someone had wanted to get her protector out of the way.

Which made him wonder...Is that someone going to come after me next?

Chapter 20

By mid-afternoon, Valerie felt the effects of her night that had been short on sleep and long on worry. She'd managed to be productive all day so far, but a cup of coffee would provide a much-needed jolt, so she wrapped up what she was doing and headed to the house for a little break.

A few minutes later, she took her mug of comfort to the back porch. Looking at Rex's empty bed, she blinked away tears.

Even though he was in good hands, his absence was like a knife to her heart.

Sipping her coffee, she willed the phone in her pocket to ring with good news from the vet. The more time that passed without any word from her, the more Valerie worried that something was wrong.

Needing to distract herself, she gazed out the window to where Dad, Derek, and the guys worked at clearing away the squash vines. The sunlight broke through the clouds, beaming onto the men like a spotlight. Funny, her photography lesson the other day had opened her eyes to the beauty that had surrounded her for her whole life. She liked seeing things through Derek's eyes.

On one of the hooks by the door, she noticed Derek's camera case. What had he said about the best way to photograph people? He liked to catch them when they didn't realize that they were being photographed. Well...he had said he wanted her to practice. She might as well practice what *he* preached. Smiling to herself, she removed the case from the hook and flung it over her arm.

Stepping out the back door, she shivered against the cold. Gingerly, she opened the latch on the case and removed the camera, then took off the lens cap and raised the device to her eye the way he had shown her. She could tell right away that the lens was smudged, something he had warned her about.

Fortunately, he'd told her he always kept lens wipes in his bag, so she opened the little pocket on the front and dug through a few items—some kind of camera cleaning tool, a memory card, his keys. There on the bottom was a soft blue cloth in a plastic cover. She quickly polished the lens and returned the cloth, then carefully aimed and took a few shots.

She checked her results in the

viewfinder. These were actually pretty good. She smiled at the thought of his face when he saw these on his camera.

Just as she was about to take another shot, the sound of her phone ringing sent her heart into her throat. She hurried back inside and set the camera on the table as she read the phone screen.

Dr. Ames. Taking a steadying breath, she tapped the green circle to answer.

"How's my boy?"

"Rex is doing fine." The effects of limited sleep were apparent in the vet's voice. "He's resting, but all his vital signs are good."

Some of Valerie's tension dissipated, leaving her trembling and weak-kneed. She looked up and mouthed, "Thank You, Lord."

"I overnighted Rex's samples to the lab in Billings." The doctor sounded serious. "I'm pleased that we got the results back already."

"So...you know what did this to him?"

"Well, yes. It's a bit of a mystery, though. There was a fair amount of bupropion in his system. Does anyone in your household take antidepressants?"

That wasn't at all what Valerie had expected. Some kind of plant or spoiled food, maybe. But a drug? "Not that I know of. My dad and I don't take anything..."

A thought stopped her cold. Had someone done this on purpose?

"You should ask everyone who works for you, just to be sure." Dr. Ames' no-nonsense tone felt daunting. "It could be that Rex got into someone's bag or maybe their car."

"Right..." She looked out again at the men in the field. Dad was always clear with their employees that they needed to disclose anything that might inhibit their ability to operate the machinery. But he hadn't mentioned if he'd asked Derek the usual questions. He wasn't technically an employee, so chances were good it hadn't occurred to Dad.

"You can take him home today," the doctor said, "but it's imperative that we figure out where the drug came from so it doesn't happen again."

After giving Valerie a few basic care instructions, Dr. Ames ended the call. None of this made sense. As far as Valerie knew, Derek was the only one who had been on the property yesterday morning, but even if he did have a prescription drug, Rex wouldn't have had access to it. And he wasn't a dog who ate just anything. Pills would have to be hidden in some kind of delicious food.

Derek wouldn't hurt Rex on purpose...would he?

That lingering question of how Derek had just happened to show up right when she'd needed help bubbled to the surface. He had witnessed for himself how protective Rex was of her. If anyone wanted to get to her, it stood to reason they would want to eliminate her *bodyguard*.

No...Derek wouldn't do anything like that. But if there was even the slightest possibility, she had to rule him out before entertaining the notion that someone else had gotten access to her dog. How could she do that?

Remembering that she had left the camera out, she quickly put it back in the bag. She was about to return it to the hook when a thought occurred to her.

His keys were in the pocket.

She stared at the bag in her hands, contemplating. The men should be occupied for some time. This might be her only chance to find evidence in his RV—if there was anything to find—but she'd have to move quickly.

After swiping the keys and hanging up the bag, she threw her coat back on, then went out the front of the house and made her way across the yard and the dirt drive. She did a quick surveillance of her surroundings to make sure no one could see her, then slipped around to the door on the side of the RV. Hands shaking, she tried the first key with no luck. But the second one easily slid into the lock, and the knob turned.

Guilt pricked her conscience. She had never done anything like this, but then again, she'd never suspected that someone was out to get her. If Derek couldn't be trusted, she needed to know.

She pushed the door open and peered inside.

For some reason, it was much cleaner than she expected. Not that she'd thought Derek would be a slob, but in her experience, men who were on their own without a woman to hold them accountable tended to let clutter accumulate. From what she could see, Derek was either very organized, or lived a pretty spartan existence. Either could be a result of all his traveling.

Reminding herself of her mission, she quickly found the bathroom and opened the medicine cabinet. Just the basics. Toothpaste, shaving stuff. No prescriptions at all. Moving swiftly, she checked the other obvious places. Bedside table. Kitchen. No drugs—or anything suspicious, for that matter.

Of course, if he'd emptied a bottle, it would be in the trash, not a cabinet. But the two trash cans she found—bathroom and kitchen—were apparently free of anything incriminating. Standing in the aisle of his kitchen space, she heaved a breath of relief. Nothing in her search indicated that she couldn't trust him.

She wanted...needed...that to be true.

Then her eyes landed on something that seemed out of place in this orderly home. A small photo was haphazardly clipped to the driver-side sun visor.

Curious, she eased forward. It was a picture of two people, the edges crumpled as if it had been handled a lot. As she got closer, her heart started to pound. Leaning on the back of the banquette dining bench, which backed up to the driver's seat, she felt an irrational feeling of betrayal.

In the photo, a beaming Derek embraced a gorgeous woman, her long, black hair wafting as if there was a breeze blowing through the beautiful natural setting in which they stood. Her head was tilted back, and he looked down at her, their eyes locked in a loving gaze.

Valerie fought back tears. The horrible feeling that she had found, not the evidence she had been looking for, but the evidence she needed, hit her like a punch to the gut. Derek had someone. An important fact that he had not disclosed.

A movement through the front windshield sent her pulse reeling. Dad and Derek were walking in from the field. Dad said something to Derek and peeled off toward the back door of the house, while Derek continued on, heading straight for the RV!

Flustered, she scanned the small space to make sure everything looked just as she'd found it. She fairly flew out the door and pulled it shut. Thinking fast, she raised her fist as if she was about to knock, just as Derek came around the corner.

He jolted to a halt. "Hey."

"Oh...hey." She feigned surprise at his appearance. "I just, um..." She fumbled for words. "Dr. Ames called. Rex can come home. I thought you might want to know."

"Fantastic." He broke into a grin.

She let out a breath. Seeing the relief in his eyes, she knew he couldn't be responsible for this.

"Does she know what made him sick?"

"Yeah...it was..." Putting her hands on her hips, she looked away. "It was a drug.

Bu-pro...something."

His eyes narrowed. "What's that?"

"Something that's in antidepressants."

"Ooh. And do you have any idea—"

"None. I mean...you don't happen to—"

"Take antidepressants? No. I don't even like to take pain killers."

Rolling in her lips, she nodded. Judging from the absence of any medications in his place, that rang true.

"So," he said, "I guess we need to visit Jeremy again. Have him add this to your case file."

"You think someone did this on purpose?"

"I don't want to scare you, Valerie. But I don't know what else to think, do you?"

Wrapping her arms around herself, she shook her head.

"Let's not worry about that right now, okay? I just need to go back to the house to grab my camera case and I can go with y—"

"No!" Why was she yelling? "I mean…I can get it." Wow, could she sound any more guilty? Shoving her hands into her pockets, she gripped the contraband keys. "I need to get the keys…*Dad's* keys. The keys to his truck."

In the seconds it took her to cut a wide arch around him and start for the house, she detected a puzzled look in his eyes. Of course, he had to wonder why she was acting like a nervous kook.

Her chest ached. He'd given her no indication of a romantic interest in her, but his lack of disclosure about having a special woman in his life felt like a lie. She had trusted him…but had she really? She'd broken into his home, after all.

He might have been less than truthful with her, but was she any better?

Chapter 21

"Hard to believe it's only three days till the wedding." Checking each item off on her order, Millie went through the last of the crates Valerie had stacked in the diner kitchen.

"Yeah, hard to believe." Rolling her sore shoulders, Valerie reviewed the invoice. Thanks to the wedding reception, this was nearly twice Millie's normal weekly delivery. She handed the invoice to

Millie. "You got room for all of this in your walk-in?"

"We'll make room." Millie smiled. "Johnny spent all week cleaning in there."

"You're both working extra hard this week."

"It'll be worth it to see Janet and Jeremy happy." Millie scanned the invoice, then gestured for Valerie to follow her to the small office, just off the kitchen. "Speaking of Jeremy, has he made any headway on your case?"

"Nothing new. And none of it makes sense." Placing her hand on her stomach, Valerie pressed against the worry that had been churning all morning. "It's like a bunch of weird coincidences that should fit together but don't."

"Does he think what happened to Rex has something to do with the other things?" Millie sat at her desk and opened the drawer to dig for a pen.

"He doesn't know." Valerie perched on

the edge of the chair next to the desk. "I mean, we have no clue how Rex got poisoned. I'm just grateful he's recovering." She was also grateful that nothing else had happened since then. They'd had a couple of days of everything seeming to return to normal.

Except that, in addition to the worry, Valerie had been plagued by a profound case of melancholia.

Millie tapped her chin with the pen. "Nobody else in town saw that red van but you and me?"

"Besides Derek, no. And whoever owns it must've left town." She ran her fingers over her eyes. "It's been a whole week, and no one's reported seeing it."

"Well, maybe that's good."

"I guess. It's hard not having answers though." And with the wedding this weekend, and the fall market next week, Valerie hated being so distracted. It hadn't been lost on her that this might have been someone's intention. But why?

"Oh, Hal was in for breakfast this morning." Millie looked up from filling out the check. "Said your truck will be ready tomorrow. That's good news."

"Yeah." Valerie wanted to be happy about that. But after what had happened, she wasn't sure she would feel safe driving it.

The back door opened and Derek and Johnny brought in the last of the order.

Millie swiveled around in her chair. "Honey, why don't you and Derek get that all put away in the walk-in?"'

"You got it, beautiful."

Johnny's chipper attitude always made Valerie smile. It was nice to see that he and Derek had hit it off. Not that this surprised her. Derek seemed to get along with everyone.

The more time she spent with him, the more he seemed like the real deal. Just a genuinely nice guy. Which made the situation with the mystery woman all the more confusing. Valerie had spent the better part of three days trying to figure out how to ask him about her without admitting she'd seen the photo.

Not that it mattered. If he had someone in his life who he wasn't mentioning, there had to be a reason. And he wasn't a romance candidate for her, so he didn't have to tell her everything.

As soon as the men disappeared into the walk-in, Millie pumped her eyebrows. "You might not have Rex right now, but I'm happy to see you're not alone."

Valerie leaned on the desk. "Derek has been a big help around the place."

"I'm guessing he makes a good bodyguard too." She signed the check. "Kevin Costner's got nothing on him."

"Between you and Carrie..." Sitting back, Valerie folded her arms. "I have to admit though, I do feel safer having him around, especially with Rex out of commission."

"Is he thinking about staying on?" Millie tore the check from the book and handed it to her.

"Don't get any ideas, Mill. He's only here for the winter." She slipped the check into her waist pack. "And I had better not need a bodyguard anymore by the time he leaves."

A flash of sadness accompanied the thought of him moving on in the spring. *Get a grip, Valerie*. Then another thought occurred, something she'd been trying to ignore. Their tax bill was looming.

Would they still own the farm, come spring?

"Dad, come on!"

Derek knelt on the floor of the Hayeses' living room, rubbing the sides of

Rex's face, and trying not to think about how lovely Valerie looked as she stood there calling up the stairs.

This was the second weekend he'd been there, and the second time he'd seen her dressed to go out. Tonight, the satiny blue pants suit she wore was perfect for the wedding rehearsal and dinner, which was where she and her dad were headed. That was, if Mr. Hayes ever finished getting dressed.

With a sigh, Valerie stepped into the living room. "I knew he'd forget how much time he needs to shower and shave and put on nice clothes. He should have come in from the field when I first told him to."

Straightening, Derek made an exaggerated roll of his eyes. "Parents. Am I right?"

She laughed. "A hundred percent." When Rex turned his attention toward her, she bent to run both of her hands across his back. "I really appreciate you hanging out with Rex tonight. I feel safer. You know...under the circumstances."

"Hey, it's my pleasure." He hadn't mentioned his lingering concern that if someone had come after Rex to make Valerie more vulnerable, Derek himself might be in the line of fire too. This had been a completely uneventful week, and he hoped his fears had been unfounded, but he was keeping his gun on him, just in case. "We're having a guys' night in. Sandwiches, kibble, and photo editing."

"Sounds like a wild time. Oh..." She took her phone out of her purse and tapped on it, then handed it to him. "Put in your number. Then I'll send you a text so you'll have mine."

He did as she asked. "Look at us, stepping into the twenty-first century." He handed the phone back to her.

"We're not *that* far behind the times."

They both turned at the creak of the stairs. Mr. Hayes appeared, looking very smart in a cream-colored cable knit sweater and blue slacks.

Valerie pressed her fingers to her throat. “My handsome date has finally arrived.”

“You didn’t think I’d stand you up, did you, sweetheart?”

“I was beginning to wonder.” She sent Derek a smirk. She’d been so standoffish to him all week that it was nice to see her showing some warmth again.

He’d attributed her coolness to the anxiety of all the incidents that had seemed to be targeting her. And he hadn’t forgotten the conversation he’d overheard about the threat that they could lose their farm. If she was worried about that, it could explain her distance.

He’d been looking for the right time to bring that up, but was it really any of his business? He was an outsider, still earning their trust.

And prying into their personal

business probably wouldn't help.

Chapter 22

All week, Valerie had wanted to talk to her friends about her discovery in Derek's RV, but they'd all been so focused on the wedding that she hadn't had a chance. So when she and Carrie had a moment to themselves in Carrie's kitchen, getting the rehearsal dinner ready to serve, Valerie had taken the opportunity to spill the beans on herself.

"I don't know, Val." Carrie placed half

a lemon in the citrus squeezer and pulled the handle down. "A picture doesn't necessarily mean anything."

"He's a photographer." Valerie sighed. "To him, photographs mean *everything*." She took her anxiety out on the carrot she was peeling. "The woman obviously means something to him if he keeps her photo...*their* photo...in such a prominent place."

"Good point. Maybe she's the reason he had to get away for a while. He could be getting over a bad breakup."

Before Valerie could respond, the back door slammed and Joe walked in from the mudroom. "Ladies." He looked between the two of them. "Don't let me interrupt. I'm just here for the salmon." He crossed to the refrigerator.

"Hey, honey..." Carrie waved her husband to join her at the kitchen island. "We should tell Valerie our good news."

"Oh, yeah." Joe removed a platter of

filleted salmon from the fridge and set it on the counter next to Carrie's lemon-prep station.

Valerie frowned, unsure if she was ready for anything labeled as "news," good or otherwise. "What is it?"

Looking lovingly at Joe, Carrie wiped her hands and linked her arm through his. "We've decided we're adopting."

Valerie felt her breath leave her. "Wha—?"

"A dog." Carrie laughed.

Chuckling, Joe shook his head. "My wife loves to try to give people a heart attack."

"I'll say." Valerie huffed out a laugh. "But a dog is still big news. What's his name?"

Carrie and Joe looked at each other, then Carrie broke into a grin. "It's Buster. After we talked about him, I felt so bad, I called animal control. They said that since Buster hadn't actually bitten anyone, they'd be willing to release him to someone who can commit to proper training. We're way out here, away from people, and there aren't any kids on the premises. Yet." She looked at Joe and gave his arm a squeeze. "Joe and I prayed about it."

Joe raised a brow. "We want to give Buster a shot at a good life. He'll be happy on the ranch."

Valerie's lower lip quivered. "You guys are the best."

"We probably have our work cut out for us." Joe lifted the platter and headed for the back door. "I'll be manning the grill."

As he made his exit, his grandmother—Mrs. Brannon—entered from the dining room carrying an empty hors d'oeuvre tray. "I'm glad he's getting the fish going. This crowd is hungry." She went to the oven and turned on the light to check on her homemade slider buns.

"Everything smells amazing." Valerie inhaled deeply as she watched Mrs. Brannon remove the lid from the crock pot. "You make the best pulled pork in the entire county."

The older woman chuckled. "I have serious doubts that you've done a tasting tour of the *entire* county, dear, but I'll take the compliment."

"It's the reason Janet is letting us host the dinner." Carrie poured the bowl of lemon juice into a larger bowl, which she was using to mix up her coleslaw dressing. "That and Joe's famous barbecue salmon."

"I swear, Carrie." Valerie shook her head. "How you haven't changed your mind about being a vegan living with these two, I'll never understand."

"It's not always easy, believe me."

"Valerie, dear, would you mind taking that relish tray out to the table?" Mrs. Brannon nodded at a large platter filled with pickles, olives, and sliced vegetables.

"Sure thing."

Valerie wiped her hands on her apron and picked up the tray. She hip-bumped the door leading from the kitchen out to the formal dining room, where Mrs. Brannon had set the table with one of her hand-embroidered tablecloths, and her white, gold-edged china that she liked to use for large dinner parties.

As Valerie placed the tray on the table, she looked through the doorway leading to the front sitting room, where some of the guests mingled in front of the fireplace. The buzz of happy conversation lifted her spirits. This was the first time all week that she'd felt even the slightest bit lighthearted.

Sighing, she let her gaze settle on the beautiful room she was in. She'd always loved this place. In fact, there'd been a time when she had dreamed of being the lady of the house. She and Joe had—in her mind, anyway—been heading in that direction. But when Carrie had arrived in Rockford, Joe's head had turned. He'd gently given Valerie the boot.

Not that Valerie held anything against either of them. They were so happy together, and it would have been horrible for both Valerie and Joe if he'd married her only because she was the best the town had to offer. She had learned her lesson, because being stuck in a bad marriage had to be just about the worst thing that could happen to a person. Better to be always-a-bridesmaid than a wife with an unhappy husband.

Rounding the table, she spotted Jeremy standing in front of the fireplace with his arm around his bride-to-be. It thrilled Valerie that both of her best childhood guy friends had found the loves of their lives. And that Carrie and Janet had become her besties. It was all working out the way it was meant to, even if it did leave Valerie with her dad as her date for events like this.

Things could be worse.

When Jeremy glanced over and saw her, he said something to Janet, who nodded and continued the conversation she was involved in with her soon-to-be in-laws. He wended his way through the guests and entered the dining room.

"Hey, Val." By the tone of his voice, he might as well have put on his sheriff's hat as he crossed that threshold. "Things are going to be hectic tomorrow and I wanted to be sure I talked to you. Since both of my deputies are groomsmen in the wedding, I'm bringing in some officers from Luxton tomorrow."

"Good thinking." Her mouth went dry. "Are you afraid something might happen?"

"Better to be safe. You know how certain people get ideas when they know half the town is away from home."

Nodding, she straightened a place setting. She wasn't sure she liked where this was going.

Jeremy rubbed the back of his neck. "And I'm assigning someone just to keep an eye on your place."

Yeah, not liking this at all. A knot formed in her stomach. "You really think that's necessary?"

"Since we still don't know what happened to Rex—"

"You think whoever it was might try something again?" The knot tightened. So much for feeling lighthearted.

He shrugged. "Until we know what's going on, we shouldn't assume they won't."

"I hate this." Not that she didn't appreciate it. She was blessed to have such a caring friend.

But...this night was supposed to be a celebration.

"Listen." She punched his arm. "I don't

want you to even think about me and my little problems until you get back from your honeymoon. Got it?"

He grinned. "Yes, ma'am. But remember, you call Bobby if you have any concerns. And I mean *any*."

"Got it. But I'm praying that Bobby has a very boring week as interim sheriff."

"Me too." He shrugged his brows and returned to the sitting room.

Valerie placed her hand on her chest, willing her heart rate to slow. She glanced up at the high coffered ceiling and prayed for her problem to just go away.

Chapter 23

The ticking of the clock on the Hayeses' living room wall and Rex's gentle snore as he slept soundly in front of the fireplace were music to Derek's ears. The perfect score for an evening of sitting at the dining room table, going through what he had for his book so far.

At the beginning of this trip, he'd missed the city sounds—sirens, rackety trucks, car horns—but now that he'd spent some time out in the country, he completely understood its appeal. A guy could really hear himself think out here.

Taking a bite of his ham sandwich, he scrutinized the tiny squares on his laptop screen that represented the work he'd done in the past couple of weeks. While he'd started with a basic premise of depicting the four seasons at various locations around the state, a more focused theme seemed to be taking shape—one he hadn't expected.

The shots of Valerie out in the pumpkin patch made him smile. What was this feeling he had when he looked at her? It felt familiar—a lot like the way he'd felt about Erin, but it wasn't quite the same. No one could replace Erin, and it wouldn't be fair to compare anyone to her. But for the first time, he started to think there might be a place in his heart for someone new.

He sat back and pinched the bridge of

his nose. What was he even thinking? He'd only known Valerie for a little over a week. But how long did it take? How long had it taken with Erin?

Setting aside that thought, he picked a favorite from his shots of Valerie. If this made his final cut, he'd ask her permission to use it in the book. How would she feel about that?

Next up were the shots from the corn maze. That had been a good day. A yearning for more days like that washed through him.

Leaning back in his chair, he stretched his arms over his head, distracted by the gallery wall across from him. It reminded him of the display he had in his townhouse back in DC. Funny, as important as photography was to him, he hadn't bothered to bring any of those personal photos with him.

Right. Except one. The one that both comforted and broke him every time he looked at it.

Maybe that was why he hadn't put any more personal photos up in the RV. The story of his own life was what he had hit the road to escape from.

Returning his focus to the screen, he clicked on one of the shots he'd snapped from the corn maze tower. What a view. He loved the unique perspective of the maze, and the glimpses of happy people moving through it. And that mountain range was stunning.

Squinting, he zeroed in on the mountains, and a shape that looked really familiar. He picked up his computer and carried it over to the gallery wall then held it next to the group shot by the lake. Sure enough, that was the same mountain range in the background, with the prominent peak—Sugar Peak—making it undeniable.

So the lake wasn't far from the Frazier farm. Which meant it would be just a short drive from here. *Huh.*

He walked back to his seat. What if he suggested to Valerie that they go there one day? Maybe in the spring, they could rent a boat and go fishing. He could find out if he liked sunfish.

As that idea settled, he continued to pick the best shots so far for the book.

Then he saw a few that he didn't remember taking. He clicked on one of them and chuckled when he recognized himself, along with Mr. Hayes and the farmhands.

Sitting back, he ran a hand through his hair. "Sneaky, Valerie. Very sneaky."

But how had she managed? If he didn't have his camera with him, it was generally in the banquette seat in the RV, where he stored his photography equipment. *Oh, right.* That would have been the day he'd left it hanging in the back porch when he went out to help pull the vines. Valerie obviously saw it and did some practicing.

Sipping his ginger ale, he picked the best of her images and moved it to the project file. The idea of having a shot of himself in the book made him feel like less of an outside observer, and more like he belonged. That felt surprisingly good.

Suddenly, Rex jolted awake. He pushed to his feet and went to the front window, emitting a low, threatening growl.

Derek's nerves snapped to high alert. "What's going on, boy?" He stood and moved to the window, then pulled the curtain back just enough to see out. All he saw in the pool of warm light coming from the fixture above the barn door was the yard, a little of the field, and his RV. Nothing that shouldn't be there, at least...not that he could see.

He moved to the side to get a look at the garage. Now that Valerie had her truck back, they'd all agreed that leaving it locked up was the best plan, unless they absolutely needed to drive it.

Rex barked, then strode urgently to the foyer. Derek stayed at the window, not sure what he was looking for, or what he would do if he saw it. Rex barked again and appeared in the doorway, his ears at high alert. It was hard to tell if he needed to go out for personal reasons, or if he'd sensed something out there that needed to be chased off.

"Okay, okay." Shaking his head, Derek started for the foyer.

The moment Derek opened the front door, Rex bolted over the porch, down the steps, and across the yard, then vanished into the darkness. Derek stepped out onto the porch, trying his best to see. Rex continued barking like the watchdog that he was, but at what, Derek had no idea.

Then a loud pop echoed from somewhere in the distance, followed by another. *Gunshots?*

The barking stopped.

"No...no." Alarmed, Derek drew his gun from his holster—an action he'd never taken aside from practice—and headed toward where Rex had disappeared into the field.

Holding his breath, he looked around, but there was no movement and no sound. If anything had happened to Rex...

Then a rustling noise turned his head. He raised his weapon and steeled his nerves.

Another rustle, louder this time. The tall grass shifted and a figure appeared. Derek steadied his gun, aiming at something that emerged from the brush.

He let out a breath. "Rex."

Rex barked and trotted toward him, apparently satisfied that he'd chased off whatever had put him on alert.

"Come on, boy." Derek took one last look around, then followed Rex back to the house.

Had someone actually fired a gun?

Now he wasn't sure. All he could think was that if anything happened to Rex on his watch, he'd never forgive himself.

And neither would Valerie.

"The wedding is going to be beautiful." Valerie sounded tired but content.

Derek stood in the foyer, watching Valerie and her dad remove their coats, while Rex did a happy welcome-home dance. The jitters hadn't quite dissipated from the strange occurrence of a little while ago, and he wasn't quite sure what to do about it.

He had called the nonemergency number for Rockford, and the woman had told him she'd send someone to patrol the area. She'd also told him that they regularly got reports of gunfire out in the country and it almost never amounted to anything. It was the "almost" that kept Derek from feeling reassured.

"Oh, and I brought you something." Valerie picked up a small bag she had set on the hall table and handed it to him. "It's a slice of Carrie's vegan apple tart."

He peered into the bag. "Vegan?"

"Don't let that scare you, son." Mr. Hayes patted Derek's shoulder as he passed him on his way into the living room. "I'm making my evening hot cocoa. Anyone want some?"

"No thanks, Dad." Valerie yawned. "I'm heading upstairs in a sec."

"Sure, I'll take a cup," Derek answered, not because he wanted cocoa, but because he thought it might afford him an opportunity to talk to Mr. Hayes alone.

"Thanks for being my date." Valerie called out.

"Thanks for asking me, sweetheart." He spoke over his shoulder as he passed through the dining room.

Valerie looked at Derek. “Did my boy give you any trouble?”

“He was great. Ate. Slept. Went out once.” Derek rubbed the back of his neck, not sure if he should tell Valerie about what had happened. The last thing she needed was one more thing to worry about, but he was concerned about tomorrow. No one would be here at the farm for most of the day and all evening. He knew their routine of leaving the dog door open, and the thought of Rex being outside on his own, after what had happened tonight, sent a shudder down his spine.

“Well, it’s late, and tomorrow’s the big day.” Valerie turned for the stairs.

“You sure you feel okay leaving Rex tomorrow?”

She turned back with a hint of surprise in her eyes. “Actually, Jeremy made me nervous, so I called Dr. Ames. She lives in town, close to the clinic, and she agreed to take Rex for the day. We can pick him up on our way home from the reception."

"Great plan." Derek felt a knot of tension between his shoulder blades loosen. "Goodnight."

With a contented smile, Valerie signaled for Rex to follow and the two retreated up the stairs.

Derek breathed easier. Rex would be safe, and Valerie didn't need to know about the possible gunshots just yet. Let her get a good night's sleep and focus on the wedding tomorrow.

He'd tell Mr. Hayes, and that would be enough for now.

Chapter 24

Sitting at the long table designated for the wedding party, Valerie scraped the last of the cake crumbs from her plate onto her fork. Under the table, she tapped the toe of her cute dyed-to-match-the-dress, closed-toe pump in time to the upbeat music.

At the sound of chairs scraping against the polished rustic wood floor of the barn-turned-event-center, Valerie realized that everyone at the head table had risen to go hit the dance floor. Everyone but her. A blush—which she hoped would be concealed by the soft lighting of the vintage chandeliers and string lights—hit her cheeks. There was nothing like being the last-woman-sitting at a dance event.

Her gaze cut across the crowded space, then landed on a table at the far end of the room where Dad sat yukking it up with his cronies. Too bad she couldn't use his hitting-the-wall as her own excuse to bail.

Not that she wasn't having a good time. It had been a beautiful wedding, and she had managed, for the most part, to put the events of the past two weeks out of her mind. But, this was the point in any wedding reception where the wallflowers were separated from the couples, and for her, it stopped being fun.

She sighed. Part of her duty as co-maid of honor was to stick around till the departure of the happy couple. And, as the photographer's ride, she was doubly obligated. She might as well make the best of it.

Aware that someone had pulled the chair next to her away from the table, Valerie caught a glimpse of teal-blue satin, identical to the dress she wore.

"Hey, girl."

As Annica Frazier smoothed the skirt of her dress behind her so she could sit, Valerie breathed a little easier. It was nice to not be the only single gal not out there boogying down, even though Annica was seven years younger than her, and nowhere near old-maid status.

Annica groaned. "I just ate two pieces of cake, and I think I'm busting my seams."

Considering that she was as slender as a blade of grass, Valerie doubted her seams were at risk.

They sat for a moment in a comfortable silence, watching the couples dancing. Aside from a few out-of-town relatives, Valerie knew most everyone, except for one unfamiliar face.

"Hey, who's Rune dancing with?" Valerie nodded toward the couple, who were doing an animated version of the Twist. "I've never seen her before."

"Rune brought a plus-one." Resting her forearms on the table, Annica leaned in conspiratorially. "Her name's Bridget and he met her on one of his delivery routes."

"He does his deliveries at night. How on earth did he meet anybody?"

"She's an ER nurse at the hospital in Dupont. She works the night shift. And she happens to take her lunch break at the same time Rune is filling the snack machines in the employee break room. "

"Lucky for Rune."

"I think, lucky for Bridget too."

"He's a good guy." Valerie was happy for Rune, but a little sad that she was a strong contender to win this game of musical chairs with all the singles her age in town. With Rune out of the running, she was one step closer to being the last of their age group who remained unmarried.

"Speaking of dancing," Annica said, "I think I'll go stir up that huddle of cowboys over there and find myself a partner." She directed her gaze at a group of early-twenty-something men hanging out near the gift table. "Wanna come?"

"No. But you have fun."

As Valerie watched Annica wending her way through the round tables and white folding chairs, she felt a little vulnerable all alone on the dais. The last thing she wanted was for one of the church grandmas to enlist a grandson who was either way too young, way too old, or entirely disinterested, to come to her rescue.

In no mood for a pity dance, she stood, steadied herself on her heels, and aimed for the table she and Carrie had set up along one wall of the large room. If she didn't run into anyone to talk to, she could pass the time tidying up the happy-couple photo display and making sure that everyone had signed the guest book.

As she meandered, she looked out at the dance floor. Janet, looking radiant in her wedding gown, danced with her son, Caleb, a picture of cuteness in his tiny ring-bearer tux. They were mugging for Derek, who had somehow managed to infiltrate the dance floor without getting trampled.

Jordan and Moe, whom Derek had enlisted as his assistants for this event, stood off to the side holding Derek's bag and various pieces of photography equipment.

When Jeremy scooped up Caleb, and started dancing with him and Janet, Derek snapped a few shots of the new family, then shifted his focus to the other dancers.

“Have you talked to him?”

Valerie jumped at the sound of Carrie’s voice. She’d been so lost in thought, she hadn’t realized her friend had sidled up next to her.

“Talked to him about what?” She feigned ignorance. “The woman in the picture?”

“No. The woman standing right here.” Carrie poked Valerie’s shoulder. “You don’t have to admit you saw the picture. Just tell him how you feel about him.”

“I don’t—”

“Don’t even try it.” She held up a hand. “I saw the way you were looking at him just now.”

“Here’s the thing...” She took Carrie by the arm and led her closer to the wall, out of earshot of the other guests. She hadn’t admitted this to anyone but Rex, and it was about time she did. “You know how God calls some people to stay single?”

"Oh, come on." Carrie tilted her head and narrowed her eyes, which were particularly blue next to the teal satin of her bridesmaid dress. "You're not saying *that's* the reason you're still single?"

"It makes sense."

"In what universe? I'm pretty sure that the way people know it's God's will for them to stay single is that they have no desire to get married and have a family. Is that the case for you?"

Valerie sighed. "No. But—"

"But *nothing.*" She gave her a little shove in the direction of the dance floor. "Go talk to him."

As Valerie started to argue, the song ended and a new one started. She recognized it as "This Will Be," one of Joe's favorites. Predictably, the man himself emerged from the sea of mingling guests, making a beeline for Carrie.

"Sorry, Val." He reached for his wife's hand. "But I'm stealing her away."

As they headed for the dance floor, Carrie turned and made a shooing gesture with her hand. "Go."

Rolling her eyes, Valerie wavered. Should she? She looked over to where Derek had been photographing the kids, but he wasn't there anymore and neither were his able-bodied assistants. She scanned the dance floor, which was full of happy couples. The bride and groom. Carrie and Joe. Rune and the adorable ER nurse. The other two groomsmen—Deputies Bobby and Kyle—had paired up with two of Janet's visiting friends.

Then her eyes landed on one of the tables directly opposite her, where Dad bent down to speak with Maggie. Looking delighted, Maggie placed her hands on her cheeks and nodded.

Narrowing her gaze on the scene, Valerie took a couple of steps forward to get a better view.

Hannah, who sat next to Maggie,

pushed her chair back as if she was about to stand, but Dad waved her back. To Valerie's surprise, Dad pushed Maggie's chair out to the dance floor. Holding hands, they danced, unimpeded by her wheelchair.

Valerie's chest tightened. What was going on?

"Do you dance"—a deep voice startled her—"or is it more of a spectator thing?"

She tore her focus from her dad and Maggie and turned to Derek, who had managed to sneak up behind her. She huffed out a chuckle. "You're supposed to be on duty."

"It's just one dance." He nodded toward Jordan and Moe, who sat at a table with all the photography equipment, downing punch like they'd been laboring in the hot sun. "I told the guys we needed a break."

He held out his palm to her, like Mr. Darcy at the Netherfield ball. Her stomach strangely fluttery, she put her hand in his, and he led her to the dance floor. While they started to move to the beat of the song—always a little graceless at first—she saw Carrie smiling her encouragement. Valerie chuckled. As if she and Derek were going to have a serious heart-to-heart with half the town huddled around them.

Just as she was getting comfortable with the upbeat dance, the song faded into a slow piano intro. All around, couples moved closer together, and Derek looked at her with a raised brow. She stepped into his hold, a little unsure but not unwilling.

The momentary awkwardness of standing so close eased into a feeling of being cared for. Through the wall of party guests, she caught a glimpse of Dad and Maggie, still swaying to the music. Dad even ventured a little spin of Maggie's chair that made her laugh. Valerie realized she hadn't actually seen the two of them interacting in quite some time. What had she missed?

"Tomorrow's Sunday." Derek's voice sounded smooth next to her ear. "We're about due for another lesson."

"Shooting and shooting." Her stomach fluttered for a different reason at the grim reminder that she might need to defend herself. "I don't want to keep you from working on your book. It's what you came out here to do."

"You wouldn't be keeping me from it if we combined that with your lessons. You have a great eye. I might want to use some of your work in the book, if you don't mind."

She frowned at him. Was he pulling her leg?

At his expectant look, she sputtered, "F-for real?" Then bitter reality interceded. "Oh, but we still don't know if someone's messing with me. Do you think it's safe to be out and about?"

"We could go someplace with people

around."

"True. One condition. We go out shooting tomorrow if you go to church with us first."

He winced and she felt him tense.

"I'm sorry." She took a half-step back, subtly distancing herself from him. "That wasn't fair."

"No, it's..." He relaxed a little and pulled her back in. "I used to go to church all the time. I just haven't in a while." He paused. "But...I am supposed to be keeping the bad guys away from you."

He turned his head and met her gaze, urging her heart into her throat. Looking into his eyes, she saw something she'd never seen there before. Something she could only think of as *longing*.

Maybe Carrie was right. Maybe this was the time to tell him how she felt.

Her thoughts blurred. All the reasons why she shouldn't feel this way about him seemed insubstantial when held up against all the reasons she should. And as they looked at each other, she tipped her head back and he eased closer until their lips were dangerously close to touching.

The song ended, and people around them began clapping.

"Ladies and gentlemen," the emcee crooned into the microphone, "at this time, Jeremy and Janet invite you to gather outside for their send-off."

Derek blinked, like he'd just woken up and was trying to get his bearings. "Right...I have to..." Releasing the hold he had on her, he pointed to the table where he'd left his equipment.

"Oh, and I have to..." Frowning, she tried to recall what she was supposed to do. "Bubbles! I'm supposed to—"

"Yeah." Visibly swallowing, he loosened his tie and backed a few steps away before making his retreat.

What was *that?* Still trying to regain her composure, she moved through the crowd of guests as they grabbed coats and headed for the tall double doors leading outside.

As Valerie stepped out into the crisp night, she saw the wedding party gathering on the wide front walkway. All except Bobby, who stood on the lawn several yards away with his phone to one ear and his hand covering the other.

"Valerie!" She turned to see Carrie coming toward her carrying a basket of bubble wands. "Here you go, sweetie." She kept moving, handing out wands from her own basket.

As Valerie started to do the same, she saw Bobby end his call and turn to scan the growing crowd. Then he headed toward her, his expression urgent.

Her stomach buckled, and she braced herself.

"Val." He moved quickly. "I just got a call from the deputy out at your place. We need to get over there." He leaned in so he wouldn't have to shout. "He just caught someone breaking into your house."

Chapter 25

It had taken all Valerie's performance skills to make it through the send-off as if everything were normal. The moment Janet and Jeremy had driven away, Bobby had taken off for the farm, and she had alerted Derek and her dad to the concerning news.

Now, some twenty minutes later, Dad pulled his truck in front of their house, next to Bobby's patrol car. Several yards away, Bobby and two officers Valerie didn't recognize stood talking to a man seated in the back of a Luxton patrol car. As Dad and Derek got out of the front of Dad's truck, one of the Luxton officers shut the door to the patrol car, and the three men approached them. As Valerie made her way out of the back seat, Bobby came toward her with his hand held up.

"Val...we want to keep you out of the guy's sight, just in case."

"Just in case, what?" She peered around Bobby, trying to get a look.

"We just want to keep you safe, ma'am." The other officer offered his hand. "I'm Deputy Grant from Luxton. And this"—he indicated the second officer—"is Deputy Barr."

Valerie nodded at the men. "Why are you afraid for my safety?"

Deputy Barr looked over at their patrol car, where the silhouette of their prisoner's head was framed in the back window. "This guy is bad news. He's been harassing women in Luxton for months. We've had lots of complaints but nothing we could actually hold him on. Till tonight. We caught him in the act of breaking and entering."

Valerie shivered, in spite of the warm wool coat she'd pulled on over her dress. Dad came alongside her, and put a protective arm around her shoulders.

"What was he after?" Dad asked. "Did he say?"

The deputies exchanged a glance.

"He's not talking much." Deputy Grant took out his phone and tapped it. "Do either of you recognize him?"

He held up a photo he'd snapped of the guy while he was seated in the car, looking disheveled and not at all pleased.

Valerie nearly choked on her own breath. "I do. I mean..." She leaned forward to be certain. "Yes, I'm sure Carrie and I saw him while we were getting gas in

Luxton a week ago. The night of the bachelorette party." *The creepy beer guy.* She'd gotten a good enough look at him that night that his features were etched into her memory.

Derek stared at her. "You didn't mention that."

"I didn't think there was a reason to." She looked at Deputy Grant. "Do you know what kind of car he drove to get here?" She scanned the yard, but didn't see any vehicles other than the ones that were meant to be there.

"I have another patrol car driving the periphery of your property. They found a beat-up old Audi sedan parked up the road a ways. Maroon colored."

"That sounds like the car I saw this guy get into. But I don't know him. How would he wind up here?"

Bobby gave her a sympathetic look. "Seems like maybe this guy had you in his sights."

"Vincent Greco." Deputy Barr continued. "He picked certain women. Made a game of following them."

"So he's a stalker." Derek's voice rumbled with anger.

"I'd say so." Deputy Barr's mouth curved downward in disgust. He turned his focus back to Valerie. "Jeremy gave us the rundown on all the things that have happened to you and why he wanted us to keep an eye on your place. It all fit in with the long list of complaints we've gotten from the other women, so we suspected it might be the same creep."

"But the tracker and the dog?" Deputy Barr shook his head. "That took it to a whole new level. The guy's actions have been escalating. We wanted to catch him doing something we could finally charge him for before it got so bad that we had something serious on our hands."

"His M.O. was always to wait for an opportunity when no one is home. But don't you worry, Miss Hayes." Deputy Grant returned his phone to his pocket. "We'll nail him for all of it. Messing with your truck. Poisoning your dog. Shooting at your house—"

"Shooting at our..." Valerie frowned. "But that didn't—"

"It did." Derek spoke calmly. "Last night."

She stared at him. "Last night? While Dad and I were gone?"

Wordlessly, Derek nodded.

"Wh...why didn't you say something?"

"I reported it, then I talked to your dad. We agreed that telling you wouldn't do anything but keep you awake all night."

Stunned, Valerie turned to her dad, who nodded slightly. As mad as it made her to be left out, she couldn't argue with the truth. She would have been a mess for the wedding.

"At the end of the day," Deputy Grant said, "we should have enough to put this guy away for a while."

Valerie's stomach buckled. "How long is a while?"

"A year at least."

"That's all?" Dad's grip on her shoulder tightened.

"Longer if we can link him to the more serious charges." Deputy Barr looked at Valerie with warm eyes. "Poisoning your dog. That's low."

"Speaking of Rex," Bobby said, "I asked Kyle to go pick him up for you. Hope that's okay."

"Oh, that's great. Thank you, Bobby."

"Mr. Hayes." Bobby gestured toward Dad. "If you'll come with me, I can show you where he broke into the back of the house."

Grunting, Dad squeezed Valerie's shoulder and went with Bobby.

"We'll be taking Greco back to Luxton to book him. I think you can rest easy tonight, Miss Hayes."

As the two deputies strode toward their car, Valerie leaned against Dad's truck for support.

Looking concerned, Derek rubbed her upper arm. "Hey, it's okay."

"He tried to get into our house." The implications of that suddenly hit her. "What do you think he would have done?"

"Try not to think about it." Derek reached out and pulled her into his arms. "I'm just grateful that he was dumb enough to get himself caught."

"Thank God." She stepped back from the hug. "I can have my life back."

"Let's get inside." He put his hand on her shoulder and guided her toward the house.

As they slowly ambled up the walkway, Valerie looked at the clear dark sky. Now that her biggest problem had finally been put to rest, maybe she could get back to focusing on the things that were really important. Like clearing enough profit at the fall market to keep the farm in the black.

And maybe figuring out the mystery of the man who seemed so intent on protecting her.

Chapter 26

Valerie made the final push to the top of the Shadow Summit hiking trail, thrilled to no longer be obsessed with looking over her shoulder.

Confident that the man who had caused her so much grief was now sitting in a Luxton jail cell, she had insisted that instead of a lesson with the gun today, she and Derek should use that time to get some really amazing photographs.

Rex ran on ahead, wagging his tail, then looked back as if to ask what the delay was. As they caught up to him and rounded the curve of the path, the vast valley appeared in front of them. Gazing out at the farmland and the distant mountains beyond, a smile pulled at her lips. Why did she never take the time to come up here?

Wiping his forehead with the back of his sweatshirt sleeve, Derek let out a low whistle. “Told you Montana was paradise.”

“You did say that, didn’t you?”

“Sure did.” Setting his camera case on a downed tree, he scanned the full scope of the view. “And you tried to pretend you didn’t already know.”

“I guess I just needed a reminder.”

She took the dog water bottle from her daypack and offered Rex a drink, which he eagerly accepted. Even though it had only been a twenty-minute hike from the parking lot, the sun was surprisingly warm.

After putting the bottle away and taking a swig from her own, she stretched and sat on the log. She watched as Derek set up his tripod, then took a camera from the case. Instead of affixing it to the tripod, he turned to her and clicked a few shots.

She made a face. "I'm starting to think anyone who spends time with you has to get over their fear of being photographed."

Brow furrowing, he jerked his head back. "I guess I don't think of it that way. I'm so used to photographing public figures."

"Well, speaking on behalf of all my fellow private citizens, it does take some getting used to." Putting her hands on her hips, she rolled her shoulders. The ordeal of the past several days had done a number on her nerves, and her muscles still felt tense.

Derek tightened the camera to the tripod. "Still a little anxious?"

"A little, but believe it or not..." She worked the kinks out of her neck. "I'm more relaxed than I've been in a while."

"It's been a rough two weeks."

"I'm just glad they caught the guy. *Vincent.*" The name made her cringe. "It's scary to think about how bad it could have gotten."

"Sounds like a lot of women will be breathing easier. What a creep."

"Anyone who would stoop to poisoning a dog is pretty evil."

"Yeah, I'm glad *Rex* is okay." He glanced her way. "But I'm even more glad that *you're* safe. I don't know what I would've..." His hands stilled, and he looked down, like he was second guessing what he'd been about to disclose.

Her stomach fluttered again, the same way it had last night on the dance floor.

When he looked her way again, he

seemed intent on avoiding eye contact. “I want to show you how to set up a landscape shot.” He tipped his head, indicating that she should join him.

Biting her lip, she pushed to her feet.

“I put on the wide-angle lens.” He stepped aside so she could position herself behind the camera. “Look through the viewfinder and think about your composition.”

Through the viewer, she found the horizon line, then adjusted the camera. “How’s that?” She stepped to the side so he could check her work.

“That looks good.” He gave her an encouraging smile. “Are you happy with where the sun is?”

“It’s in the sky where it belongs.” She shrugged her eyebrows. “I’m pretty happy with that.”

He smirked. “You should consider a career in comedy.”

Returning his sarcastic look, she

stepped behind the camera again. Now that she could focus on something other than watching her back, she needed answers from Derek. If he did have someone back home—a girlfriend, or worse, a *wife*—she needed to know before she invested any time and energy into one more dead-end dream.

Moving the camera again so the lighting would be more off-center, she contemplated how to broach the subject. *Hey, you wouldn't happen to be married, would you?* seemed a little abrupt. Maybe a more indirect approach would encourage some casual mention of the people in his life.

"Tell me the most exciting place you've ever been."

He chortled. "You mean, besides right here?"

"I'm serious." Putting her eye to the viewfinder, she acted like she was focusing on the lens. But her true focus was on probing for answers.

"From a photography standpoint, I'd have to say Machu Picchu."

Her breath caught, and she snapped her gaze to him. "Beautiful place." Satisfied that his response had been purely coincidental, she returned her eye to the camera. "Or so I've heard."

"What about you? What's the most exciting place you've ever been?"

"I've never been anywhere."

"I'm sure that's not true."

"Okay, fine. The most exciting place I've been is Boise, for an interstate exchange program in 4-H."

He paused. "Boise's nice."

"It's not Machu Picchu." She took a picture, then stepped back for him to check her work. "My mom used to get old, discarded travel magazines from the library. We'd go through them together and cut out pictures of places we wanted to go."

"Nice." He picked up the tripod and moved a few feet to the left. "So, why have you never gone anywhere?"

"My mom and I always talked like we would someday. I'm not really sure what we thought would happen to make *someday* different than every other day. The farm always came first. And when my mom died..."

He glanced her way. "She took the dream with her?"

She stared at him, a knot forming in her throat. Looking down, she nodded. She hadn't ever actually thought of it that way, but how else could she explain it?

"You should do it." Derek's tone was compassionate. "Pick a place you really want to go, and start planning."

"That's an old dream." She shook her head. "I'm pretty much resigned to staying in Rockford and running the farm." Assuming, of course, that they didn't run it into the ground, which seemed to be more of a possibility this year than ever.

"That really what you want to do?"

Her chin trembled. "There's nothing wrong with—"

"N-no..." He held up his hand. "I'm not saying there's anything *wrong* with it. I think it's amazing. I'm just honestly asking if it's what *you* want, or if it's for your parents."

"Oh." Folding her arms, she shifted her weight from one foot to the other. "No one's ever asked me that before. I'm not sure I ever considered that there was a difference."

"Give it some thought."

She sighed. If she'd been making decisions based on a false assumption, maybe she needed to ask God what He wanted for her. "I'll give it some prayer too."

He winced again, only this time it was more subtle, almost like a conditioned response.

"You have something against prayer?" Now it was her turn to wince. That question had come out sounding more accusatory than she had intended. "I mean…I know you went to church with us this morning. But you did that for me. Whenever I mention church, or praying, you make a face. Don't you believe in God?"

Facing her, he rolled in his lips, like he was thinking through his response. "I used to. But I guess I stopped."

"Why?"

Looking away, he huffed out a resigned sigh, then held a hand out toward the log.

Bracing herself, Valerie crossed back to it and sat, wondering if she was about to hear more than she had bargained for.

He sat next to her. "I…um…well, I used to be really active in church. That's where I met my…" He shut his eyes. "My fiancée."

Her stomach dropped to her toes. The

woman in the picture. "Oh..."

He glanced at her briefly, holding up a palm as if to indicate that there was more. "Erin." He smiled fleetingly. "She was...so on fire for the Lord. Her job was at a rehabilitation center for homeless people who had addictions. She was all about serving people in need. She was always—" He swallowed. "—always going out to wherever the people were and taking food or whatever was needed."

"Wow." Valerie's hands shook, not sure if she felt more impressed or intimidated.

"So one day..." He went on, his voice low. "...a little over a year ago...she told me she was going with a team to a homeless encampment. We have more than our share in DC. She did this pretty regularly, but for some reason, I felt like I needed to go with her that day. I hadn't ever done that before. Hadn't ever felt that...I don't know...*nudge* before."

He drew in a long breath before continuing. “So we were there, handing out blankets and other things. I heard some yelling and I turned around and there were these two guys fighting with each other. One of them drew a knife. I looked for Erin and she was just a few feet away from me...closer than I was to the fight. I reached for her, but before I could even move, she just...went down.”

“Oh no.” Instinctively, she put her hand on his arm.

He smiled briefly in acknowledgement of the gesture, then went on. “It was pretty much a blur, but the next thing I knew, I was at the hospital. Sitting in a waiting room.” His look grew distant, like he was mentally in that room again, not sitting on a log with her. “Not that this probably made a difference, but it wasn’t the best neighborhood, so it wasn’t the best hospital. But people from our church came. And people from Erin’s work. We all prayed for days. But then…" He shrugged. "She died anyway. I couldn't understand how God would let her go into that dangerous situation, doing *His* work, and then take her home even though we were all begging Him to let her stay."

She placed her hand on his. "That was the big thing that happened that made you decide you needed a change?"

"Yeah." Nodding, he ran his sleeve across his eyes. "So, you wanted to know why church isn't my thing anymore. It's because God and I aren't really on speaking terms."

She squeezed his hand, almost wishing she hadn't pulled this story out of him, but relieved that she had. Now, she knew who the woman in the picture was. *Erin.* Someone Valerie probably would have been friends with if life had worked out differently.

Wanting to say something that might help, she turned to face him directly. "You know, I used to blame God about my mom."

He glanced at her, then looked down, smiling sadly. "You don't anymore?"

"No. Because somehow, while I was questioning my faith, my dad's faith just kept growing. I saw him really leaning on the Lord. And even though he was still sad and struggling, he seemed to find peace. I figured that must be why."

Eyes still distant, he nodded. "Well, I'm glad that helped you. Both of you. I'm not sure I'll ever get there."

Sitting in silence, she felt a cool fall breeze kicking up around them. She wondered for the millionth time why things had to happen the way they did. But sometimes, it had to be enough to trust that God knew, so she didn't have to.

She had learned two important things about Derek. He was single—although the thought of getting involved with someone who was still grieving a lost love was more than she wanted to contemplate—and he was wavering in his faith.

When it came to Derek, all signs appeared to be pointing her back to her vow of singleness.

Chapter 27

Now that his job as unofficial bodyguard had come to an end, Derek assumed he'd be spending less time with Valerie. All alone that evening in his RV, he couldn't help but feel like he'd missed an opportunity.

He had been paging through the Montana guidebook, getting ideas for places he'd like to photograph. He studied the map of Rockford and its surrounding area. He could pretty easily pick out the Hayeses' farm. From there, he traced the route they'd taken to do deliveries. He found what must be the Fraziers' farm, then figured out how to get to the lake Valerie had talked about. *Hidden Lake*. Funny, it was just a little ways off the same road the Frazier farm was on. He made a mental note to check it out if he was up that way.

Picking up the plate that had held his pathetic single-guy dinner, he stood from his small dining table and took the two steps required to get to the kitchen sink. He squeezed a drop of soap on the plate, wondering what Valerie was doing right now. After everything he had shared with her today, he wouldn't blame her one bit if she had solidly placed him in the friend zone. What woman would want to start a relationship with a man who was, for all intents and purposes, still emotionally attached to his late fiancée?

He rinsed the plate and set it on the drainboard.

Grief was a funny thing. Just when it seemed to be settling into a palpable undercurrent, it hit again with the force of a tsunami. He had told himself that leaving DC, where memories of Erin lurked around every corner, would facilitate healing. The truth was, he had hoped he'd just forget.

Folding his arms, he leaned against the counter. What had Mr. Hayes said to him that night they'd played Scrabble? Something about time healing all wounds, but some scars always aching. Maybe the key to moving on was accepting that the ache would never go away. Maybe, he could even learn to embrace it.

Glancing in the direction of the house, out there beyond his windshield, he thought about Valerie again. He knew this was a big week for the Hayeses, with the fall market coming up next Saturday.

Knowing how important it was that they make as much profit as possible from that event, Derek had promised himself he wouldn't let them try to talk him out of helping out as much as he could. He had no idea how close they might be to actually losing the farm, but he needed to do his part. If there was one thing he had learned from Erin, it was that helping other people was always the right thing to do. Even though it had led her to being in the wrong place at the wrong time, it hadn't been because her intentions were wrong.

As predicted, it had started to rain. He had no idea what that meant for the work plan tomorrow, but he braced himself for a muddy morning.

It was only seven thirty, but he'd bet Mr. Hayes was making his bedtime hot cocoa right about now. And Valerie was probably settling in with a book. Something suspenseful, he'd bet, even though she kept saying she needed to give her nerves a break and switch to a lighter genre.

The night was young and he didn't feel like going to sleep yet. Maybe, if the downstairs lights of the house were still on, he could go over and share some cocoa and watch the evening news.

He sauntered over to the windshield, just to take a look. Placing his hand on the back of the driver's seat, he leaned over to pull the blind up under the rearview mirror. As he did, something fell from the back of the sun visor. He looked down to where the picture of him with Erin at Yosemite had landed on the floor.

He bent to retrieve it, then slid into the passenger seat, staring at it.

His heart broke every time he looked at this picture. That had been a good day—one that he would give anything to go back and relive. But he couldn't. No amount of wishing would change anything. His only options were to stay stuck in this place of sadness, or move ahead, taking some of the sadness with him, but also finding brand-new reasons to be happy. And maybe, if he was patient and didn't act like a total knucklehead, Valerie could be one of those reasons.

Feeling convicted, he retreated to the bedroom. He opened the cabinet next to the bed and placed the picture on the shelf. He could still take it out when he wanted to look at it, but he didn't need to cling to it out of fear of losing the memories of his time with Erin.

He closed the cabinet. It was time to leave the past where it belonged, and open himself up to new opportunities.

Normally, Valerie didn't watch the evening news with her dad, but tonight, she wanted the company. As the final report—a human interest piece about a cat befriending a goat—wound down, Valerie sipped the last remnants of her cocoa and thought about her conversation with Derek that afternoon.

"Hey, Dad." She considered. "Did you ever want to do anything other than run the farm?"

Dad drew his head back slightly. "Like what?"

"I don't know." To be honest, she didn't even really know why she was asking. Maybe as part of finding the answer for herself. "Did you ever want to explore the world?"

Taking a draw from his cup, he considered this like it was a foreign concept. "Never had the urge to wander." His expression softened. "Guess I always felt like everything I could ever care about was right here."

Valerie smiled. It was a sweet answer, and knowing her dad, completely sincere.

"What brought this on?" He shifted slightly in his easy chair. "You thinking about going somewhere?"

Was she? She hadn't expected that question. "I guess I've just been talking to Derek a little too much." She chuckled. "He's been everywhere, and I've been—"

"Don't say *nowhere*. You've been where you were meant to be."

"Boise?" She wiggled her eyebrows, but her heart sank at the melancholy suggestion that her world was destined to be as small as it felt.

"So you haven't traversed the globe," he went on. "Doesn't mean it will always be that way."

She looked at him, hoping he'd elaborate. But he just yawned and checked the clock.

"Big week ahead." He lowered the footrest of his chair and pushed to his feet. "I'm hittin' the hay."

"Yeah, me too." She grabbed his cup

before he could reach for both of them. “I’ll get these. Sleep well, Dad.”

She sauntered to the kitchen, trying not to tax her brain too much with this new puzzle. As she washed the mugs, she gazed out the window. A light rain had been falling for the past hour, which was always good news for the fields. She leaned a little to her right, taking comfort in the soft glow from Derek’s windows. Even though she no longer needed a bodyguard, she felt safer having him out there. But she’d better not let herself get too used to that.

A few minutes later, she climbed the stairs, pausing on the landing to look out the little window. In the time it had taken her to finish up in the kitchen, the wind had kicked up outside, which made being inside feel all the cozier.

Once in her room, she stepped into her closet to pick something to wear tomorrow. From the corner of her eye, she saw the box that had been sitting there gathering dust for ages. Seventeen years was a long time to keep a dream stashed away, out of sight but not really out of mind.

Drawing in a fortifying breath, she bent to pick up the box, and carried it out to her room. Rex lifted his head from where he had settled on his bed, then, seemingly satisfied that his services weren't needed, he relaxed. She set the box down on the big braided rug that her grandmother had made for her, and lowered herself next to it.

"Oh, God." She looked up. "Is this where I'm meant to be? Or do You have something else for me?"

Gingerly, she removed the lid from the box, waving away a puff of dust that wafted upward. Instantly, her eyes welled at the sight of the photos, mostly cut from magazines. Some of them still had remnants of tape on the corners from their time spent gracing the wall above her bed. Others had tiny holes from the pushpins used to affix them to her bulletin board.

She lifted them individually from the box, smiling at the memory of the conversations she and Mom'd had over each. So many places. London. Thailand. Spain.

Then the one that had been her favorite. She sputtered out a laugh as she lifted the magazine cover featuring Machu Picchu, which she'd kept for years taped to the wall next to her window. Something about the electric blue of the mountains and the vibrant green grass had drawn her in. It looked familiar enough but so exotic and different. Like Montana's distant cousin on the other side of the world. After finding that cover, she had told Mom that would be her first choice as a travel destination.

Why had packing all of this up after Mom's death felt like the right way to honor her?

Reaching into the box again, she felt her eyes prickle. She'd forgotten about her collection of craft ideas. She picked up a picture of a fall centerpiece made of dried flowers and leaves. All her designs for the items she'd made to sell had been inspired by craft magazines. Together, she and Mom had made such plans for the shop they'd wanted to open together someday.

Wiping her cheek with her sleeve, she sputtered out a little laugh. They had dreamed of going far away, but they had put just as much importance on their plans for staying right here. Both had been equally important.

Maybe she needed to reword her prayer. Maybe it wasn't that God had something *else* for her. Maybe what He had in mind for her was something *more.*

Leaning back on her heels, she examined the array of images she'd spread out on the rug. She rolled in her lips, then stood and got the tape from her desk. She crossed to the wall by the window and taped the Machu Picchu magazine cover to the wall. She stood back. It looked comforting, and familiar, and right. She smiled. Her mom wouldn't have wanted her to give up her dreams.

A loud *snap* startled her from her thoughts. She paused, waiting, but heard nothing more. Rex hadn't stirred, but whatever she had heard had come from outside, on the other side of the house.

Adrenaline coursed through her like the trickle of a spring thaw. She opened her door and peered out. Everything was quiet, except for the rain and wind outside. The only light upstairs was the soft glow of the bathroom night-light spilling out into the hallway. Dad must not have heard the sound, because there was no light under his door, and she didn't hear his footsteps on the creaky floor.

She padded down the stairs to the mid-floor landing and drew back the lacy curtain covering the small window. Grateful for the utility light on a post outside that softly illuminated the back-yard area, she saw the source of the noise. A large branch had fallen from the mountain ash tree. She let out a breath. Even though they kept an eye out for weak limbs, this wasn't an uncommon occurrence in even a light windstorm. She made a mental note to have the guys haul the branch away and to make sure the tree hadn't been damaged.

She was about to go back up when something else caught her attention. Leaning in, she did her best to see through the water-spotted glass. It was a light, way off in the distance. That was their property, pretty much as far as the eye could see. But where exactly...

The farmhouse. She'd looked out this window a million times, and she knew exactly where the house sat. As she watched, the light moved then disappeared, then reappeared a bit to the right.

She gasped. It looked like a lantern, or maybe a flashlight, that had moved from one room to another. She stood back for a moment, pondering what to do. When she looked up again, the light was gone.

Was she imagining things?

Chapter 28

Sitting in the passenger seat of Valerie's truck, Derek wavered between reassuring her that there was no cause for concern, and validating her decision to have Bobby and Kyle meet them at the farmhouse this morning.

"The only people who have any business over there would be Jordan and Moe, since the house sits next to the Christmas tree grove." Gripping the steering wheel with one hand, Valerie used her other hand to tame a bit of hair that had escaped from her ponytail. "But there's a staff bathroom at the back of the barn. I can't think of a reason for them to go into the house, especially at night."

"I'm sure there's an explanation."

Twisting her mouth, she glanced at him, probably thinking that comment was as unhelpful as he realized it sounded.

After last night's rainstorm, the morning had dawned cold and relatively clear. It had left this road, which they had accessed from the same main road they used to get to the Hayeses' house, a little on the muddy side. But Valerie's old truck seemed to handle it with ease.

As the house Valerie referred to as *the original farmhouse* grew closer, he saw a white barn—smaller than the red barn next to the Hayeses' place, and maybe in need of some repair. The house itself was larger than he'd expected, not to mention more ornate. While the home occupied by Valerie and her dad had simple-farmhouse charm, this one had more of an *East of Eden* feel to it. All it needed was a picket fence and it would look like it had been lifted out of a posh, if a little neglected, Victorian neighborhood.

Derek breathed easier seeing the patrol car parked in front of the small garage. Even though he'd brought his gun, he felt better having the trained professionals going in ahead of them.

Valerie pulled up behind the empty patrol car. They got out, and Derek waited for Valerie to come around to his side.

She checked the screen of her phone. "Bobby texted that the back door wasn't locked and that we should wait out here."

"Is that unusual? The door, I mean?"

Her eyes darted around like she was ultra-aware of her surroundings. "Dad might've forgotten to check it the last time he was here. He does that at our place too.

He gets distracted by things he's working on and doesn't want to lock himself out." Slipping her phone into her pocket, she looked toward the house. "I hope we're not wasting their time."

"If they thought it was a waste of time, they wouldn't have come." At least, that was Derek's assumption. It didn't take a genius to see that Valerie's group of lifelong friends cared about each other. She was lucky to have Jeremy and Bobby on her side.

Folding his arms, he got a better look at the house. The soft-gray wood siding looked a little chipped, and a couple balusters were missing from the railing on the wrap-around porch. Apart from that, there were no real indications that the house had been abandoned. Of course, from this vantage point, he couldn't see the damage to the roof.

"Our own personal Grey Gardens." Her voice sounded sad as she squinted against the morning sun.

"Doesn't look *that* bad." From what he remembered about the infamous estate that had been inhabited, but not maintained, by some distant relatives of Jackie Onassis, that seemed a little exaggerated.

She gave him a side-eyed glance. "You haven't seen inside. The upstairs is pretty sad." Looking away from the house, she pointed at a stand of evergreens. "That's our Christmas tree grove. I always wanted to turn this part of the property into a real Christmas tree farm. I wanted to live in this house and turn the barn into a little store that I could keep open year round."

So she *did* have a dream. Had she been inspired by their conversation yesterday? "Doesn't seem like it would take a whole lot to make that happen." He smiled. "What's stopping you?"

She huffed out a chuckle. "Money."

"That's what small business loans are

for. What else?"

"What *else?* Isn't that enough?"

"Look, money will always be an issue. You can't let it be the thing that stops you from moving ahead."

Shifting her weight from one foot to the other, she frowned and smoothed out her ponytail. "Even if I could get the money..." She paused, and gave a long blink. "There are *so* many other things that need doing first, before I can even think about—"

The front door of the house opened, and Bobby came out onto the porch, followed by Kyle, who looked much older in his uniform than the *kid* Derek had met at the wedding. Kyle pulled the door shut and shook it to ensure it was locked, then followed his partner down the steps and started inspecting the area around the house.

"Morning," Bobby called out as he crossed to them. "Well, apart from that door being unlocked, we didn't see any signs of anyone being in the house."

Valerie rubbed her arms. "No footprints or anything?"

"Mudroom floor's not too clean, but I figure that's from when your dad stops by from time to time. Nothing out of the ordinary. You say it looked like a flashlight?"

"Maybe. Or a lantern."

Bobby nodded. "And you've never seen anything like that out this way before?"

"No. I mean, I'm sure we would've noticed."

Clicking his tongue, Bobby scanned the landscape. "I'll have a patrol car keep an eye on things the next couple of nights. If it wasn't so far from town, I'd suspect vagrants, but like I said, it doesn't look like anyone's been staying here."

The way Valerie chewed her lip, Derek knew that answer hadn't brought much reassurance.

Bobby seemed to sense that too. "Sorry I don't have a better answer, Val. But, hey, this should cheer you up. Deputy Grant has been grilling Vincent Greco. He's not admitting to much but he did say he has a prescription for Wellbutrin, also known as bupropion."

Valerie's face brightened. "What Rex got poisoned with?"

"Says he takes it to help him quit smoking."

Derek frowned. That seemed like good news, but why would Greco tell them that if he knew it could implicate him in the poisoning charge, especially if he wasn't owning up to anything else? "So, he just offered up this information?"

Bobby shrugged. "Grant said he asked the guy if he was on anything and that's what he said. Must've tossed some tainted meat or something in the yard to get Rex to eat it."

"It's awful to think about." Valerie

shuddered. "So, he's not admitting to messing with my truck?"

Bobby shook his head. "Don't worry. They've been trying to pin him down for so long, they're more focused on the things they have evidence to support, which is all the things he did in Luxton, and of course breaking into your house. Once they have that nailed down, they'll press him more on the other things that happened in Rockford."

"So...the things that happened to *me*..."

"Well...yeah, but—"

"Hey, Bobby."

They all turned at the sound of Kyle calling from the side yard of the house.

"You might want to come take a look at this."

Derek felt his stomach clench as he and Valerie followed Bobby to an overgrown area several yards from the house. A walkway led from the back door, like maybe there used to be a shed or something over that way. Kyle directed their attention to the ground on the other side of some bushes. There, in the fresh mud from last night's rain, was a prominent set of tire tracks.

Valerie gasped. "Someone parked a car here last night."

"Bigger than a car. I'd say a truck. Or maybe..." Bobby knelt to get a closer look. "...a van."

Derek's gaze cut to Valerie. The way her face paled let on that she was thinking the same thing he was.

Chapter 29

Two days had passed with no word from Bobby about Vincent Greco or a possible intruder in the original farmhouse, and Valerie had been too busy getting ready for the fall market to worry about either. But sitting in bed reading a new novel from one of her favorite authors, her nerves were on edge. Seemed her own experiences of the past several days were still a little too fresh for a suspense novel to feel like entertainment.

Closing the book, she thought about the heroines in these stories. They always started out in their safe little world, but none of them stayed there. They'd get caught up in a harrowing adventure that would lead them to their dream. Dream job. Dream life.

Dream man.

She heaved a sigh. Should she try to be a little more like these women? Terrified of facing the scary monsters, but doing it anyway? In these books, no matter how crazy the situation got, there was always a way out. Maybe she should adopt that perspective. With a little courage, her own monsters might not be so scary. What was she so afraid of, anyway?

After setting her book on the bedside table, she leaned down and pulled her travel and craft box from its new home under her bed. Sitting crisscross, she put the box in front of her and removed the lid. The last couple of days, she'd allowed herself to daydream again. It had been years since she'd thought of her vision for the far corner of the farm, and she had forgotten how thorough her childhood plan had been.

She removed the map she'd made, probably at about age ten. It was actually pretty impressive. Her colored-pencil rendering was rough, but surprisingly realistic. Of course, it would need some fine-tuning, but maybe Derek was right. All she needed was a business plan with actual costs and projected profits. Instead of feeling daunting, the thought energized her.

Once they got their property taxes paid, maybe she and Dad could apply for a business loan. In her mind, that had started to sound feasible. Annica had been telling her lately how profitable the corn maze had gotten for her family, and how she kept thinking of ideas for expansion.

Valerie's idea wasn't all that dissimilar.

She laid out some of the craft ideas she'd particularly liked. Her vision had always been that she could sell whatever she had time and inspiration to make, but also to feature wares from other artisans. Part of the appeal, even when she was a kid, had been to create an opportunity to help other people. They could even donate part of the proceeds to charity.

And it wasn't like she'd be forging unchartered territory all by herself. She could make a list of people in the community who would support her idea, and maybe even want to help. Maybe she and Annica could bounce ideas off each other, and do some joint marketing. Their farms were only a few miles apart, so it wasn't unreasonable to think they'd share a customer base.

Of course, Dad would need to be convinced. They were full business partners, after all, and they did everything together. It was probably best to fully prepare herself before she mentioned it to him. If he saw that it wouldn't make their financial problems worse, which she knew would be his concern, and would ultimately increase their profits, of course he'd agree.

Her phone buzzed, startling her. She looked at her screen and smiled as she answered. "Hey, Derek."

"How's the book?"

"Uh...what book?"

"Don't think I'm being creepy or anything, but I saw that your light was still on, so I figured you must be reading."

"You're almost right. I was reading. You'll never guess what I'm working on now." She gave him a quick rundown of the one eighty she'd done since they'd talked about her farm plan yesterday.

"I'm proud of you, Valerie. What can I do to help?"

His offer warmed her heart. It was

good not to feel alone in this. "You've already helped more than you know. But thanks. I'll keep you posted."

After a few minutes of small talk, they said goodnight and ended the call. Derek was a good guy. Maybe she shouldn't write off that part of her dream just yet.

Motivated by her rush of inspiration, she brought up a search engine on her phone and typed in *how to write a business plan*. If she did a thorough job before presenting her idea to Dad, he'd know she was serious about it.

And if he knew how much it meant to her, how could he say no?

On Friday, Valerie and Derek had gotten their market booth set up so quickly, that Valerie had decided to stop by Maggie's house to check on her. Since Derek had borrowed her truck and taken Rex with him to get some photos, Maggie had invited Valerie to stay for tea.

Assuming that the offer had been motivated by her finally having live-in help, Valerie was surprised to find that it was Hannah's day off. Maggie had put together a lovely tea tray for them all on her own, and they were having an enjoyable visit.

Valerie hadn't intended to tell Maggie her entire idea for the farm, but once she'd gotten started, Maggie's interest encouraged her to keep talking.

"It would be a lot to take on." Sitting in Maggie's small but tasteful dining room, Valerie took a sip of lemony tea from a delicate blue-floral teacup. "But I really think it would pay off."

"It's a wonderful idea, dear." Maggie topped off Valerie's cup from her matching teapot. "But I'm wondering...have you..." She bit her fuchsia-glossed lip. “Have you spoken with your father about it yet?”

Valerie shook her head. “Not till I have my business plan written.” She had gotten to the point where she would need to dig into Dad’s files in his office to get some solid numbers, but she wanted to wait for a time when he wasn’t around. “So, if you see him—” She twisted her fingers over her mouth. “—mum’s the word.”

“Of course.” Maggie smiled, but her eyes seemed sad.

Valerie felt a flush cross her cheeks. “Oh, Maggie. I’m sorry. I know the original farmhouse used to be your home. I didn’t mean to be insensitive.”

“Don’t be silly.” Maggie waved away her concern. “I’m thrilled to think of that house having a new lease on life. I have my memories, of course.” Her gaze grew a little distant as she sipped her tea. “Some good. Some...well...” She looked down, her eyes getting misty. She shook herself out of her rumination. "At any rate, you should talk to your father. It's high time he—"

The chipper chime of her doorbell cut into their conversation, giving Valerie a start.

She moved to stand. "Would you like me to—"

"Oh, no. You enjoy your tea." Maggie unlocked the wheels of her chair and backed away from the table. "Can't imagine who that is."

As Maggie left the room, Valerie wondered what she'd been about to say. It was high time Dad did *what?*

Hearing the muffled sound of a male voice in the foyer, Valerie strained to hear. Since she couldn't make out the words, or recognize the voice, she assumed it was some neighbor she didn't know, or maybe a delivery driver.

Taking a sip of tea, she studied the lovely room, and what she could see of the living room through the doorway. Even though she had visited Maggie a handful of times, it had been a while. She'd always assumed that Maggie lived off disability, and was incapable of doing much beyond the basics. But now that she thought about it, there was nothing in her small but inviting home that supported that assumption. Until recently, she had been a virtual shut-in, but she'd made a lovely home for herself to be shut in*to*.

A low buzz drew her attention to her cell phone. She retrieved it from her waist pack and found a text from Derek—a smiley emoji and a picture of her boy playing with a stick by the river.

She was about to reply with a heart emoji when Maggie's voice rose in volume.

"...never seemed to bother you before" came through crystal clear, sounding civil but angry.

Valerie stilled, trying to make out the man's response, but the voices ceased and the front door closed very loudly. She glanced up as Maggie wheeled back in, agitation puckering her brow.

Concerned, she sent her reply then put her phone away. “Is everything okay?”

“Fine. It’s just...” Lips pursed, Maggie seemed to search for words. “I find it odd that someone could want nothing to do with a person for years, then suddenly show up at their door.”

“Who was it?” A car engine roaring to life drew Valerie’s gaze to the dining room window. All she could see was a rear bumper of the vehicle as it pulled away from the curb.

“No one important.” Maggie poured more tea into both their cups. “My late husband’s family never amounted to much. He himself was...well, face it. He was, sadly, cut from the same cloth.”

Valerie’s hand froze in place over the plate of lemon wedges. While she’d overheard more than one conversation between her parents that let her know neither of them cared much for that rotten kid Zak's parents—Daniel's brother and sister-in-law—she'd never heard anyone say anything negative about Daniel Kaufman. He'd been her dad's lifelong best friend, and Valerie had been under the impression that the world had lost a regular saint the day he died.

Squeezing the lemon into her tea, she pondered how to respond. It didn't feel like her business, but if Maggie needed to talk about it, she wanted to encourage her. "What do you mean?"

"We were married so young. Consider yourself fortunate, dear, that you didn't do that."

A nerve pinched in Valerie's chest at the reminder that, at thirty, she was past the point of being physically capable of marrying young.

"There are certain things a woman should take the time to...*discover* about a man before marriage. The biggest test is, how does he behave when he doesn't get his way?"

"Makes sense." She swallowed an unintentionally large gulp of the hot liquid, then coughed before adding, "I take it your husband didn't pass that test?"

"Let's just say, he wasn't the man I thought I had married. And we were so isolated out there on the farm. I thank God to this day for your sainted mother. She was a good friend. I wore a trail through the fields between our house and yours."

Valerie smiled slightly, in spite of the melancholy story. "I remember that trail. Mom and I would walk it too when I was little."

"Yes. Coming to check on me, although I'm sure you were too young to realize. Your mother saw what I was up against. She worried."

Worried about what? Not wanting to

pry, Valerie sorted through the swirl of questions she didn't know Maggie well enough to ask. "Did my dad? I mean, he always talks about Daniel like he could do no wrong."

"Well, they started out as friends, but then they became business partners." Maggie sighed. "I don't want to speak for your father. You might want to ask him." She shrugged her graying brows. "Would be interesting to know how much he'd tell you."

Valerie felt flustered. Twice today, Maggie had hinted that Dad might have things on his mind that he'd never shared with her. It was disconcerting to think of him having parts of his life he didn't include her in.

Especially if it had anything to do with the farm.

Chapter 30

Sitting across from Valerie at the dinette in his RV, Derek tried to recall the last time he'd had anything that even remotely resembled a Friday night date with a woman. It had been a very long time.

Not that this should be considered a date, but when Valerie had asked for his input on her business plan, he'd figured inviting her over for dessert would be a better option than sneaking up to her room while her dad did the dishes. He knew how important it was that Mr. Hayes didn't see the plan until she felt fully prepared, so the dining room in their house seemed a little too exposed.

Looking at her laptop, which she'd positioned at the end of the table in front of the window, he read over her bullet list of goals. "You'll have to make sure the property is zoned for this kind of business."

"I already thought about that." She minimized her plan on the screen. "I sent Annica an email and she forwarded the most recent zoning info." She brought up a document she'd downloaded. "She's a great resource."

Glancing over the document, he nodded. "Good. So you'll know what you're up against when you apply for all your permits."

"There's so much more to this than I realized when I was an idealistic ten-year-old."

"Good thing you didn't know." He uncapped his bottle of water and took a swig. "No kid would ever have a dream if they had to worry about red tape."

"Yeah." Interlacing her fingers together, she stretched her arms across the table and looked around the small space. "Your place is nice. I mean...tiny, but very homey."

"You think so?" It was a little beige for his taste, but he appreciated the practicality of a neutral color scheme. "You're actually the only guest I've ever had. You and Rex." He reached down to pet the dog, who had somehow managed to stretch out on the floor next to them and not take up the entire width of the walkway.

"Really?" Looking away, she clicked her nails on the Formica tabletop. "Actually, I have something to confess."

By the seriousness of her tone, he

figured he should give her his undivided attention, so he stopped petting the dog and sat up straight. "Sounds serious."

She let out a jittery chortle. "You might want to run for the hills after I tell you what I did."

"I doubt that, but...go on." He braced himself, trying not to guess what this might be about.

"Remember that day last week when you came back from helping my dad, and I was knocking on your door?"

He tracked back in his memory. "Yeah...?"

"I had kind of..." She slumped down, like she might want to hide under the table. "...broken into your RV." She winced, waiting for his response.

His eyebrows shot up. "You did...what, now?"

"Maybe not *broken in*, exactly. More like, I borrowed your key."

As she rapidly relayed how she had

checked his RV for signs that he might have been responsible for Rex's poisoning, it dawned on him that her story filled in some gaps he'd all but forgotten about.

"Then you almost caught me. I shouldn't have done it." She looked at him with puppy-dog eyes filled with remorse. "But you were at the farm the day of the poisoning. I didn't know you all that well yet. I mean, now I know you'd never..." She cast a gaze at Rex, whose back legs pumped like he was dreaming of a Preakness win. "I'm so sorry."

He nodded slowly. "I already knew."

"You...*knew?*" Straightening, she leaned forward on her elbows. "I've been torturing myself with guilt. But you knew, all this time?"

"I didn't *know* know, but you seemed so flustered. Then when I saw the pictures you took with my camera, I knew you probably saw my keys in my bag."

"Why didn't you say anything?"

He lifted a shoulder. "Guess I figured I might have done the same thing. Someone was messing with you. You didn't know who you could trust."

"I'm so embarrassed."

"Don't be." He thought for a moment, then added, "But I hope you know you can trust me. I wouldn't hurt Rex. Or you."

Their eyes met. Something flashed in hers that was gone so fast, he wondered if some fleeting emotion had caught her off-guard. Not just friendship or gratitude. Something more.

More like...*longing*.

The buzz of his phone snapped him out of his thoughts. He reached for his back pocket and glanced at the screen. "Huh."

"Who is it?"

Tapping on the Answer button, he gave her a wink. "Hello, sir." He enjoyed the curious look she aimed at him as he listened to the voice on the other end.

"Thank you. I understand. Yes, sir. Goodnight." He ended the call and set the phone on the table. "That was your dad."

"My dad?"

"He wanted to remind us that tomorrow is the big day. He thought we'd like to know he's turning in."

"Why did he call you and not me?"

"He issued a warning that I had better be a gentleman and walk you home before your curfew." He chuckled at the notion. "You have a curfew?"

"Not since I turned eighteen."

"Well, I'm guessing it's been reinstated."

"Parents. Am I right?" With a roll of her pretty brown eyes, she shut her laptop and shoved it into her bag. "He has a point though. Tomorrow starts bright and early. Thanks for all your help."

"It's the least I can do after I forced you to wipe the dust off your old dreams." He stood to clear their bowls.

"Yeah, they were pretty dusty." When she moved to stand, Rex pushed to his feet and gave a long stretch. "And thanks for the dessert." She reached for her coat, which she'd draped over the back of the front passenger seat.

"I'm glad I could wow you with my ability to make pudding from a box."

"I have nothing against pudding no matter what its origins are."

He grabbed his own coat from where he'd tossed it on the banquette and shoved an arm in a sleeve as he reached for the door. The moment it was open, Rex bounded out for his evening field frolic.

Valerie followed, a little more dignified than her canine companion. A light snow had started to fall, and she tipped her head back, eyes closed, waiting for Derek to finish putting on his coat so he could shut the door.

As they started toward the house, the two windows at the back of the upper floor went dark.

"Dad's down for the count." She hiked the strap of her bag higher on her shoulder. "I think I'll take advantage of the opportunity to grab that financial information I need from the computer in his office."

"Just don't stay up too late." He shoved his hands in his pockets. "Tomorrow's the big day."

"I'm sure it won't take me long to find last year's tax return. Dad's pretty organized. I can email it to myself and go over it later."

"You want me to text you if his bedroom light comes back on?"

She smirked. "Like we're spies on a secret assignment?"

"Exactly."

"A girl goes on one reconnaissance mission, and suddenly she's Mata Hari." The smile she sent him reflected his own teasing attitude. "It's not like I'm doing something behind his back. I'm an equal partner in the business."

"I know. I just thought the spy angle sounded intriguing."

"I'll be fine. But thanks for the offer. If he comes downstairs, I'll hear him. You know how creaky those stairs are."

They reached the bottom of the porch steps and Valerie whistled out into the darkness. In a moment, there was a rustling sound and Rex galloped toward them and up the steps.

Valerie turned to Derek, and for a moment he wondered if this had almost felt like a date to her too. But when she reached for the handrail and took a step up, he figured that was his answer.

"Don't you stay up too late either." She smiled. "Tomorrow's the big day." Her teasing tone mimicked his.

"One of the biggest of the year." He returned her smile. "Or so I've heard."

Eying him in a way that made him

seriously want to ask what she was thinking, she slowly turned and made her way to the door. He watched until she and Rex were safely inside, then turned for his own home-sweet-home. Tipping his head back, he felt the icy flakes hit his face.

The thought crossed his mind that snow wasn't the only thing in the air.

Chapter 31

Valerie removed her coat, feeling a floaty sensation that she desperately wanted to quash. It was that same feeling she used to get whenever she'd spent time with Joe, before Carrie had arrived and everything had changed. It wasn't a bad feeling, but that was the problem. She didn't want to assume that Derek was ready to move on.

Or if he was, that he wanted to move on with *her*.

Holding up a hand to let Rex know they weren't going up just yet, she crossed to the bottom of the stairs and listened. Confident that the only sound she heard was the gentle *tick tick* of the living room clock, she treaded lightly into Dad's office.

Once Rex had followed her in, she turned on the desk lamp and fired up the computer. Considering how much she hated sneaking, even when it was for a good reason, she wanted to make this quick. At least this time, she was sneaking around in her own home, not Derek's RV.

He'd been unbelievably understanding about her confession. The fact that she felt such a weight lifted off her shoulders was probably a good indication that her little foray into criminal trespass had been the wrong thing to do. Also, if she hadn't done it, she never would have seen the photo of Erin on Derek's sun visor, and therefore wouldn't have noticed its absence tonight, and wouldn't be feeling all fluttery right now.

She rubbed her eyes. Why was life so confusing?

After pulling Dad's comfy wheeled captain's chair back from the desk, she sank into it. The clock in the living room struck the half hour, jarring her out of her thoughts. Eight thirty wasn't late, but considering that she'd be up extra early tomorrow to get her morning chores done before they loaded the trucks, she'd better stay focused.

An image of her, Dad, and Rex standing in front of the barn popped up on the screen, the way it had since the day they'd bought this computer. She clicked the Documents icon. One of these days, she'd persuade Dad to show her his bookkeeping system, but in the meantime, it couldn't hurt to at least familiarize herself with it. She found a folder named *Financial.* Within that, he had set up a file for tax returns, and one for expenses, so it seemed pretty straightforward. If she ever needed to take over the books, it shouldn't be hard to figure out.

After navigating to the tax returns, she opened a browser and brought up her email. She hit Compose and put her own address in the To box. Then she attached the most recent tax return and the one before that, just in case.

What else would she need? Might as well attach last year's expenses too. The total would be on the return, but it would be helpful to see a breakdown.

After attaching it and hitting Send, she decided to take a look at it now, to be sure it had all the information she needed. She went back into the documents and clicked on the file labeled *Expenses* for the previous year,

It came up on the screen and she scanned the list of categories. Dad was so organized, and fortunately skilled at math. It seemed doubtful there'd be any fat to trim, but maybe she'd see something Dad hadn't thought about.

She was about to close the file when something grabbed her attention. Her stomach rolled over as she stared at one of the entry lines. This couldn't be right.

Her elbows hit the desk and her hands flew over her mouth.

Why would Maggie Kaufman have received money from the farm every quarter of the past year?

She stared at the numbers. No. Something had to be wrong here.

"What are you doing?"

At the sound of Dad's voice, Valerie whipped around so fast that she almost tipped the chair over. He stood in the doorway in his pajamas and robe, hair askew like he'd been sleeping, looking at her with an expression she'd never seen on his face before. Surprise. Confusion. And was that...anger?

"Dad...I..." Where to begin. She

swallowed hard, her actual reason for being there lost in a haze of confusion and betrayal. "W-why did Maggie get money from our farm last year?"

His eyes flashed wide, then his brows furrowed. He stormed toward the desk in a way that made her push the chair back to get out of his way. He reached for the mouse with hands that were visibly shaking. In a flash, the document vanished and the image of the three of them in front of the barn appeared once again, only this time, their happy faces seemed mocking.

"I don't know what you think you saw—"

"What I *think* I saw?" She stood. "Dad, I have eyes. I know exactly what I saw."

"You shouldn't be in here."

Valerie's legs turned weak, and she almost sank back into the chair. She wasn't a child. Why was he treating her like one?

Hands still shaking, he jabbed at the keyboard in an apparent attempt to shut down the computer. “It’s not your place to go poking around—”

“N-no…” She crossed her arms in front of herself. “Don’t try to make it look like I did something wrong. This is my business too.”

“You don’t keep the books. I do.”

“But I’m an equal partner. I have a right to know every detail.”

“Then ask. ’Steada sneaking around.”

“I wasn’t…” Except that she had been. Not in the way he seemed to think, but still.

Her thoughts scrambled, and tears pushed at the backs of her eyes. Suddenly, she was six years old, being scolded for touching the wet paint on the fence even though she’d been warned not to.

She stood there watching in stunned silence as Dad jerked wires out of the back of the computer, like he thought that was an actual security measure. She had been the one to set up the computer in the first place. She'd taught him how to use it. And now...

After disconnecting the keyboard, he shoved it into one of the desk drawers. Valerie couldn't stand to watch any more. The last thing she wanted to do was to run up to her room and slam the door like an out-of-control brat, but that was exactly what she felt herself about to do. She turned and bolted from the room and up the stairs. Once Rex had followed her into her room, she gave the door a satisfying shove.

She flung herself onto the bed, allowing the tears to come. The worst part wasn't that her dad had given money to Maggie without telling her. *That* she could handle. The worst part was that instead of giving her an explanation, he'd turned on her, doing everything he could to distract her, blame her, and avoid answering the question.

What was really going on here? And how long had it been happening right under her nose?

Chapter 32

All the way into town, Derek listened to Valerie talk about the unexpected entry she'd found in last year's business expenses. Her dad had paid the woman named Maggie a quarter of their entire profit for the year. As much as Derek wanted to offer an explanation that would make her feel better, he couldn't come up with any that made sense.

"If he had just explained why he gave

her all that money without telling me—" She pulled her truck into the parking lot behind the post office and across the street from the park. "—then we could have talked about it. But he treated me like I was a..." Her sentence faded as she parked and shut off the engine, then gripped the steering wheel like she might rip it right off its column.

"Like you were a child?" Reaching past Rex on the seat between them, Derek put his hand over one of hers. "I know you don't want to hear this, but you *are* his child."

She opened her mouth to protest, but he continued.

"I'm not defending him. I'm just saying that maybe he needs some time to remember you're an adult now."

"And his business partner." She fired a look at him. "It was a lot of money, Derek. Money we needed. That we *still* need."

"I know." He squeezed her hand before

letting go. "So let's focus on making today profitable."

Her jaw firmed as she looked past him, and he turned to see Mr. Hayes's truck pulling up next to them.

She drew her hands across her face, like she was wiping away tears she hadn't let herself shed. "We have work to do."

She got out, followed by Rex, then slammed her door, something that seemed out of character. Derek got out and shut the passenger door with extra care, wondering if he was going to spend the day trying to absorb her emotional discharge by tempering his own.

He reached over to help remove the tarp they'd covered their load of produce with, but she had already unhooked her side and come around to his. So maybe she was going to siphon her emotions into physical labor. That seemed more in character and definitely more productive.

By the time Derek had folded the tarp,

Valerie had already started loading one of the hand trucks they'd brought. Since she seemed to have snapped into capable-woman mode, Derek turned to give Mr. Hayes a hand.

Expecting a nod or some sort of instruction, Derek was surprised by Mr. Hayes's silent focus. He sighed. Might as well follow their lead and forgo the small talk. He pulled the second folding cart from the back of Valerie's truck and got to work.

He'd barely gotten the first crate loaded when Valerie zipped the down vest she wore over a flannel shirt, then tilted her own hand truck back and stepped close to Derek.

"Tell Dad we'll take the first load while he keeps an eye on the trucks."

Before he could respond, she and Rex were off like a shot, headed for the park.

Derek grunted. *Seriously?* She expected him to act as intermediary between them? He'd do it this one time—mainly because she was already halfway across the parking lot—but he'd have to make it clear that it wasn't going to fly. If she wanted her dad to remember she was an adult, she'd need to resist the urge to act like a petulant teenager.

Shaking his head, he finished filling his cart, then pushed it toward Mr. Hayes. "I'm just going to run this to the booth while you—"

"Keep an eye on the trucks." He shot him a hooded look. "I heard."

Derek heaved a breath. *Great.* Mr. Hayes obviously knew that Valerie had told Derek what had happened, and now he was aiming his irrational anger at him too.

Not wanting to discuss it while there was so much work to be done, Derek set off for the park. True, he was a temporary tenant of the farm, and whatever was going on would naturally impact him, but he had no intention of being inserted in the middle of a family dispute.

As he crossed the street and entered the park, his mood lifted. Other vendors—many of whom he'd seen yesterday during set-up—were at various stages of unloading their wares and filling the booths. The air, more wintry than autumnal this morning, crackled with the anticipation of the day to come, and the snow accumulating in the clouds overhead.

Starting down the walkway that bordered the grassy area, a small playground, and a bandstand, Derek admired how the colorful Hayes Family Farm sign stood out. As he got closer, he could see Valerie unloading her crates from the hand truck. Some she placed directly onto the riser-like front of the display area. Others, she emptied into decorative baskets. By the way she worked, he could tell she had a vision for the display.

“Morning, Derek.”

Derek greeted the Frazier boy—Chad, if he recalled correctly—who’d called out to him. He worked with two other young men who looked like they must be his brothers, setting up their booth right next to the Hayeses’. By the looks of it, they’d be peddling corn, decorative cornstalks, and homemade jam. The three were chipper and cheerful this morning, so at least Derek would have someone to talk to today.

Rex greeted him as he parked his cart, but Valerie barely looked up.

“Since you know what you’re doing here,” he said as he began transferring his own load to the sidewalk next to her, “why don’t you keep at it, and your dad and I can unload the trucks.”

By the way she looked at him, he knew a don’t-tell-me-what-to-do protest was already forming on her tongue, but she snapped her mouth shut and paused in her placement of a tomato.

She cocked her head and gave him a slight smile, the first he'd seen from her all day.

"Okay." Her eyes drifted back to what she was doing, like she had realized his offer wasn't an implication that she couldn't do it all herself, but a reminder that she didn't have to.

Then she straightened, looking around. "I left my waist pack in the truck. My phone's in it."

"I can grab it." After setting the last of his crates on the stack, he held out his hand for her keys.

As she reached into her pocket, the rattle of a cart drew their attention to Mr. Hayes, coming their way with an ambitiously full load. Just ahead of him, Annica Frazier carried a box that was practically half the size of her small frame.

Shoving the keys at Derek, Valerie

huffed. “He’s supposed to be keeping an eye on the trucks.”

“My dad’s watching ours, so he said he’d keep an eye on yours too,” Annica offered as one of her brothers took the box from her and she lifted a red-checked tablecloth out of it.

With an exaggerated sigh, Mr. Hayes parked his cart, swapped it for the one Derek had just emptied, and immediately left again.

Derek shook his head. It wasn’t even eight AM, and already he felt like it had been a full day.

Chapter 33

By midmorning, Valerie had gotten used to working around her dad as if he weren't there, and he seemed to be doing the same with her. It astounded her that he hadn't realized yet how irrational his behavior had been last night, and that he owed her a big, fat apology.

She tried not to think about what her options would be if that apology never came.

Derek had made it clear that he wouldn't act as go-between in their little family squabble—a stance as understandable as it was annoying. Logically, she knew she'd appreciate his mature approach to the situation sometime after today, but for right now all she wanted was to wallow in self-righteousness.

That, and to sell a lot of produce.

Fortunately, the snow was holding off, and the crowd so far had been even bigger than usual. They'd been doing a steady stream of business, which definitely took her mind off her troubles. If only the dark little voice in her head would stop popping in to remind her that the partnership she'd thought she had with her dad all these years had been a lie. That it didn't matter how much profit they made today if Dad's attitude was that he could do whatever he wanted with it without consulting her.

Now, as Valerie finished bagging an order for a young couple who had come all the way from Helena just for the market, she looked up to see a welcome lull in their stream of customers. It was good timing, considering that, in addition to her normal morning coffee at home, she'd enjoyed an apple pie latte that Derek had brought her from the Need-a-Little-Pickup coffee truck. She was due for a break.

Since the booth was a reasonable size for two people, Derek had taken it upon himself to "work the crowd," giving out samples to passersby, and stepping in when she or Dad needed a break.

Trying to catch Derek's eye, she noticed Carrie and Joe on their way toward her. Walking obediently on a leash alongside Joe was a dog who looked suspiciously like a clean, well-behaved version of Buster. She cast a look back at Rex, who had curled up on his blanket next to their space heater, taking a little break from the hard work of being a dog.

She clasped her hands together as her friends approached. "He's like a brand-new boy."

"It's amazing what a little love and discipline will do." Joe instructed him to sit, then rewarded him with a treat when he did. "I've worked with him some, but he's pretty much been hanging out, being a ranch dog."

Carrie beamed. "This is his first time out in a crowd, and he's acting like a graduate of canine finishing school."

"And get this, Val." Joe pointed over his shoulder with his thumb. "We walked right by Crystal over there. She and Buster didn't even notice each other."

"Yeah," Carrie said, "but I still think Buster was pretending. I can't imagine sending him back to her now."

"Not a chance." Joe chuckled, then something caught his eye. "Hey, while you ladies talk, Buster and I are heading over to Rusty's booth." He nodded toward a display of ranch wear. "I could use a new belt buckle."

Carrie blew Joe an air kiss. "Get Buster a kerchief."

As Joe set off, Derek returned with an empty sample plate. He greeted Carrie, then handed the plate to Valerie. "I successfully gave away all the apple slices."

"So that's why we had a run on the Honeycrisps." Valerie set the plate on the counter and removed her apron. "Hey, do you mind spotting me? I'm going to powder my nose."

"Take your time." He looked over at Dad, who was helping Margaret Owens pick out a bunch of carrots. "We men will hold down the fort."

"Great." She turned her focus to Carrie. "You want to walk with me?"

She nodded, then waited for Valerie to

slide through the narrow space between their booth and the Fraziers'. As they started toward the park's restrooms, Valerie let out an unintentional sigh.

Carrie eyed her suspiciously. "Something going on with Derek?"

"What? No." Chuckling at her friend's assumption, Valerie cast a look back at Dad, who was chatting happily as he bagged up Margaret's carrots. "It's Dad. I'll fill you in later." As much as she wanted to tell Carrie, she didn't want to risk someone overhearing. "At least mundane family drama is better than being stalked."

"Yeah." Carrie's nervous chuckle turned into a frown. "Hey, have you heard any more from Bobby?"

"He called a few days ago. The sheriff in Luxton is still building his case. Greco's not admitting to anything, but he had a pattern. Each of the women in Luxton had complained about him giving them a hard time just a few days before they had some kind of vandalism or a break-in at their house."

"Huh. So he broke his pattern with you."

Valerie shoved her hands in the pockets of her vest. "What do you mean?"

"I mean, you didn't see him until the convenience store. The strange things started happening to you a few days before."

"Well, yeah. But—"

"And all the other women live in Luxton. You don't do deliveries that far. When would he have seen you before that night?"

"No idea."

"So if he messed with your truck, *then* happened to see you on his home turf, where he gave you a bad time and followed you to your house, he was breaking his pattern."

"I guess." She paused, having no idea

what to make of that observation. "You think that matters?"

Carrie shrugged. "Maybe not." Her brow furrowed. "There's something else though. The night you saw him at the gas station, he was already in the store when we walked in, right?"

"Yeah...?"

"He didn't follow us in. Does that seem strange to you?"

"Maybe he followed us there then went inside while we were pumping gas."

"Why would he do that, though? I mean, for all he knew, we were going to pay at the pump and leave. If he was following us, wouldn't he have waited to see where we were going?"

Valerie's temple started to throb as they arrived at the short line outside the door to the ladies room. "You think they're not going to be able to prove he's responsible for everything?"

"I'm not saying *that*. It's just..." Rolling

in her lips, Carrie waved it off. "I'm overthinking it." She jolted like she'd just realized how much time had passed. "Hey, I should go find Joe before he starts looking for me." She took a couple of steps backwards. "See you tonight for the talent show?"

"We'll be here." Valerie waved as Carrie disappeared into the crowd.

Folding her arms, she turned back to join the movement of the line. Carrie had a point, but Bobby had seemed so certain that everything was lining up.

Or had he? Now that she thought about it, he had said everything they were sure that Greco had done to the other women was lining up. They knew he had broken into the farmhouse because he'd been caught red handed. But beyond confirming that Greco had a prescription for bupropion, Bobby hadn't said anything about the other things that had happened to her.

But the incidents had stopped when they'd put Greco behind bars. He had to be responsible for her truck, and for Rex, and maybe even for the gunfire Derek had heard.

Didn't he? Except that, if he wouldn't admit it, and they couldn't prove it, would they ever know for sure?

Terrific. Now Carrie had her overthinking it too. Or maybe Valerie just wanted to take her mind off her "mundane family drama," which she felt helpless to do anything about.

Chapter 34

In the few minutes since Valerie had left with Carrie, Derek and Mr. Hayes had seen a steady stream of business. Derek hadn't fully appreciated until today how excited people got about farm-fresh produce.

"These will make a delightful tart." A small, fifty-something woman held open an almost full reusable shopping bag, her round cheeks lifted in a smile.

"Sounds delicious." Derek nestled a clear plastic bag of pears between a sack of potatoes and a garlic braid.

As she tapped her chin and continued to study their offerings, Derek noticed that Hannah was pushing Maggie down the walkway, headed in their direction. He groaned inwardly. It hadn't occurred to him that Valerie might have to face Maggie before the issue with her dad got resolved.

He scanned the walkway behind them, grateful that there was no sign of her yet. With any luck, the line at the restrooms would be long enough to keep her away until Maggie moved on.

"Maggie!" As they neared the Fraziers' booth, Annica called out. "You look so stylish. I love your coat."

"Why, thank you, dear." Maggie smoothed the front of her short, beige coat. "I've had it for years, but I've hardly worn it."

"Everything comes back in style." Annica sounded chipper, which seemed to be her norm. "I love the bell sleeves."

Curious about that name, Derek glanced over to see that her sleeves were—not surprisingly—shaped like a bell from the elbow down.

While Hannah perused the Fraziers' jam selection, Maggie wheeled herself over to the Hayeses' booth. Mr. Hayes had just finished with a customer, and he greeted Maggie as she came to a stop near his end of the stand.

While Derek helped the pear-tart woman decide between the curly kale and the Swiss chard, he noticed Mr. Hayes leaning forward on the edge of the booth, intently focused on Maggie, whose look had turned somber. Their voices were low, but when Derek moved closer to grab a bunch of basil, he couldn't help but overhear.

"...showed up at my front door again

yesterday." Contempt radiated from Maggie's tone.

"What does he want?" Mr. Hayes's voice came out in a low growl.

"I have no idea. I made it clear that I want nothing to do with any of the Kaufman family at this point."

"If he comes around again, I want you to tell me." Cutting his gaze toward a group of teens who noisily passed the booth, Mr. Hayes appeared to remember they weren't alone. "We'll get the sheriff involved if we have to."

The sheriff. That sounded serious.

Whatever was going on, it was none of Derek's business. But, as he tallied the total for his customer, he couldn't help but wonder if whoever Maggie was so concerned about had something to do with the reason Mr. Hayes had been giving her money behind Valerie's back.

"Looks like diamonds."

Valerie had been so lost in thought as she took advantage of a late-afternoon lull to restock the greens, that she needed a beat to realize that Derek had spoken to her. She glanced up, having no idea what he was talking about.

Using his chin, he pointed toward the row of trees that lined the opposite side of the walkway, and the puffy clouds beyond. "It's snowing."

"Oh..." Her gaze tracked upward. "So it is." Turning her attention from the sky, she perfected the placement of a bunch of kale and moved on to the heirloom tomatoes.

"You seem distracted." Derek wiped away the dirt that had accumulated on the counter where they kept their cash box and receipt pads. "You talk to your dad at all yet today?"

"Not a word." She sighed. The dance of anger with her dad had been as exhausting as it was pointless. It had come as a relief when he'd taken a break to help his friend Tom scour the market in search of an anniversary gift for his wife. "It's not just that, though."

That caught his attention. "What else?"

Stilling her hands, she contemplated. Ever since her conversation with Carrie earlier in the day, she hadn't been able to shake the feeling that something just wasn't adding up. "Do you think there's a chance that Vincent Greco isn't the guy?"

Folding his arms, Derek leaned a hip against the counter. "What do you mean? They caught him trying to get into your house."

"Yeah, I know he's *that* guy. But..." She looked away, trying to get a handle on what she was even thinking. "He didn't follow us into the store."

Derek stood straight, his expression turning serious. "Okay. So?"

"If he was the guy who put the tracker on my truck and tried to kill my dog, wouldn't he have been following us, not already in there buying beer?"

"You're saying you think he might not have done it?"

"I'm saying I don't know if it makes sense to assume. Bobby didn't say..." She stopped. Why was she forgetting to include the most important One in this conversation? The One who knew what was happening and what would happen. God knew what she needed to do about Maggie and Derek. He knew if Greco was guilty, and if he wasn't, who was.

"I need to pray about this."

Derek looked away. "Yeah. If that'll make you feel better."

"It's not about making myself feel better."

"Okay." He tipped his head from side to side. "We can agree to disagree."

Pressure built behind her eyes. *Is that my answer about Derek?* How could she hold out hope for a man who had no faith? If she wanted her faith to be the cornerstone of her life, why would she settle for a relationship with a man who had so easily walked away from God?

From the corner of her eye, Valerie saw someone moving in their direction at a rapid clip. Reluctantly, she pulled her eyes from Derek and saw that it was Hannah. Her stomach buckled, but she quickly noted that Maggie wasn't with her.

Thank goodness, because her nerves could only take just so much. Facing Maggie like everything was normal might send her over the edge.

Turning to Derek, she held up a hand to put a cap on the topic. "Agree to disagree. And about Greco...I'm sure I'm just worrying about nothing."

His gaze lingered on her like he might not be so sure, but a couple with two young kids were enthusiastically perusing the pumpkins, so he turned his attention to them.

Hannah fell in line behind a few customers buying corn at the Fraziers' booth, then, catching Valerie's eye, she shifted closer to her. "Hi, Valerie. I missed you when we came by earlier." As one of the corn customers stepped away, Hannah moved forward, still talking to Valerie. "I got distracted and I totally forgot my jam."

"I'm glad you came back." Annica reached under her counter and produced a bag, which she handed to Hannah. "I was going to run it over to Maggie's house."

Valerie wanted to smile, but it came out forced. "M-Maggie's not with you?"

She felt a light touch to her arm and looked at Derek, who gave her a supportive nod. An acknowledgement of what he probably knew she was thinking.

"Oh, I left her watching some kids juggling." She pointed in the direction she'd come from. "I don't want to leave her for long."

"I'm so glad she's getting out more." Annica moved as close as the confines of her booth would allow, so she didn't have to shout over a rowdy group of middle schoolers passing by. "She was so smart to hire you."

"Oh, we have the Hayeses to thank for that." Hannah grinned at Valerie. "Mr. Hayes is the one who hired me."

Valerie's forced smile faltered. That couldn't be true. Dad would have told her.

Her heart sank. Apparently, there was a *lot* Dad hadn't told her.

A jumble of questions bubbled into her throat, but when she opened her mouth, no words came.

"Well, I should go." Hannah clutched

the bag of jam. “I need to get Maggie home.”

“She won’t be here for the show tonight?” Annica asked.

“I think the shopping has worn her out. She’s ready for a good night’s sleep.” Hannah lifted a wave and made her retreat.

Derek dipped his chin close to Valerie’s ear. “I’m guessing you didn’t know.”

Jaw tightening, she shook her head. “Add that to the list of things I didn’t know.” She looked over at Rex, who was sleeping on his back, legs in the air. Suddenly, a tremor shot through her system. This had gone on long enough.

Firming her resolve, she removed her apron. “Would you watch the booth for a few minutes? I need to find my dad.”

“Valerie. I think you—”

“I can’t take any more.” She gritted the words out quietly, through clenched teeth.

"He has some explaining to do."

Derek reached for her arm as she turned to go, but the two kids chose that moment to hoist their pumpkin picks onto the counter, ready to pay. She took advantage of the opportunity to duck out. This should only take a few minutes. The way she felt, she was going to find Dad and get some answers if she had to drag them out of him.

He owed her that much.

Chapter 35

Valerie's head swam as she searched the crowd for Dad's navy-blue coat and distinctive plaid ear-flap hat. At the opening between the booths where the sidewalk cut over to the street, she saw him by the curb, helping Tom Cooper throw a tarp over one of Walt Duncan's hand-carved rocking chairs in the back of Tom's pickup.

As she marched up to him, Dad saw

her, and his cheerful demeanor instantly faded.

"Tom." She greeted their old family friend. Nodding at the rocker, she added, "Elaine will love it."

"Hope so." Tom patted the side of his truck. "Now to get 'er home before Elaine gets back from her mom's." With a tip of his hat, he moved to get into his truck.

Valerie turned to her dad. "We need to talk."

Eyes widening, Dad looked around. "We should get on back—"

"Derek can manage for a few minutes." She kept her voice low, but her emotions simmered. "I need some answers."

Closing his eyes, he slumped into his shoulders. When his eyes opened, he looked around self-consciously. "Let's walk." He started for the crosswalk, away from the crowd.

Aware that the snow wasn't letting up, she took her wool beanie out of the pocket of her puffy vest and pulled it on as they crossed the street. Once on the other side, Dad turned left, which made sense. That led them toward Rockford Street, but away from where the majority of the people were coming and going from the market.

The moment they were a reasonable distance from any passersby, she dove in. "Hannah said you hired her for Maggie? Is that true?"

His eyes tightened, but she saw a hint of guilt in them. He held up his hand as if the gesture would stop her questioning. "Calm down."

Heat filled her cheeks, those two words having the opposite effect of what they commanded. "You know what would calm me down? You telling me the truth. I already know you gave Maggie money. Did you hire Hannah for her too?"

He glanced around, his chin trembling, then shoved his hands in his pockets and crossed Rockford Street. He continued up the side street, further away from people.

Just past the opening to the alley, he let out a long breath, eyes focused on the sidewalk ahead. “Yes.”

A fire burned in her gut as she waited for him to elaborate. When he didn’t, she pressed him. “Why?”

He walked a few more yards, then stopped, hanging his head. They’d made it half a block from the park, up the residential street. If anyone was curious, at least they wouldn’t be able to overhear.

Moments passed, and she sensed that he was either praying, or calculating how little he could get away with telling her. Finally, he opened his mouth to speak.

“Because I’m responsible.”

Confused, she stared at him. Was he honestly expecting her to know what that meant?

“For what, Dad? For Maggie?”

He half-turned to face her, his mouth opening and closing like a fish. Then, he glanced up, eyes glistening. "For the accident."

Oh. The blood drained from her face. Of all the possible answers that had flitted through her mind, that hadn't made the cut. How on earth could he be responsible for the accident that had left Maggie unable to walk, and had killed her husband—Dad's best friend?

Her gloved hand covered her mouth. What was this can of worms she had ripped open?

All she could say was "I-I don't understand."

He cleared his throat. "I, um...I found out that Daniel wasn't who I thought he was."

That seemed to go along with what Maggie had said yesterday. That Daniel wasn't the man she thought she had married. She nodded, encouraging him to continue.

"You were so young. You probably had no idea about our problems."

She'd been five at the time of the accident, but he was right. Before it happened, everything had seemed fine. All she recalled after the accident was sadness and a lot of people coming and going. Then Mom explaining to her that Daniel wouldn't be there anymore and Maggie would need a chair with wheels to help her get around.

"Daniel and I were equal partners in the farm. I managed the crew and he handled the money. It worked out great for the first few years." He paused, then looked up as if he had just noticed that they were being snowed on. He took a few steps, putting them under the shelter of Marjory Trainor's oak tree.

"A little before the accident," he continued, "I noticed something was wrong with the farm's finances." He winced, maybe seeing the irony in that. "Long story short, I figured out that Daniel was skimming money."

"Oh..." She held her tongue. Now that he was talking, she didn't want to discourage him.

"It was fall, just about this time of year. I tried to have it out with him, but he denied it. Stormed out of the house. The next day, Maggie told your mother that they were going to the cabin for a while. I don't think Maggie knew the situation, but I suspected Daniel was going into hiding, and I wasn't supposed to know where he was."

"Did you go to the sheriff?"

"We were friends. I thought I should try to work it out first. If he needed the money..." Closing his eyes, he gave his head a small shake, as if to get himself back on track with the story. "I just wanted to talk to him, so I got in the truck to drive to the cabin. It was a rash move, considering that it was snowing and almost dark. You know how that road is out to the cabin."

Curvy and narrow. She remembered. "So...did you talk to him?"

"Never got the chance. The snow started coming down worse. I was waiting for the weather report to come on the radio, but I started to lose the signal. I looked down to adjust the dial." He swallowed. "I only had my eyes off the road for a few seconds. But when I looked up, there were headlights in front of me. I must've drifted into the other lane, because the oncoming truck swerved to keep from getting hit. It spun and went off the road, down into the ravine."

"Oh, Dad. That's awful."

He ran his gloved hands over his eyes. "That's not the worst of it." He let out a long breath. "I didn't stop."

She stared at him. What was he saying?

"You didn't just pay her last year, did you? You've been paying her a quarter of our profits for...for how long?"

He held for a long beat. "Twenty-five years."

Anger boiled fresh. She turned her back on him, not wanting to look at the pain in his eyes right now, because her own pain was all she could manage.

That explained it all. Why they were always so broke, even when the sales were coming in. Dad had been paying Maggie a share of their profits for all these years.

An unbearable sense of betrayal hit her like a freight train. She had dedicated her life to keeping this business running. Worked tirelessly, hardly ever taking any time for herself. And all this time, Maggie had done nothing for the business but she'd gotten a quarter of the profit?

The full weight of Dad's deception hit her. "People have been overpaying us because they don't want us to lose the farm." She turned her head to look at him, her body slowly following. "Did you know that, Dad? Our customers...friends...have been donating their own hard-earned money to keep us from going under. While you've been paying a quarter of our profits to someone who doesn't even do anything to keep our place running."

"She can't help, Valerie. She's disabled."

"She's in a wheelchair, Dad. She's not paralyzed. She's more capable than you think."

He worked his jaw, the argument seemingly drained out of him. "Look, we can talk about this later. We need to get back."

As right as he was, she was in no mood to walk with him. "You go on. I need a minute."

He nodded. She watched as he turned to go, then flipped up his collar and hunched his shoulders against the falling snow. He seemed so vulnerable—not the strong, capable father she'd always known him to be.

When he was a half a block ahead, she shoved her gloved hands into the pockets of her vest, and trailed behind him. Tears threatened, but this was no time to let herself cry. Everything that she had hoped for in her life was on the brink of destruction. Now that she understood that so much of their profit was being paid as indirect hush money, how could she hope to create a financial plan that would lift them out of the red, much less allow her to expand the way she had dreamed of doing?

Where did that leave her? Did she even want to stay in business with her dad, now that she knew he'd been lying to her for practically her whole life?

And then there was Derek. Just when she had started to get her hopes up about him, he'd shown her how ill-matched they were. Spring would come, and he would move on with his exciting life, leaving her here with nothing but a dog and a sad failure of a life.

Just past the opening to the alley, something stopped her. An erratic pounding noise...coming from the alley.

Turning to look, she took a couple of careful steps back. Her breath caught. Halfway down the alley stood a van. *The* van. The same one she'd seen before.

No...it couldn't be.

Her heart racing, she moved a little closer, straining to listen. It sounded for all the world like the pounding was coming from inside the van. She looked around, but the only people to be seen were a half a block away and across the street. She reached for her phone, but... Oh, man. Why had she left it in her apron pocket back at the booth?

After determining that there was no one else in the alley, she crept closer, trying to see through the back windows. It was no use. Even if it were possible from this distance, they were caked with dirt.

The closer she got, the more certain she was that the frantic pounding was coming from the van. Cupping her hands to one of the back windows, she peered in.

On the floor inside the van, she saw someone sitting, hands tied behind them, pounding on the wall of the van. As her eyes adjusted to the dark inside, Valerie realized who it was. Her heart nearly stopped.

Maggie!

Chapter 36

Derek had managed to hold down the fort on his own for what had seemed like at least half an hour. When Mr. Hayes entered the booth and grabbed his apron, Derek glanced down the walkway, which was starting to resemble a winter wonderland.

"Did Valerie find you?"

"Hm?" Mr. Hayes grunted. "Oh...uh, yeah. She'll be along in a minute."

Derek sighed. He should let it go at that, of course. What went on between the Hayeses was none of his business. Still, he'd been part of their household for the past couple of weeks. And he'd committed to helping with the farm for the rest of the winter. Didn't that make this at least partly his concern?

Before he could compose an appropriately nonintrusive question, an older woman came up to Mr. Hayes, inquiring about the best way to caramelize beets.

Thankful that he hadn't had to field that one, Derek looked up to see Bobby approaching in his deputy uniform.

"Hey, Bobby. Don't they give you a day off?"

"Not till the boss gets back." His face turned serious. "Say, do you know where Valerie is? I wanted to give her a heads-up about something."

"She should be back soon. Something

about her case?"

Bobby sighed. "The sheriff in Luxton is dropping the charges against Greco for everything that happened here in Rockford except the break-in at the farm."

"Dropping the charges?" Mr. Hayes joined in as the customer picked through the beets. "Why?"

"Guy's got an alibi. He was in Idaho the week her truck got messed with. Taking care of some outstanding tickets so his license didn't get suspended. That night Val saw him at the gas station, he just got back to town that day."

"What about Rex?" Derek asked. "That didn't happen till two days after."

Bobby was shaking his head before Derek reached the end of his sentence. "He got into a fight that Saturday night. Spent the better part of Sunday in the same jail cell he got put back into the very next week."

Derek's stomach clenched. So,

Valerie's concern had been well-founded.

"The thing is, it fits his M.O. He sees a woman, maybe gives her a hard time, then follows her home. Goes back later and digs up her flowerbed, or spray paints her garage door. Or breaks in. Anyway, I wanted to tell Val we still don't have this solved, so she should watch her back." As he spoke, the radio on his coat lapel crackled something about kids doing wheelies in the snow at the high school. He spoke into it, then turned back to Derek and Mr. Hayes. "Gotta go. Would you tell Val what I said?"

"Sure—"

"—Yeah, of course."

Derek watched as Bobby blended into the crowd. The sense of unease he felt himself was coming off of Mr. Hayes in waves as the older man rang up the customer's purchase. Where was Valerie?

The moment the customer stepped away, Mr. Hayes turned to Derek, his lip quivering. “I don’t much like the sound of that.”

“Me either. I’m calling her.” Derek reached into his back pocket, but instead of his phone, he felt something else brush his fingers. Valerie’s truck keys. He held them up. “I forgot to give these back to her this morning.”

“Least that means she didn’t go far.”

Derek retrieved his phone from his other back pocket and brought up her number. No sooner had he tapped it, than he heard a buzzing sound. He looked down at her apron sitting on the counter.

He looked over to see Mr. Hayes staring at the apron, concern filling his eyes.

Derek grappled with a growing unease. “I don’t suppose she changed her mind about carrying the gun.”

Mr. Hayes shook his head. “It’s locked up at home.”

Feeling something brush against his

leg, Derek looked down to see Rex standing next to him. His ears were straight up and alert.

He bent to pet him, a sense of urgency building. Wherever she was, she was without her keys, her phone, and her guard dog. Add to that the possibility that the person who had been harassing her was still out there, and he had a pretty solid case for the disquiet building in his gut.

He turned to Mr. Hayes. “Rex and I are going to look for her. She comes back here, tell her to call me.” He looked down at Rex. “Let’s go find your mama, boy.”

“Maggie!”

Maggie’s head snapped in Valerie’s direction, her eyes filled with terror. She stopped pounding and struggled to speak, but Valerie could now see that she was gagged.

Shaking, Valerie rattled the door handle, but it wouldn't budge. "I'm going for help." She tried to keep her voice low in case whoever had done this was nearby. "Hang on!"

The way Maggie's head shook, Valerie was sure she was asking her not to leave, but what other choice did she have?

Darting back out of the alley, she nearly slid on the snow-covered sidewalk. She ran, intending to alert the first person she could get to. All she needed was a phone so she could call for help.

At the corner, she glanced down the main street. Someone was walking, but they were near the end of the block by the diner. Then a movement. A woman had just closed the trunk of her car and was coming around the driver's side. Hannah!

"Hey!" Dashing toward her, Valerie called out.

Hannah's head jerked up, confusion furrowing her brow.

Valerie waved for her to come with her. "It's Maggie!"

Hannah looked around, a dozen emotions flicking across her face. "Wha...where?"

"In the alley. Do you have your phone?" Valerie started back toward where she had come. "Call for help!"

Hannah hesitated.

"Come on!"

Seeing that Hannah had reached into her pocket and taken out her phone, Valerie hurried back around the corner to the opening of the alley.

"She's in the back of that—"

The brake lights of the van popped on, and it started moving.

"No...no!" Her thoughts blurred. "We need to follow them!"

"Get in my car!" Tapping at her phone, Hannah jogged back the way they'd come.

Valerie broke into a run. By the time she got to the corner, Hannah had opened the driver's door of her car and had her phone pressed to her ear. Catapulting herself at the passenger door, Valerie turned her head just as the van appeared at the corner by the diner. It took a left onto Rockford Street, away from them, and toward where the street became the highway.

She stumbled to get into Hannah's car. "Hurry!" Twisting in her seat to keep the van in her sights, she quickly fastened her seatbelt.

"Th-that's right..." Hannah struggled to keep her phone by her ear as she backed the car out of its space and made a U-turn. "We're following the van now."

"Tell them it's the same van I reported two weeks ago. Jeremy has a file." She reached for Hannah's phone. "I can talk while you drive."

"Thank you." Hannah tapped the

phone and set it in her lap. "She said to keep a safe distance and she'll call back. She's sending someone."

Valerie's thoughts were muddled. Were they doing the right thing? If she had her own phone, she could call Dad. Or Derek. Or anybody. Why didn't she have any numbers committed to memory?

As Derek weaved through the throng of happy shoppers, trying to keep up with Rex, he realized that his canine buddy had his nose to the ground. Not just doing his usual sniffing-out-a-rabbit meander. He was on a trail. Could it be Valerie's trail?

Keeping Rex in sight, Derek scoped the area, to no avail. He asked a few people if they'd seen her, getting either a "Sorry, no," or an answer that confirmed the direction that Rex was taking him.

So…trust the dog.

After crossing the street and heading up the block, Rex retraced his steps, leading Derek first into the alley, then back to the main street, where he stepped off the curb and stopped. Looking up at Derek, he barked, turned in a circle, and barked again.

"What's going on, boy?" Derek studied the prints in the snow. It was pretty easy to see that someone had gotten in on either side of a car that had then backed out and made a U-turn. Why would Valerie get into a car? If she needed to go somewhere, wouldn't she have told them?

Unless…

His chest burned. Unless she hadn't gone willingly.

His mind raced. He needed to call Bobby. He reached for his phone, again finding Valerie's truck keys.

"Come on, boy." Retrieving his phone from his other pocket, he took off toward

Valerie's truck. If he was right, and Rex's nose was to be believed, he needed to figure out where this car had gone before their only hope got buried in the snow.

Chapter 37

Valerie's heart felt like it was going to pound right out of her chest. Hannah was doing an impressive job of keeping her distance behind the van, but when it took the turn onto McGregor Road, Valerie started to worry. What if the driver knew he was being followed, and he was deliberately leading them someplace isolated?

"You're sure dispatch hasn't called us

back?" For the millionth time, she kicked herself for not having her own phone. "Maybe we should call them again."

After turning off the highway onto McGregor, Hannah eased to a stop. She lifted her phone and tapped it. "No service." Rolling her lips, she set it back in her lap. "What should we do?"

Valerie's mind raced. If the dispatcher—probably Peggy, since it was the weekend—had sent a car like she said, they should wait here to direct them. But if they let the van get out of sight, there were so many roads leading off McGregor, Maggie could be lost. The snow was coming down harder now. How likely would it be that the police would be able to follow the van's tracks?

She strained to keep the van in view. What should they do? There were a few small farms along this road, but everyone was at the market, so there was no hope of stopping to use someone's landline.

She realized Hannah was still waiting for an answer. "I think we need to keep going. We'll most likely be able to get cell service past the Frazier farm. That's not far. Then, we can let dispatch know where the van is headed." Of course, the weather wasn't working in their favor. And it would be getting dark soon.

As Hannah started forward again, Valerie tried to make sense of this. "Why would anyone want to take Maggie?"

Hannah shrugged. "Maybe she has a secret fortune?"

Valerie pressed against a knot forming in her stomach at the reminder of Maggie's financial situation. Not exactly a fortune, and not even enough for Valerie to hold a grudge over.

Please, God, show us what to do, and protect Maggie.

The van had rounded a curve and disappeared from sight, but the sign for the corn maze came into view.

"The Frazier farm is just up ahead." Valerie held out her hand for Hannah's phone. "I should keep checking for service."

Hannah picked up her phone, but instead of handing it to Valerie, she tapped the screen. "Still nothing." She returned it to her lap. "Can you see the van?" She pointed to the right. "Is that it heading down that road?"

Valerie twisted a look at the fields to the right, but she wasn't sure what road Hannah meant. "There isn't a—"

When she turned again, her heart jumped into her throat. Instead of holding the phone in her hand, Hannah held a gun.

And it was pointed at Valerie.

"Nine-one-one," the female voice on the

line said. "What's your emergency?"

"This is Derek Bradford." Derek hit Speaker and held the phone in front of his mouth. "I need you to tell Bobby that I think Valerie is in trouble."

"Val Hayes?" The woman's tone slipped out of professional and into personal. "I've got Bobby and Kyle dealing with some kids at the high school. Our Luxton officers got called back there on a bank robbery. I can let Bobby know, but it might be a few minutes."

"Have him call me. Tell him I'm following some tire tracks up the highway heading north."

Ending the call, he pulled to the shoulder and brought up Mr. Hayes's number. After tapping on it, he checked the side mirror for traffic and started moving again.

When the call went to voicemail, Derek groaned. He knew the man kept his phone on him, but since Derek hadn't noticed him making a practice of checking his messages, it wouldn't surprise him if he kept his volume turned down. He'd leave a quick message, just in case.

"Mr. Hayes. This is Derek. Has Valerie come back? If she does, have her call me. Rex and I are looking for her. And Mr. Hayes...?" He didn't want to unnecessarily cause a panic, but better to be safe. "I'm starting to worry."

"Wh-what are you doing?" Heart pounding, Valerie twisted in her seat, putting as much distance between herself and Hannah as she could. Instinctively, she held her palms at shoulder level, like a criminal surrendering.

"Shut up. I need to think." Hannah's face had turned cold and steely, nothing at all like the sweet woman Valerie had thought she was. "You should have just stayed out of it."

"What do you mean? Out of what? Hannah, I don't know what you—"

"I told you to shut up!" Nostrils flaring, Hannah kept her hand that held the gun—which, now that Valerie got a good look at it, was on the small side and had a fuchsia barrel— surprisingly steady. "We had a plan. If he wasn't so stupid."

Acid rose in Valerie's throat. Who was she talking about?

"What kind of plan?" She kept her voice low, like Hannah might keep talking without noticing that Valerie had ignored her command to keep quiet. "Is this about Maggie?"

Huffing out contempt, Hannah gave her a side-eyed glance. "What do *you* think? We might have to go back to our original plan." The woman tipped her head to the side. "Too bad for you."

"I don't understand what this has to do

with me."

"You don't own that whole farm, you know. Half of it's supposed to be ours."

Ours? Who was this woman, really?

Hannah shook her head. "We didn't want to hurt you, you know. We just wanted to scare you."

"Okay. Well...y-you've done that." Valerie fought to keep breathing. "Now what?"

She raised the gun, as if Valerie might have forgotten it was there. "We'll figure it out when we get there."

Valerie shrunk back, assuming the *we* who would do the figuring out didn't include *her*.

Where are we going? would be the obvious question, but she was fairly sure it would be wasted on the obvious answer—*You'll find out when we get there*. They were still on McGregor, but there was no sign of the van, a fact that no longer seemed to bother Hannah. So, obviously, she knew their destination. Whatever time Valerie had before they arrived, she needed to use wisely. Maybe she could appeal to the woman's humanity. Talk her out of whatever this plan was.

"Hannah..." She gentled her tone, trying to appear sympathetic. "I know you don't want to hurt anyone. You're a nurse."

Hannah blew out an ugly snicker. "Only because people told me I could make easy money as a nurse. What a joke that is. I spent five years cleaning bedpans and changing bandages. What's easy about that? And the money's not enough to make up for it." Letting out a breath, she shook her head. "When I found out about the farm..." Her tone turned dark, almost like she'd forgotten Valerie was there. "I don't care so much about the revenge. I just want the money."

Revenge? It suddenly hit Valerie. Did this have something to do with Daniel's accident? But how did Hannah figure in with that?

"Hannah, we don't...have any money."

The woman chuckled. "I know how much that farm is worth. Even just the part that's supposed to be ours. We...well, *I* just want our fair share."

Unless there was something else to this story that Valerie had been kept in the dark about, there was no way any share of the Hayes Family Farm would fairly be owed to Hannah.

Was there?

"I don't understand. You said my dad hired you through an agency in Billings."

"Yeah, you ever hear of *Caring Hearts Caregivers?*"

The mockery she infused in that name made Valerie wince. "N-no."

Glancing at Valerie, Hannah smirked. "Neither had your dad. He fell for my little marketing campaign. Didn't even realize the woman he talked to on the phone was the same woman the *agency* sent out as an in-home caregiver." She shook her head. "Gull-i-ble."

"That's..." Valerie swallowed the word *appalling*. Her only hope was to try to make this disgusting woman think Valerie was on her side. "That's really smart of you. But...why Maggie?"

"Be*cause*." She bit off the word as though it did all the work of answering the question. To Valerie's surprise, Hannah took a deep breath and went on. "We knew about the deal. We knew how Daniel died, and that half of the farm is supposed to be ours. We figured, why wait who knows how long so we can collect on a small part of it, when we can go for what we never should have lost because your dad—"

She hit the brake, muttering a curse word and looking around like she had forgotten to pay attention to where she was going. When she put the car in reverse, Valerie glanced back, realizing they'd driven past the farmland and into the woods. Then when Hannah stopped and shifted into Drive again, it dawned on Valerie where they were going.

Her stomach dropped at the implication of why they might be headed to the lake.

Chapter 38

Even through her down vest, Valerie felt the barrel of Hannah's pistol prodding her to keep walking. Hannah had parked in a clearing, and had kept her gun trained on Valerie as she got out and crossed around to the passenger side. After telling Valerie to put her hands on her head, Hannah had instructed her to get out and go where she told her.

Valerie was pretty sure she could see

the lake through the trees on the other side of the road, but thanks to the snow and the darkening sky, nothing struck her as familiar. She'd spent a few vacations at this lake as a child, but had never been here at this time of year. In the waning afternoon light, all she could see were trees, falling snow, and the gray area that she assumed was the lake.

Her chest ached at the thought of her dad teaching her to fish at this lake. Why had she been so mad at him earlier?

At a break in the trees, she could see a structure down by the water. Probably a boathouse. To her relief, she saw the van parked a ways past that. Whatever was going on, at least she still had a hope of helping Maggie. If she hadn't been too mad to walk back to the booth with her dad, how long would it have taken for someone to notice Maggie was missing?

"That way." Hannah jabbed the right side of Valerie's ribcage, forcing her to veer left, away from the lake. Nearly stumbling on something—probably a rock or a tree root—she looked down to catch herself. When she looked up again, her breath caught. There was a cabin. Not just any cabin, but one that looked familiar. Front porch with stone columns on each corner. Porch swing. Big front door. She was almost certain this was the cabin that belonged to Daniel's family.

Now her surroundings made sense. The boathouse. The clearing where the kids used to play while the moms sunbathed. The spot right over there where they'd all posed for the picture.

And it tracked with Hannah's ramblings. It also tracked with Maggie's concerns about whoever had been at her house yesterday. Was that person the one who had taken her?

Now that Valerie had her bearings, she tried to remember everything she could about this place that might help her form an escape plan, but her memory felt foggy. Surely it had a phone. In the kitchen, maybe? If she could get to it, she could tell the nine-one-one operator where they were. That was something, anyway.

She started up the front steps. The warm glow coming from the windows would seem inviting under different circumstances. The place gave her the chills, but all things considered, it was a more encouraging option than the boathouse.

As Valerie reached the front door, Hannah gave her a shove with the gun. "Go in."

She followed the barked instruction, and her heart sank. It was no warmer in there than outside, and the glow in the windows came from candles placed around the room. No electricity. So probably no phone either.

The layout was exactly as she remembered. A staircase on the left of the entryway. Straight ahead, a door led to the kitchen. Hannah gave her a shove through the doorway to the right, which led to the living room.

There, Maggie looked up from where she sat in a straight-backed chair, her arms behind her and the gag still in place. Her eyes were wide with fear, and Valerie detected some discoloration on her cheek, like she'd been hit.

A man knelt at the fireplace, positioning logs. He whipped around, then sprang to his feet. Whatever Valerie had been expecting, he wasn't it. He was maybe in his early thirties with scraggly, brown hair, dressed in jeans and a denim jacket, like he hadn't quite planned for the weather.

Seeing them, his eyes blazed. He stormed toward Valerie. "What are *you* doing here?" Stopping just short of where they stood, he turned on Hannah. "What is *she* doing here?"

Hannah huffed out a breath so close to Valerie that she could see the wisp of vapor next to her ear. "When you decided to go rogue and become a kidnapper, you should have thought that maybe someone might notice."

Valerie studied the man's face as he flicked his narrow-eyed gaze from Hannah to her then back to Hannah. She knew that look.

"Zak...?"

Daniel's nephew had apparently grown up into an adult version of the obnoxious bully he'd been as a kid. He turned his manic gaze on her and she braced herself for what he might do.

But after a moment of staring her down, his eyes darted back to Hannah. "What are we supposed to do with her?"

"I don't know, genius. You're the one who wanted revenge."

Why did Hannah keep using that word? Did Zak want to get back at Dad for his uncle Daniel's death? He'd been, what? Seven? Twenty-five years was a long time to hold that kind of grudge.

And how did Hannah figure into this? Was she his girlfriend? His wife?

Running a hand through his wild hair, Zak looked around. He jabbed a finger toward Hannah. "Stay here." Then he stomped off, into the kitchen from the sound of his footsteps.

"Idiot," Hannah muttered.

Making eye contact with Maggie, Valerie tried to communicate reassurance. Their captors were at odds with each other, and they apparently didn't have a plan. If Valerie could figure out a way to play one off the other...

Zak's heavy stomp sounded behind her. "Hands behind your back."

Grateful at least for the opportunity to lower her hands and let the blood flow into her fingers, she did as instructed, and immediately felt rough rope dig into her wrists. As he pulled it tight, she resisted as best she could, hoping for a little give so the blood flow to her hands wasn't cut off altogether.

Please don't let him gag me.

A small request, but the thought of having some greasy rag shoved into her mouth made her stomach turn.

"Sit over there." He shoved her toward an armchair, which sat at a diagonal in the corner next to the front window.

She did as he said, finding it impossible to get comfortable with her arms tied behind her. Zak wrapped a long rope around her and the chair back, securing it in a knot behind her.

When he started pacing, running both hands through his hair, she sighed in relief. No gag. *Thank You, Jesus.*

Shivering, Valerie hoped he'd pick up where he'd left off with building the fire, but he continued his frantic pacing. The way he moved, Valerie had to wonder if he was on something.

He stopped his movement long enough to poke his finger in Hannah's face. "That was a real stupid thing to do, bringing her here."

Valerie cringed at the abusive way Zak spoke to Hannah. It was awful, but knowing how he'd always treated Valerie when they were kids, she shouldn't be surprised.

Hannah snarled. If his attitude bothered her, she didn't show it. "What was I supposed to do, let her call the sheriff on your sorry self? It would've come out that you're my boyfriend and we'd both be in jail."

He stopped moving and stared at her, apparently at a loss for an argument against her logic. "Okay." He held his hands up at face level, like he was trying to think. "We can still do the thing—" He tipped his head in Maggie's direction, causing her eyes to get even wider. "—only we do it here instead of at her house. That would make sense, right? She was part of the family."

Valerie felt sick. What were they planning to do to Maggie?

"Think, Zak." Jutting out one hip, Hannah waved the hand still holding her pink gun. "How would she have gotten here? She can't drive."

"Right." His eyes darted around, then landed on Valerie. "She brought her. We just need to steal her truck and leave it here."

"We're going to go back into town and find where she parked, and what? Hotwire it? You suddenly a car thief too?"

"I don't see you coming up with a plan."

Hannah shoved her gun into her waistband. "Whatever we do, we have to move." She pointed at Valerie. "Someone's probably noticed she's not wherever she's supposed to be. They're going to be looking." For the first time, Valerie saw doubt and fear in Hannah. She was starting to panic.

But was she right? Would Dad be worried? Would Derek?

"Sheesh, calm down." Zak touched his fingertips to either side of his head. "All we really need to do is wait it out long enough, then we sneak her back into her own bed"—the callous glance he gave Maggie was bone chilling—"where you conveniently 'find' her in the morning."

"What about *her?*" Hannah snapped at Valerie like a rabid dog. "I think your little bribery plan has been ruined."

"Yeah." Zak looked Valerie up and down like she was a problem that needed to be solved.

"You can't let her talk, Zak. She knows too much."

"You think I don't know that?" Zak paced again. "You just stay in town and do whatever you'd do under these..." He flicked a hand at Maggie. "...circumstances. Then go back to Billings. Let me worry about her." He shot a glance at Valerie that, if looks could kill, would have done her in. "I come back for the reading of the will. We take the money. We sell the house in town. We sell our part of the farm. Boom. Life's good." Zak's face eased into a full smile. "In fact, this works even better. The old man will fold if his little girl goes missing. 'Bout time he paid for cheating me out of my full inheritance."

What on earth was he talking about? Was he the heir to Maggie's estate? Bratty little Zak?

"Yeah. That could work." Hannah looked around. "Where's the stuff?"

"Kitchen." He headed out of the room.

Hannah moved to follow, then turned and cast a pensive look at their two captives. "Don't try anything." Sputtering out a guffaw, like that struck her as funny, she followed Zak.

Valerie waited a moment, then spoke to Maggie, keeping her voice low. “Are you okay?”

Maggie closed her eyes, probably to stop herself from rolling them at the inane question. Of course she wasn’t okay. But she nodded.

“I’m going to think of something. Don’t worry.” Valerie scanned the room, trying to figure out how they could get untied. Her mind paged through all the books she’d read where the hero or heroine came up with some ingenious way of getting free. Unfortunately, she didn’t see any sharp edges that she could use to saw through the rope. When she struggled, the knot only seemed to tighten, and there was no way she could slip out of it.

But even if they could get free, how would they get away? Valerie hadn’t seen Maggie’s wheelchair anywhere, and she couldn't just leave her. This problem was too big for her to solve.

Right now would be a good time for some divine intervention.

Chapter 39

Derek struggled to see through the snow hitting his windshield. Thankfully, there hadn't been any other traffic going in this direction on the highway in the few minutes he'd been traveling, but still, it was hard to tell if he was following the right set of tracks.

Casting a glance at Rex sitting next to him, still on the alert and even more focused than Derek, he questioned the wisdom of this search. He didn't know Valerie well, not as well as he would like to. But failing to come back to the booth, even if she was upset, didn't seem like something she would do.

Follow your gut. He remembered hearing at some point in his life that the feeling in your gut was the voice of God. That had given him comfort at the time. Strangely, it brought him comfort right now.

The fact was, he didn't know Valerie's whereabouts or if she was in trouble, but God did. If he believed that, it followed that he still believed in a higher power. Not just any power, but his Lord and Savior, Jesus Christ. King of kings and Lord of lords. Why had he stopped believing? How had he ever thought that he could do this life without Him?

Keeping his eyes fixed on the road, he felt an overwhelming urge to talk to God. He hadn't prayed since the day Erin died.

Even before that, if he was honest with himself, he'd always been more focused on asking for a blessing on his own plans than seeking God's will. Maybe this was a good time to make a fresh start.

"Dear Lord." He cleared his throat and dove in. "I'm sorry I stopped believing. Please. If it's Your will that I find Valerie, show me where to go. Whatever's going on with her, she needs You." He paused, swallowing his pride. "*I* need You. I always have."

Blinking against a sudden blurriness, he struggled to see through the increasing snowfall. A sign up ahead on the left had an arrow pointing to a turnoff to the right. As he got a little closer, he squinted. It looked like the vehicle he was following had taken that turn, but it was hard to tell for sure. As he slowed, he glanced at the hand-painted sign, which read simply *Corn Maze*.

He'd studied the map of the area. Now

at least he knew where he was.

Between praying and racking her brain, Valerie kept an ear tuned to what she could make out of the conversation going on in the kitchen. Putting together the bits and pieces, she still didn't understand what was going on.

"If you had done your homework..." Hannah's voice surged, then got muffled again. "...figured out from the start...weren't even *in* her will."

She caught Maggie's eye, but the woman looked more confused than Valerie felt.

"...I would've convinced her..."

"...didn't even want to see you, Zak. Besides..." Something crashed, like they were putting away dishes. "...sick of waiting forever."

Valerie scanned the room. A wispy curtain covered the front window, making it difficult to see out. The candles on the table in front of the window, on the mantel, and on the table next to Maggie didn't give off enough light for her to be able to make out details of the room.

Before she could come up with an idea for getting them free, she heard Zak and Hannah on their way back from the kitchen.

"...wheelchair's in my trunk." Hannah was back to sounding more angry than afraid. "You would have just left it there on the sidewalk, which would've been *real* smart."

Valerie's stomach soured. Was that what Hannah had been doing when she had seen her at her car? Putting Maggie's wheelchair in the trunk? If she had come around the corner a few seconds sooner, she would have questioned that.

Rethinking those few moments, she

recalled another detail. Something had seemed odd about the person she had seen hurrying up Rockford Street. He was wearing a denim jacket in a snowstorm. A minute sooner, and Valerie would have encountered the two of them together. Would the situation have gone differently?

Zak strutted in, carrying something black—a folder, maybe. He set it down on the side table next to the chair Maggie was in, then walked around behind her and started untying her hands. “We need you to sign something for us, Aunt Maggie.”

Hannah carried something pink. A makeup bag? She tossed it on the couch, which was adjacent to Maggie’s chair, then unholstered her gun and aimed it at Maggie. “Don’t try anything.”

When Maggie’s hands were free, she drew them around in front of herself, then rubbed her wrists. Zak opened the folder and set it in her lap, then shoved a pen at her, but instead of taking it, she gave him an angry glare.

"Come on," he said. "Just sign it."

"Take the gag off." Valerie didn't realize she'd spoken until Zak and Hannah snapped their heads in her direction. "I mean...you can't expect her to cooperate with that thing in her mouth."

The two exchanged a silent agreement, and Zak removed the gag.

Maggie made a sour expression and coughed a few times. She lifted the folder, then held it away so she could focus on its contents. "What is this?"

Zak huffed out irritation. "It's a will, obviously. Agreeing that you're leaving everything to me, like Uncle Daniel wanted."

"What? He never would've—"

"My dad said Uncle Daniel would've left it all to him, and then it would've gone to me."

"That's not—"

"Sign it!" Hannah turned the gun from Maggie to Valerie and took a couple of long strides toward her.

Valerie shrank back.

"I'm sick of wasting time." Hannah's normally tidy ponytail had loosened, adding to her madwoman persona. "So just sign it, or you're going to watch Valerie die and we're going to make it look like you did it."

Valerie's heart was in her throat. She stared at Hannah, then looked over at Maggie, who had been stunned into inaction. Valerie gave her a little nod. At least if she signed the paper, that would buy them some time. Maybe Derek had alerted Bobby.

Her hope sank at the realization that even if they were looking for her, there would be no reason for them to look here.

Maggie quickly scribbled on the document. Hannah lowered the gun, giving Valerie a moment to exhale, and casually turned it back on Maggie.

Zak took the document and held it up, examining it. Then, looking triumphant, he closed the folder. "Now we just replace that old will with this."

"The will that's in my desk?" Maggie fired an accusatory glare at Hannah. "You got into my personal files?"

"It was right there." She sat on the couch next to the makeup bag. "The file drawer wasn't even locked."

"It shouldn't have to be. It's in my home."

Zak yanked Maggie's arms behind her back and started retying her wrists. "I told you I could just forge her signature."

"That wouldn't fool anyone." Hannah shivered. "You couldn't even build a fire? It's freezing in here."

"Poor you. It's always about *you*." Zak continued tying Maggie's wrists, while he argued with Hannah. "Why are you such a nag?"

"Why do you think?"

After holstering her gun, Hannah unzipped the bag and took something out of it. A cold shiver ran down Valerie's spine. *A syringe.*

Maggie's eyes bulged. "What are you—?"

Zak slid the gag between her lips and tied it again, turning her question into a frantic murmur.

Hannah glared at him. "How am I supposed to get to her arm now?"

"You're the professional." He sneered. "Figure it out."

While Zak returned to setting the fire, Hannah rolled her eyes and undid the top buttons of Maggie's blouse. Then, in spite of Maggie's resistance, she slid her blouse and coat sleeves down far enough to reveal a portion of her upper arm. She removed a cap from a vial and edged closer to Maggie.

"Now, sweetie." She weirdly reverted

into caring-nurse mode. “This isn’t going to hurt.” She pulled the plunger of the syringe back. “It’ll take a little while, then you’re going to get sleepy. You’ll drift off and just never wake up.”

“What are you giving her?” Valerie’s voice shook.

“Abacephen.” Hannah lifted one shoulder in a shrug. “It’s a heart medication, but in a large enough dose, it makes the heart slow down till it just stops beating.” She jabbed the syringe needle into the vial and turned it upside down. “Funny, it doesn’t show up in the blood postmortem.”

“Hannah, wait.” Valerie needed to do something. “You don’t want this on your conscience. We can work something out. You and Zak can live in the old farmhouse if you want to.”

She wrinkled her nose. “That smelly old place? Zak took me there one night. Not my style.”

Valerie saw anger overtake the fear in Maggie's eyes, and she couldn't blame her. The thought of these two poking around on their property was sickening.

"Hannah, don't!" Valerie's voice rasped. "You'd regret it for the rest of your—"

"Shut *up!*" Zak sprang to his feet, reaching into his back pocket.

As he surged at Valerie, she caught a flash of something red in his hand.

"No, please don't—"

He shoved the bandana into her mouth and tied it so tight it cut into the corners of her lips. She tried to scream, knowing it was futile.

"That's better." Casting her one more murderous glare, he returned to his task at the fireplace.

Pulling the plunger back, Hannah frowned at Zak. "Do you even know what you're doing?"

"I think I know how to light a fire,

okay?" He lit a long match and touched it to the kindling, igniting a blaze.

Huffing out disgust, Hannah removed the needle from the vial.

Valerie closed her eyes and prayed a desperate prayer. When she opened them, Zak was on his feet, warming his hands in front of the fire, and Hannah held the needle inches from Maggie's exposed arm.

Smoke started puffing from the fire into the room.

Hannah coughed. "Oh for the love of..." Lowering the syringe, she waved her other hand in front of her face. "You didn't open the flue, you moron."

He knelt down and made a feeble attempt at reaching through the smoke, then flapped his hands and launched into his own coughing fit.

"I can't believe you." Hannah set the syringe on the coffee table and stomped across the room. She shoved the curtains open and flung the window sash up.

Valerie shivered as a burst of cold air gusted in, blowing out one of the candles on the table.

Zak stood, still waving away smoke. “Got it.”

“Bra-vo.” Hannah stomped back to the coffee table and picked up the syringe. She stabbed it into Maggie’s arm and pushed the plunger.

Valerie blinked against smoke and tears, saying a silent prayer for God to remove the effects of the drug.

“That’s done.” Hannah tossed the syringe back into the bag. “Now what?”

“I don’t know.” Zak coughed. “I can’t think with you harping at me.”

“You can’t think because of this smoke, you moron. I need some air. And at least there’s heat in the van.” Hannah started for the door. She stopped and glared at Zak. “Are you coming?”

Zak cast an assessing look at Valerie, then at Maggie. Shoving his hands in the pockets of his jacket, he grunted and followed Hannah from the room.

Valerie heard the front door slam. She could still hear the couple arguing through the window, but their voices grew quieter as they walked toward the van.

She had to think fast. At least the open window was helping clear the smoke, but another gust of wind blew in, threatening to freeze them. Worse, when she glanced at the window, she saw that the wind was blowing the curtain in, dangerously close to the candle flame.

Valerie shot a look at Maggie, whose focus was on the curtain as she struggled against her binding, but then she cast her own panicked look at Valerie. *She sees it too.*

The wind kicked up again, only this time, the curtain touched the flame, igniting the fabric.

Inside her head, Valerie heard herself scream.

Chapter 40

Derek drove as fast as he could, considering the snow and his struggle to see the tire tracks on the road ahead. When he reached the Frazier farm, he pulled over. No surprise that the house was a dark shadow against the gray sky. The whole Frazier family was in town at the market. Where Valerie should be.

He checked his phone and groaned. No service. Which explained why he hadn't gotten a call back from Bobby.

But...hang on. Hadn't Valerie said something about rich people living up this way? If he remembered correctly, she had said there was a tower, so if he kept going, he should be able to get service.

Starting forward again, he decided he'd at least keep driving till he could talk to Bobby. He was on what amounted to a wild goose chase, with nothing more to go on than Rex's canine intuition and his own gut. He glanced at Rex, who was as alert as ever, eyes focused on the road ahead. Could they both be wrong?

Not a minute up the road, his phone buzzed, startling him. Stopping the truck, he looked at the screen. His heart jumped to his throat at the name.

He tapped the screen. "Mr. Hayes."

"Derek...where are you? Have you found her?"

His hope sank and he started driving again. "No, not yet. I let Bobby know."

"I'm worried. You don't suppose this has something to do with Maggie, do you? Valerie's so mad at me. Not that she shouldn't be."

"You think she took off because she's mad?"

"Thought she mighta gone to talk to Maggie herself. Only Maggie's not answering her phone either. Now I'm worried about the two of them, to tell you the truth."

Derek thought about the conversation he'd overheard earlier. "Mr. Hayes...I might be way off, but...I heard Maggie say something about someone maybe harassing her?"

"Her late husband's no-good nephew. Never trusted that kid." He clicked his tongue. "That's what's got me worried."

Derek looked up at the road. The snow had eased up some, and he could just make out the lower part of the mountain range ahead. A thought struck him. "I need to call Bobby."

"All right. Keep me posted."

"You do the same. Oh, and Mr. Hayes...?" Derek swallowed hard. "I'll be praying."

He heard an intake of air as if Mr. Hayes might be fighting back emotion. "Me too, son."

Keeping an eye on the road, Derek's hand shook as he tapped the screen and checked his missed calls. Three from a number he didn't recognize, which he assumed must be Bobby. Not bothering to check voicemail, he clicked on the number.

The thought of Valerie being in danger stirred something in him. A primitive desire to protect someone he loved. He was falling in love with Valerie. He'd be a fool to keep denying it.

Bobby's voicemail picked up. Was he out-of-range too?

The second Derek heard the beep, he

spoke. "I think I might know where Valerie is." He'd been powerless to save Erin. He couldn't fail Valerie too. "And if I'm right, she's in trouble."

Valerie watched in helpless horror as the flames chewed the curtain and spread to the wall on the far side of the window. A peripheral movement drew her focus to Maggie, whose whole upper body was thrashing. Then, to Valerie's amazement, Maggie pulled first one arm free, then the other. She quickly reached up to untie the gag, which she flung to the floor.

"I-I can get to you," Maggie called out. "J-just hold on!"

Struggling futilely against the ropes that held her, Valerie prayed as Maggie braced one hand on the table and the other on the chair next to her. With unexpected grace, she eased her body to the floor, then used her arms to crawl toward Valerie.

Valerie checked the progress of the flames, which were now working their way to the wall directly across from her. Bracing her feet against the floor, she tried to move the chair, but it was just too heavy. She screamed encouragement as Maggie made it to her side of the room, then pulled herself to a sitting position and worked at the knot behind the chair. Once Valerie felt that rope fall, she twisted so Maggie could reach the one binding her wrists.

With a blessed sense of relief, she pulled her arms free and dug at the knot in the bandana. She sputtered as she cast the thing aside and knelt next to Maggie. "I've got to get you—"

"Get me to that rug." Rolling onto her stomach, Maggie pointed to a rug in the entryway. "Don't worry about hurting me.

Just pull." Face to the floor, she stuck her arms above her head, Superman style.

With no time to lose, Valerie did as instructed. Once she had Maggie on the rug, she picked up the corners and pulled with everything in her. She flung the front door open and kept going. At the top of the stairs, Maggie reached for the balusters to help lower herself down. When Valerie had her on the ground, she stopped to catch her breath.

"Valerie!" Maggie twisted a look back at the house.

Valerie followed her gaze to see that the fire had gone through the wall and made its way onto the porch. She glanced in the direction of the van. There was no sign of Zak or Hannah, but it would only be a matter of time before they were alerted to the situation.

"That way, sweetie." Maggie gripped the rug and used her chin to point to the other side of the cabin.

As she pulled Maggie over the snowy, rugged ground, Valerie racked her brain. It had been years since she'd thought about the long summer days spent playing around this cabin. There had been a shed back this way. She recalled hiding in it once during a game of hide and seek. Once they were around the corner, she turned and looked. Yes! It was still there.

"Just a little further," Valerie said, fighting to catch her breath. "Can you make it?"

"I'm game if you are."

The sound of voices spurred Valerie on. She prayed that their captives wouldn't get close enough to see the distinctive trail she and Maggie had left in their wake.

Once at the shed, Valerie tugged the door open. She heaved Maggie inside and shut the door behind them. Enough light entered through the spaces between the slats that Valerie could see a shovel in one corner and some paint cans.

They could still hear the muffled shouts. "The will is in there!"

Zak's bellow came as a bitter reminder of where his priorities lay. He didn't care that he'd left two women tied up inside a building that was now on fire.

"Valerie." Maggie pushed to a sitting position and leaned against the wall of the shed. "You have to go. Don't take the road. It'll take too long."

Valerie crouched next to her. "Maggie, I—"

"If you cut through the woods, it's a straight shot to the main road. From there, you can get to a place where someone can help, but stay out of sight."

"I can't leave you."

"I'm fading, honey. Better for one of us to get away. Go while you can."

The yelling continued, mostly indiscernible, but it sounded like Hannah and Zak were distracted for the moment and hadn't realized she and Maggie had escaped.

"I…I'll get help. I'll send someone." That was, if she even made it out herself undetected.

"That would be lovely." Maggie nodded. "I'd…prefer not to go this way, if at all possible."

"You have to go in and get it!" Hannah's shriek echoed through the night.

"Maggie…" Valerie clutched the woman's hand. "I'm so sorry."

"None of this is your fault, dear."

"I know, but…" But she had spent what would probably be the last day of Maggie's life resenting her, and that seemed worthy of an apology. Swallowing a sob, she moved to stand.

"Wait…" Maggie lifted a hand. "You can't let them destroy the original will. I don't want Zak to have anything. It's all meant to go to you."

Valerie caught her breath. “M-me?”

“Who else? I don’t have much, but what I have should by all rights go to you. Your father looked after me, and I know it came at a cost to you.”

Valerie felt a warm tear slide down her cheek. “I’m so sorry about my dad. You should know he’s regretted causing the accident for all these years.”

Maggie frowned. “He didn’t cause it.”

“But...he said Daniel had to swerve because my dad’s truck was in the wrong lane.”

Her eyebrows shot up. “That was your father in that truck? I never knew...”

“You two never talked about it?”

She shook her head. “Well, no. Not to the extent that.... Oh, honey, you have to tell him that’s not the way it happened at all.”

More indiscernible shouting sent Valerie’s heart racing, but she kept her focus on Maggie. “Tell me quickly.”

"Daniel and I were here at the cabin. He was upset about something, but he wouldn't say what."

Valerie bit her lip. Maggie didn't need to know about the money.

"He'd been drinking. He said he needed to talk to your father and that he didn't want to wait. It was snowing. A night like tonight. But against my better judgement, I got into the truck with him. He was driving too fast and he kept drifting into the wrong lane. I was warning him and he was telling me not to nag him. He hit the gas and flew around a curve and there was another truck coming. But it was our truck that was in the wrong lane, not that one. Daniel swerved to get back into the right lane, but it was slick and we rolled. That's what your father needs to know."

"Zak!" Hannah let out a high-pitched shriek.

Zak let fly some breathy curse words.

"They're not in there!"

"What's not?" Hannah's voice raged. "The will?"

"No!" Zak cursed again. "The women."

Valerie snapped a look at Maggie, whose eyes were glistening. Valerie pulled her into a hug.

"I'll be praying for you." Maggie released her from the hug. "Go."

Reluctantly, Valerie stood, then pushed the door open and peered out. She could still hear Hannah and Zak, but she couldn't see them. She slipped out and crept quickly into the woods.

As she darted from tree to tree, she looked up. There were no stars...nothing to help her get her bearings. She'd have to rely on Jesus—her true North Star.

Chapter 41

Knowing he might lose his connection again, Derek had written down the directions he'd gotten on GPS from where he was to Hidden Lake. He had almost missed the sign for the reassuringly named Hidden Lake Road, which he'd now been traveling for several minutes. The next step would be to find the cabin, but he'd cross that bridge when he got to it.

It was still snowing lightly, and he optimistically hoped that what looked like tracks ahead of him weren't just ruts in the road.

Rex whined and shifted in his seat.

"You okay, boy?" He ran a hand across the scruff of the dog's neck. "Sure wish you could talk."

Rex answered with a bark, followed by another whine. He was sensing something, and Derek had a sinking feeling it wasn't good.

Then something caught his attention. He sniffed the air. Smoke? He rolled the window down halfway. Definitely smoke.

As he came around a curve, it became clear where it was coming from. It was a cabin, with flames shooting out the windows on one side.

Barking now, Rex stood, chomping at the bit to get out of the truck.

Derek looked to the right, to a dark area that was probably the lake. There to the left of a clearing was a shape that must be a boathouse, and not much further, parked among the trees...was a van.

His gut told him he'd been right. This was the place...but was he too late?

Valerie moved as quickly as she could through the woods, taking care not to trip over a root or slip in the snow. An ongoing prayer repeated in her head—*Please keep Maggie safe and alive. Please don't let them follow my tracks*.

It seemed unlikely that Zak and Hannah would realize they couldn't fix this, and just drive away. But God was in control, and she had to trust that He heard her pleas.

The snow had stopped falling, depriving her of the notion that fresh snowfall would make it harder to follow her tracks. She kept moving. It had to be, what? Six? Seven o'clock? The thought brought little comfort. Any of the farms that were close might provide some shelter while she waited, but no one would return home till well after nine. And the people who owned big chunks of land with a mega mansion in the middle were surrounded by security fences and probably patrolled by shoot-first-ask-questions-later drones.

She stopped, leaning her hands against a tree while she caught her breath. Then, peering around the tree, she saw an open space ahead. She had reached McGregor Road. And not where she expected to come out—further up with more woods to navigate—but the part of the road that was surrounded by fields. She was nearly to the Frazier farm! If she could just get there, she could rest and find some place to get out of the cold for a few hours.

A few hours... Her heart ached at the thought of Maggie holding on in that cold shed. Hannah had said it would take a little while for the drug to stop her heart. A few hours seemed like an eternity.

Another thought, even worse than the one before it, tried to drown out whatever hope she had. The shed seemed like a safe distance from the cabin, but what if the fire kept spreading in spite of the snow? The thought was too much for her to even entertain.

She had no choice but to keep moving. If she mustered enough strength, she could cut across the field ahead and come out at the Frazier place.

Taking a deep breath, she pushed back from the tree, but before she could go forward, a distant sound stopped her. The night was so silent, but...there it was again. A snapping sound, coming from the woods behind her.

She had to run. If they were following

her, her only hope was to outdistance them.

When Derek opened the driver's side door to the truck, Rex bolted out right over him. Nose to the ground, he took off around one side of the cabin.

"Valerie!" Derek did his best to see through the cabin windows as he jogged toward it, but there was no sign of life. Could she be inside, unable to answer?

Rex's bark alerted him to what looked like a rough path in the snow, like someone had dragged a shovel. He followed it around the side of the house and found Rex standing next to a small shed. He hurried to it and flung open the door.

His breath caught at the sight of someone slumped over on the floor. The glow from the fire illuminated the small area enough for him to see that it wasn't Valerie.

"Oh...Maggie..." He knelt down next to her, lifting her face. Seeing no signs of life, he reached for her wrist. He felt a pulse. Weak, but still there. He needed to get help.

The sound of Rex barking drew him to his feet as he reached for his phone. No service again. And he had no idea if Bobby had gotten his message.

He looked toward the woods behind the cabin, to where Rex's bark was coming from, though Derek couldn't see him. Had he found Valerie? But the way his bark grew quieter made Derek think the dog was on the move. Tracking her into the woods? He had to get help for Maggie, but he needed to get to Val. He held his phone above his head, giving it one last chance to connect.

"Drop it."

He pivoted to see a woman approaching him, with a gun aimed at him.

Was that...Maggie's nurse? His thoughts raced. Did she think that he had something to do with whatever had happened to Maggie? *What on—?*

"I said drop your phone!"

"Okay, okay." Not wanting to trigger an irrational action, he slowly set the phone down in the snow in front of him. "Hannah, I just got here. I had nothing to do with—"

"Shut up!" She shrieked. Her eyes were wild, not like someone who had been through a trauma, but like someone who wasn't in their right mind.

He needed answers, and fast. "Where's Valerie?"

She firmed her gaze. "Last time I saw her, she was in there." She tipped her head toward the cabin.

His heart jumped to his throat as his

gaze darted from one window to the other. On this side of the building, there was still hope, if he could get inside.

"Don't even think about it."

That confirmed his suspicion. She hadn't been a victim along with Maggie and Valerie. He had to reason with her.

"You're a nurse. How could you—"

"Right. I'm a nurse. Not because I love humanity. Humanity blows."

He winced. "You're not in this alone, *are* you? Who's helping you?"

"None of your—"

A bark, louder than before, came from behind Derek. He heard a crunching sound that told him Rex had come back for him. He turned his head just enough to see a dark form emerge through the trees with another bark.

"Aw, that..." Letting out a curse word, Hannah lowered her gun toward the figure.

Without thinking, Derek barreled into

her, just as the gun went off. She tumbled backward into the snow, and he lunged for the hand that still held the gun. With her other hand, she landed a punch to his nose that sent him reeling. Her hand slipped from his grasp and she put the gun in his face, forcing him back on his haunches. Staring her down as she got her feet under her, he raised his hands.

Then, a movement behind her stole his focus. He looked up to see Bobby and Kyle creeping forward, weapons drawn. He lifted his gaze over her shoulder. When she flinched, he surged to his feet and grabbed her hands with both of his.

"Police! Drop your weapon!" Bobby shouted.

Hannah whimpered, still struggling against Derek's grasp, then she folded, lowering her arms.

As Bobby holstered his gun and reached for his cuffs, Derek forced the pistol from Hannah's hands.

"Where's Valerie?" Bobby demanded as he cuffed Hannah behind her back.

"I don't know." Hannah sobbed.

"She does know." Derek caught his breath. "She said she's in the cabin."

"I said she *was*." Hannah looked up, eyes pleading. "But she got away."

A bark echoed from behind him and Derek turned to see Rex taking a couple of steps toward the trees, then looking at Derek and barking again. Derek thanked God for keeping the dog safe from Hannah's irrational shot.

"I'm following Rex." Derek retrieved his phone from the snow, praying the flashlight would still work. "Maggie's in that shed and she needs help."

Bobby lifted Hannah to her feet. "You go. We'll call for backup."

Gripping the small gun, Derek took off after Rex. A clear set of footprints in the snow, alongside Rex's back-and-forth paw prints, renewed his hope.

Chapter 42

Valerie ran without looking back.

By the time she made it to the fence that edged the parking area of the Fraziers' farm, she was nearly sick from exertion. She scooted into the space between the fence and an oak tree to catch her breath. When she peered around the tree, terror seized her. Clear on the other side of the field, a dark figure moved, trailing her steps.

The snow was giving her away.

Staying still, she watched the figure. Only one of the pair had followed her, and it looked like Zak. She had to think fast.

Praying that the tree would conceal her, she climbed over the fence. Then, crouching so that, with any luck, her movement would be at least somewhat obscured, she gripped the top rail, and planted her feet on the bottom rail. As quickly as she could, she shimmied along the inside of the fence, keeping low. She was banking on her observation that Zak wasn't the brightest bulb in the box. When he lost sight of her footprints, she hoped against hope that he wouldn't notice that snow had been brushed off the fence rails. That might buy her enough time to get to safety.

Reaching the corner of the fence, she dared to sneak a peek at the field. To her alarm, Zak had picked up speed and had made it nearly to the fence. She dropped to the ground, grateful for the lack of outdoor lighting on this side of the barn, and slinked the rest of the way along the fence line. Once confident that she was out of his sightline, she stood on the fence again, this time shimmying from a standing position so she could move faster.

But move to where? There was no place to go where he wouldn't find her eventually.

She heard Zak let out an expletive, which probably meant he'd gotten to the place where it hopefully looked like she'd either vanished or been raptured. Her eyes darted around.

From her vantage point, she could see the snack bar and game booths. If she could get into the snack bar, she could find something to use as a weapon. They had to have knives in there. She hurried around to the back of the building and tried the door, but it wouldn't budge.

A noise coming from the direction of the barn made her freeze. Listening, she turned her head to see Zak walking through the middle of the parking area. So he hadn't followed her fence line trail, but he was headed toward the buildings.

Trying not to panic, she looked around. There was a small window on the side of the game booth building, and it was slightly open. At her feet, she saw a couple of discarded wooden crates. She grabbed one and set in on the ground beneath the window. Taking care to be as quiet as possible, she stood on the crate and shoved the window open. Using all the upper body strength she could muster, she hoisted herself up, then through the small space. To her relief, she felt a surface close to the window on the inside. A table. She eased her weight onto it, heaving out a breath.

After a moment of recovery, she pulled herself to her knees and yanked the window closed, wincing at the dull *thud* it made. She twisted the lock, not that it would help much if Zak saw her footprints outside.

Now what? She could hide in here. But she needed something she could use as a weapon.

The narrow backstage area didn't offer much help. There was the table and a couple of chairs. A wastebasket. Hooks on the wall next to the back door. She slipped through the opening leading to the games in the front, struggling to see in the dim light. What were the games? Nerf bowling. Ring toss. And...wait...

Holding onto the counter on her left for guidance, she made her way to the game on the end. *Yes*. To her right, the row of plastic ducks stood in line, waiting to be shot by the corks fired from the air guns. On her left, she felt for one of the weapons, and removed it from its stand. She twisted off the little air tube, which was the only thing tethering it to the counter. Holding up the plastic gun, she noted that it felt considerably lighter than an actual one, but even at this close range, without good lighting, the thing looked real. They had always looked real enough to make her shy away from this game. But now...she thanked God. If she had to be a sitting duck, at least she was armed with a decent decoy.

After pocketing the gun, she felt her way around to the backstage area. A quick shake of the door knob assured her that it was locked. If Zak realized where she was, he'd have to work to get to her.

Think, Valerie. Had she learned nothing from all her years of reading? In every suspense book, the heroine always wound up in a crazy situation, and she always found the way out.

There's always a way out.

The words came into her head, not as a thought, but more like a message spoken in the Spirit. There was always a way out.

What did she need? Help, of course. A way to let someone know where she was. But since she didn't have her phone, and it seemed unlikely that she could break into the house without Zak seeing her...

But that wasn't the only phone. *Oh my gosh.* Why hadn't she thought of that sooner? *The name of the Lord is a strong tower.*

She had to get to the tower.

Saying a quick prayer for guidance and protection, she undid the lock on the door and quietly opened it. A quick look told her that the walkway between these buildings and the fence that edged the corn maze was clear. She pulled the door shut, then taking care not to leave a print in the snow, she reached for the top rail of the fence. She planted first one foot then the other on the bottom rail. Next, she swung one leg over, then the other, and took a long stride into the corn field. A couple more steps in, and she felt sufficiently concealed by the corn. She moved carefully toward what she knew to be the center, trying to minimize the rustling of the stalks as she crept through them.

She stopped, listening. The only sounds she heard were a soft breeze blowing through the maze, and the distant bark of a dog. Her heart ached. What she wouldn't give to throw her arms around Rex right about now. She wondered for the millionth time if he knew something was wrong. Surely Dad and Derek were looking for her, but where would they even begin?

Finally, she came out of the thicket onto a trail in the maze. She looked around, but from where she stood, she couldn't see the tower. She couldn't see anything but cornstalks all around her, shifting and moving in a very unsettling way.

Overhead, there were still no stars visible, but what she could see was that the sky was still lighter to the west, where the sun had gone down just a little while ago. That might at least help her from getting too disoriented.

Since she hadn't left footprints that would easily clue Zak in to her presence in the maze, it felt safe to stay on the path. Even so, as she made her way through, she intentionally darted down a few dead ends, sometimes even walking sideways or backwards. That would throw him off, if he did look for her in here. Of course, why would he? This seemed like a crazy place to trap herself.

Finally, she looked up and saw the tower silhouetted against the sky.

Thank You, God.

So close. Darting around the last bend, she almost ran into one of the support pillars. She just needed to get to the top. Gripping the handrails for all she was worth, she started up the steep stairs. The last thing she needed was to slip on one of the rungs. Once she cleared the top of the corn field, she kept her head on a swivel, watching for any sign of movement. Seeing nothing, she kept going.

Finally reaching the top, she crouched down and scooted across the floor to the far side where the phone glistened in the dim moonlight. Letting out a warbly breath of relief, she reached up and grabbed the receiver from its cradle with a shaking hand.

Please work...please work!

The sound of the phone ringing through to the other end was like a balm to her pounding heart. "Answer, Annica," she whispered. "Please."

"Hello?"

Closing her eyes, she sagged with relief. "Annica. It's Valerie."

"Valerie?" Muffled music played in the background. The piercing pitch sounded like the high school band. “Where are you? People are worried.”

Even keeping the phone pressed to her ear, the sound seemed amplified. Suddenly, she was very aware of how she might be directing Zak right to her. She needed to hurry.

“Is Derek at our booth?

“No. It’s just your dad. Where are you?”

“Listen. I need you to tell my dad to send someone to the cabin to help Maggie. And tell them to hurry.”

“Okay, but...what cabin? Val, I can barely hear you.”

“Daniel’s cabin. Tell him *I’m* in the tower in the maze.”

“What? Sorry, it’s hard to hear. You’re where?”

“The tower in the maze.” Valerie pressed the phone to her head. Had she heard something? The phone was so loud, she knew it could give her away if Zak was close enough to hear. “Zak and Hannah took us."

"I'm not sure I—"

"Shh." She listened, certain that she'd heard something from down below. A pinging sound. She kept her voice low. "I have to go. Please tell my dad."

Hating to cut herself off from the outside world, she carefully set the receiver in its nest.

She heard another creak, this time for certain.

Someone was climbing up the stairs!

Relying on Rex's sense of smell and his own flagging sense of direction, Derek trailed behind the dog as he wended a zigzagging course through the woods. Aside from some confusing footprints in the snow, there had been no sign of Valerie. Derek had no idea where they were, and he was starting to wonder how deep these woods were.

Finally, Derek saw Rex take off at a sprint, like he'd been shot out of a cannon. Moving as quickly as he could, Derek could see that the dog had stopped and was looking back at Derek. He came out of the woods, and stopped short. They'd made it to a road. Which road, he wasn't sure, but unless he missed his guess, it looked like the main one he'd taken before turning onto Hidden Lake Road. That was encouraging.

As he started across, something caught his eye. There were tire tracks, of course. But it looked like there was another set of footprints—bigger than the set they'd been tracking. Someone had walked down this road, and recently. He followed where they led—right to where Rex stood. Then they continued on the other side of the fence.

Derek's sense of urgency kicked up a

notch. It appeared that someone else had been tracking Valerie.

A buzzing in his pocket had him fumbling for his phone, which he'd stopped using as a flashlight so he wouldn't drain the battery. He must have stepped out into an area with either wi-fi or cell service.

He tapped on it, and saw that he had a missed call from Mr. Hayes. He hit Play.

"Derek?" Derek strained to hear Mr. Hayes's voice, backed by some kind of band music. "Annica got a call from Valerie. She says to tell you that Valerie said something about a tower. Do you know what that means?"

A tower? Wait...

He looked around. On the other side of the road, he saw what had stopped Rex. A fence ran perpendicular to the road, and past that was an open space, like a field.

The tower.

He knew where she was.

Chapter 43

Hearing each step on the rungs of the ladder, Valerie drew the fake gun out of her pocket and stood. There was only one way up and one way down. At least...she turned slightly and looked over the edge...only one way she was willing to consider.

An undeniably loud creaking sound jarred her and she whirled back around, but her hand was shaking so badly that the gun slipped out of it, then hit the floor with a clank. She looked down, but couldn't see it in the darkness. In her confusion, she shifted her feet, but one of her boots connected with something. In a horrible moment, she realized she'd kicked the lightweight toy, sending it skittering.

Aware of the imminent approach of her stalker, she knelt down, feeling the floor, but not finding the gun.

She panicked. *Where is it?*

Her eyes tracked to the edge of the platform and she realized there was a good four-inch gap between the floor and the bottom of the railing. The platform extended out a few inches past that. *Oh no...no...*

Another *creak.*

She glanced toward the stairs, then back to the floor. Getting on her hands and knees, she lowered her face far enough to see through the gap. There! She saw it, teetering on the edge of the platform. She slid her hand under the railing, willing it to stop trembling long enough for her to get a grip. The cold plastic touched her fingertips.

"Ya lose an earring or something?" Zak's ugly guffaw was as grating as it was terrifying.

With a burst of determination, she grabbed hold of the gun and drew it toward her. Turning to face Zak, she scrambled to her feet.

He stood at the top of the stairs, hands in the pockets of his denim jacket with one knee cocked.

Hands shaking, she gripped the gun, trying to remember what Derek had taught her. Hold it steady and with confidence. *If someone's threatening you, you want them to believe you're willing to shoot them.*

And if he didn't believe that? Well, in this case, *willing* was one thing. *Able* was another.

Steeling her gaze, she raised the gun like it had more weight to it than it actually did. Then, clutching it with both hands, she aimed it right at his smirking face.

Instantly, the smirk fell, and he jerked his hands free, raising them in surrender. Which gave her hope that he was unarmed. And, hopefully, outwitted.

"Okay, come on." He eased one foot down a step. "You don't wanna—"

"Eh, eh, eh." She signaled with the gun for him to move away from the stairs. "You're not going anywhere."

"Look." He took a couple of obedient steps away from the staircase. "I didn't want to hurt you. I just wanted to scare you."

"Why? What do you have against me?"

"It's not you. It's your dad. I wanted him to pay." He lowered his hands, getting a little too comfortable.

"Hands on your head!" She firmed her grip on the gun.

"Okay, okay." Spitting out the words like bullets, he complied. "What do you want from me?"

"I want an explanation, Zak. Why did you put the tracker on my truck?"

He licked his lips, then let out a long breath. "I just wanted to put you in a helpless position. I messed with your truck, but I didn't know how long it would take for it to die. I figured you're out in the boonies so much it was bound to happen on some lonely road. I wanted the tracker so I could keep tabs on you if I had trouble following you."

"And the plan was...?"

"Alls I was gonna do was come by and offer you a ride. Then take you someplace...you know...isolated, and tell you to give a message to your dad."

"What kind of message?"

"You were supposed to talk your dad

into giving Uncle Daniel's part of the farm back to Aunt Maggie or I was gonna expose your dad's part in the accident."

For real? "That was really stupid, Zak."

He puffed out a breath, probably annoyed at her for being right.

Now that she had him talking, she started to feel bolder. "You thought you should inherit half of our farm? Why would you think that?"

Avoiding eye contact, he worked his jaw. "When my uncle Daniel died, I heard my dad tell my mom that your dad was responsible. That he ran Uncle Daniel's truck off the road. He said that he worked out a deal with your dad. My dad would keep quiet about the accident, and your dad would keep Aunt Maggie as a partner in the farm. Dad figured Aunt Maggie wouldn't live long and that he was gonna inherit her half of the business. He planned for all those years for that ship to come in."

"That's..." What? *Stupid? Sad? Gut-wrenching?* No, this was no time to get soft. "That's too bad. Your dad didn't know that my dad bought Daniel's share?"

"Nobody told us." He sneered. "I didn't find out till last year when my..." He looked away, blinking. "When my dad died. I told Hannah I guessed it was gonna be *our* ship coming in, since Mom was already gone and Dad missed the boat."

Valerie frowned. "Go on."

"Hannah thinks she's so much smarter than everyone else. She did some kind of *title search*, and that's how we found out Aunt Maggie only owned half of what we always thought." He shook his head. "I got so mad. I needed to make it right. Then Hannah got it in her head that we could speed things along. She said in her *professional opinion*, my aunt didn't sound like she had any of what she calls *quality of life*."

Valerie felt her stomach roil. "So you planned to poison her."

"Yeah. Except after Hannah got the job, she decided she should go poking around and see if she could find the will. 'Just to make sure.'"

Amazing how this guy put a sarcastic sass into his depiction of every action of Hannah's that was actually smart. Still pure evil, but at least one of them had thought things through.

"You found out you weren't named in her will."

"That happened last week. We had to change our plan."

That explained why there hadn't been any incidents for a week. Why she had found it so easy to believe that the culprit had been jailed.

"So you decided you'd, what? Show up at Maggie's door and convince her she should leave everything to her loving nephew?"

"I didn't think that would be any big deal. She didn't need to be so stubborn. She just..." He gritted his teeth. "She ticked me off, you know? I saw her sitting there today, waiting for Hannah, and I thought, I'll give her another chance. One more chance to do the right thing. I went up to her, all friendly and everything. She told me to leave and I tried to be nice, but she just...she was asking for it, you know?"

He looked at Valerie like he expected support, but all she could think of was the purple splotch on Maggie's cheek. This man was a monster.

"Anyways," he went on. "After I...you know. She looked like she was gonna scream or something. I couldn't let her draw attention like that, so I just picked her up and carried her to the van. Stupid woman. She didn't have to make it so hard."

Valerie recoiled. How could he have such a cruel, entitled attitude? "What happened then?" He started to lower his hands and she jabbed the gun forward. "What happened?"

Jerking his arms up again, he whimpered. "I-I went back around the corner to where Hannah's car was. She was standing there staring at the empty wheelchair. I told her real quick what happened, and she just said we needed to take Aunt Maggie to the cabin and figure it out from there."

"Why not just take her to her house?"

"Because. Someone might've seen us. Stupid, nosy neighbors." His gaze grew distant. "I just want what's mine. If Mr. Hayes pays for what he did, then..."

"Then what, Zak? You can feel good about yourself?"

After a few rapid blinks, he swallowed hard and looked down.

"You're never going to find peace unless you forgive my dad. And forgive your dad for misleading you."

His head snapped up. "*Forgive?* Seriously?"

"I know it probably sounds backwards to you. But you can't fix anything by taking revenge. What you're really looking for is the feeling you get from forgiving."

Slowly nodding, he let his gaze grow distant again. "Yeah...I need to forgive. Make everything right." His eyes met hers. "That's really smart. Thank you, Valerie." He looked around, like he was letting the concept sink in. "I need to start by forgiving *you*."

"Me?" She narrowed her eyes at him. "Okay, but—"

"Yeah." Still nodding, he jutted out a knee. "I need to forgive you...for being such a controlling hag—"

He lunged at her, going for the gun. Valerie shrieked and stumbled back. Before she knew what was happening, he had wrested the gun from her hands and held it to her face. Then he frowned and looked at it.

"What in the...?" He held the grip between his thumb and his index finger, scowling at it. "You seriously thought you could scare me with a toy?"

Terrified, Valerie slowly moved her hand toward the phone, but it was just out of her reach.

Zak looked at her hand. "Ah, no way."

He flung the toy gun into the night and struck her hard across the side of her face, sending her stumbling backwards. Before she could catch her balance, he shoved her against the railing. She felt it give.

Her attempt at a scream came out as a garbled choke, and she realized that he'd wrapped a hand around her throat. He bent her back over the railing, muttering a blur of curse words. Fighting a nauseating dizziness, she flailed, pushing against his arms, but she was no match for his determination.

He raised one arm up, and she could

see his hand fisting high above his head. "You're gonna die, and nobody's gonna—"

A guttural roar echoed through the night, stealing Zak's attention. He loosened his grip, but only slightly, as he looked around, confused. In the next instant, there was an ear-piercing *bang*, and Zak released his grip on her.

Gasping for air, she grabbed hold of the railing on either side of her and drew herself up. She caught a dizzying glimpse of Zak faltering back, then heard a second *bang*. His shoulder jerked, the momentum sending him tumbling backward. He seemed to try to catch himself, but it was too late. He fell against the railing behind him with so much force that it broke, sending him over the edge.

Still struggling for life-affirming breath, Valerie stood there, stunned. The roaring continued, morphing into something familiar. Barking. Her head spun. Was she imagining it?

Then the *clang clang clang* of someone running up the stairs jerked her out of her stupor. A moment later, a man appeared at the opening in the floor.

Hardly able to speak, she stammered out, "D-Derek...!"

He took the rest of the steps and bounded toward her, then enfolded her in his arms. "You're okay." Gripping her shoulders, he pulled away from the hug and studied her. "Are you okay?"

Shaking all over and blinking against a torrent of tears, she nodded.

He pulled her into his arms again. "Thank God."

"You found me." Her voice sounded weak and she leaned in to him, barely able to support her own weight.

"I had to. You needed me." He shifted to speak into her ear. "There's something else. I remembered I need God. I don't know how I could've forgotten."

Valerie swallowed a sob. In spite of

everything she'd been telling herself for the past few weeks, she couldn't deny it anymore. She loved this man. He was the one for her.

"Hey...you stay away from me!" The muffled shout from the ground below was followed by a guttural growl that would be terrifying if she didn't recognize the source.

She pulled back from Derek, who, judging from the urgent look in his eye, shared her thought. He grabbed her by the hand, and together they rushed down the stairs. They hurried around the side of the tower, to where Rex stood, his back arched and his tail down. He growled at Zak, who lay on his back across a section of cornstalks, waving an arm at Rex.

Valerie whistled. Rex snapped his head in her direction and bolted for her, nearly knocking her over.

"Whoa, baby." Valerie laughed, throwing her arms around her good boy, who licked her face with abandon.

As soon as Rex would let her, she moved to where Derek now bent over Zak, who had a dark splotch on the shoulder of his jacket. He looked up at Derek and shook his fist. “You shot me in the shoulder, man!”

“That’s what I meant to do.” Derek’s voice sounded remarkably controlled. “You’re lucky I’m a good aim.”

As Valerie looked down at Zak, she detected the distant wail of a siren. She gripped Derek’s arm. “Are they going for Maggie? Derek, Maggie’s at the cabin. She—”

“I know.” He straightened, grabbing her arms. “I was there.”

“You were? H-how—?”

“I’ll tell you later. Bobby and Kyle called in about Maggie, and they got Hannah.” He reached into his pocket and produced a small gun.

She squinted at it. Was it...*fuchsia*

pink? "You...you *were* at the cabin."

"Yeah." He handed it to her. "Keep that on him while I see if I can get a cell connection."

Zak moaned.

"Help's coming, Zak." Derek took his phone from his pocket and started tapping at it. "Try not to move."

As Derek stepped away, Zak settled his head back, probably resigned to his fate.

Valerie trained the very-real-feeling gun on him. "Hey, one more question. Why'd you poison my dog?"

"Pretty obvious." He aimed a look at Rex. "He wasn't gonna let me get near you."

She looked down at Rex, who leaned against her leg. *So true.*

"Hey." Zak's voice was weakening. "I got one more question too."

Keeping the gun pointed at him, she raised an eyebrow. "What is it?"

"You mean what you said about

forgiving?"

She nodded. "Of course."

Zak looked up at the sky as the sound of sirens grew louder. "Then I hope you'll forgive me."

Her breath hitched. "You're going to be okay, Zak." She hoped that was true. "Just hold on."

Epilogue

Eighteen Months Later

From the driver's seat of her snazzy new-to-her Ford Ranger, Valerie glanced over at Derek. He seemed lost in thought as he watched the familiar scenery pass by on their way home from doing their morning deliveries.

Keeping one hand on the wheel, she reached the other one over to take his. "What are you thinking about?"

"Just how beautiful Montana is in the springtime." Squeezing her hand, he smiled.

She had to agree. "It's my favorite time of year."

Ever since Derek had traded his Washington, DC, assignments for a freelance travel photo website, her life had been busier than ever. They split their time between working the farm and traveling to fun and picturesque locations. Now that they were no longer paying a quarter of their profit to Maggie, they could afford to employ their farm workers year round, and hire extra hands during the harvest season. It helped that the tree farm had been profitable in its first year, thanks to Jordan and Moe's management and planning.

"By the way," she said. "Thanks for helping me get my work done this morning."

"My pleasure." He brushed his thumb

across the back of her hand. "You know the best part about doing deliveries together?"

"You mean—" She sent a flirtatious glance his way. "—besides getting to spend time with my handsome husband?"

"Yeah, besides that." His playful tone turned serious. "You don't have to be out on the road by yourself."

"Mmm." She wasn't about to argue. While she felt capable of caring for herself, it was good to also feel protected. "But I do meet the most interesting people that way."

"I hope you're talking about *me*." He lifted her hand and brushed a light kiss across it. "I think about that every time we pass the spot where we first met."

"You do?" Sentimentality sent a rush of warmth through her chest. "You are such a romantic."

Their relationship might have gotten off to a rough start, but ironically, the actions of a few bad people had changed her life for the better. If it hadn't been for Zak and Hannah plotting against her family, Derek would have driven right on by. Now, while *they* sat in prison, *she* was living her dream-come-true.

She didn't even have to worry that Vincent Greco might make a return appearance after doing the meager year he'd been sentenced to. In a failed attempt to break out of jail, the dummy had nearly killed a deputy. For that, he had been charged with first-degree attempted murder and had received a life sentence. Bad news for ol' Vincent, but good news for the community.

As she took the turn off the main road, she blew a kiss to her old truck, which had become her tradition ever since retiring it. Now, it was the centerpiece of the display at the driveway entrance to the Hayes Country Store and Christmas Tree Farm.

A minute later, as they approached the

original farmhouse—*their* house now—her spirits lifted at the sight of some cars in the parking area next to the barn.

"We have customers." Still a thrill, even though their store had been open for business for a couple of months now.

She pulled her truck next to the garage and shut off the engine. Before moving the sun visor up, she smiled at the picture that Derek had clipped there. It was the two of them, grinning like a couple of lovesick teenagers, with the ruins of Machu Picchu in the background. A sigh slipped from her lips. It had been the honeymoon of her dreams.

"You know..." Derek undid his seatbelt. "I think we should include Greece in our trip this summer. Those photos should sell like tiganites."

"Tiganites?"

"You know...Greek hotcakes."

She sputtered out a laugh. "Your humor's getting a little syrupy." She gave him a wink. "You can do butter."

"Ha ha."

"But...Greece, huh?" Resting her elbow on the console, she batted her eyes. "That *is* on my list."

"Name me a place that *isn't.*" He ran his hand through her hair and moved closer.

Closing her eyes, she leaned in. But her eyes popped open as she felt Rex insinuate himself between them from the backseat.

Derek laughed. "Buddy." He ruffled Rex's neck. "You don't have to take your job so seriously."

As Rex backed off in anxious anticipation of his door opening, Derek leaned over and gave Valerie a lingering kiss that took her breath away.

Returning to reality, they got out of the truck. Valerie tipped her head back, enjoying the feel of the sun on her face. The sound of crunching gravel drew her attention to her dad's truck coming up the road. She met Derek and Rex at the back of her truck as Dad pulled in next to them.

Valerie leaned against Derek and scratched Rex's head as they waited for him to emerge. "Hey, Dad. What're you doing on this side of the farm?"

Dad removed a cooler from his passenger seat. "Can't a man bring lunch to his wife?"

Valerie chortled. "Only if you brought enough for us too."

"Yeah." Derek raised his eyebrows and reached for the cooler lid. "What've you got in there?"

"Sandwiches. My signature egg salad. And I did bring enough for you"—he playfully flicked Derek's hand away—"but you'll have to wait, son."

Derek reached for Valerie's hand, and while Rex ran off to have a field frolic, they followed Dad into the store.

From behind the front counter, where she was ringing up a purchase for a customer, Maggie looked up and gave them a warm smile.

Dad blew her a kiss, and pointed to the cooler, then to the door to the employee break room. Maggie responded with a thumbs-up.

At the display of Derek's photography book, Valerie straightened the copy that sat on a stand for customers to page through. When a young couple turned their attention to the display, Derek greeted them and struck up a conversation.

Valerie looked on with pride as he answered their questions about the book. What he had originally envisioned as a book of nature and wildlife shots had wound up as a tribute to life in a small Montana town. As he'd worked on it, he'd realized that his focus had shifted. It had been shaping up to be less about the beauty of the landscape, and more about the beauty of the people.

Seeing that Maggie's customer had collected her bags and was on her way out of the store, Valerie went over to check in with Maggie.

"How's the day going so far?"

"Business has been steady all morning." Maggie tidied a rack of homemade lollipops, which sat next to the register. "I sold two of Derek's books. I'll be needing more signed copies soon."

Ever since Dad had married Maggie last summer, she had been handling the finances for the farm. Valerie had quickly realized there was no better choice to manage the store than her new stepmom. As it turned out, she had a real head for business.

Just as the couple Derek had been talking to brought their purchases to the counter, the bell over the door jangled. Valerie turned to see Annica hip-bumping the door open so she could enter without the use of her arms, which were full of boxes.

Ever the gentleman, Derek hurried over and took the boxes from her.

"Thanks, Derek." She dipped her head toward the door. "I've got a load in the car. I'll be right—"

"I got it." Derek set the boxes on the end of the counter, then headed back out the door.

Looking impressed, Annica joined Valerie. "Hey, Val. I hope you can use some more stuff."

"Your *stuff* has been really popular so far." Valerie had been impressed by Annica's productivity with her vintage apron and pillow creations, which had added color and variety to the store's inventory. "I'm sure we can sell whatever you bring us."

A few moments later, the bell jingled again, signaling both Derek's return, and the departure of the young couple.

"Where do you want these, Maggie?"

Derek's arms were full of even more boxes than Annica had already brought in.

"Better leave them on the counter." Maggie pointed a fuchsia-tipped nail. "I need to restock the shelves after lunch."

"I can do it, Maggie," Annica offered. "I'll even watch the store while you take a break."

"You don't mind?"

"I'm secretly in training for you to hire me part-time this summer. I need something to do when Chad takes over managing our snack stand."

"That, my dear, is an offer I cannot refuse." Maggie beamed.

"I'll tell Mr. Hayes you're on your way back." Derek pointed his thumb toward the break room, then addressed Valerie. "I'll go grab our lunch."

As Derek retreated to the back room, Maggie reached under the end of the counter that they had built low to make it easier for her to work. She produced her beige car coat—on a hanger and covered in plastic from the dry cleaner—and set it on the counter. "I hope this works out well for you."

As Annica reached for the coat, Valerie slammed her hands down on it. "You're not giving away that coat! It saved our lives."

Annica smiled. "I love that part of the story. You're a superhero, Maggie."

Maggie waved off the compliment. "More like a survivor. And you don't have to worry, Valerie, dear. Annica is just borrowing it."

"Good." Valerie released her hold on the coat, allowing Annica to take it. "Because if I ever get kidnapped again, I'm wearing this coat."

It really was the best part of their story. When Zak had tied Maggie's hands the second time, she had thought fast by taking advantage of her wide bell sleeves. Her foolhardy nephew had been so busy arguing with Hannah, he hadn't noticed that Maggie had put her fists together but spread her wrists so she'd be able to slip her hands free.

"Thanks, Maggie." Annica draped the coat over her arm. "I should have a prototype done next week."

Shifting her attention to a row of hand-drawn gift cards that needed tidying, Valerie said, "You're expanding your collection?"

"I figured I might as well." Annica shrugged. "It gives me a nice break from thinking about rototilling and side-dressing."

Maggie chuckled. "You farmers do speak your own language. I've missed it."

"You're one of us now." Valerie reached across the counter and squeezed Maggie's shoulder.

They shared a loving look as Maggie patted Valerie's hand, and the door to the back room opened.

Derek emerged, carrying a couple of sandwiches wrapped in parchment and two bottles of lemonade. He handed one of the bottles to Valerie. “It’s a beautiful spring day. I was thinking we could give the lovebirds their privacy”—he winked at Maggie—“and take our lunch to the front porch.”

“Sounds perfect.”

A few minutes later, Valerie and Derek relaxed in the porch swing with Rex settling contentedly at their feet, and unwrapped their egg salad sandwiches. As Valerie gazed out at the field and the mountains beyond, a question stirred.

She turned to Derek. “You ever miss city life?”

He chuckled. “I’d be lying if I said I don’t occasionally miss the amenities.”

“Lime bikes and Ubers?”

“I was thinking of restaurants and museums, but yeah those too sometimes. *But...*” He draped an arm around her shoulders. “I get my fill of that when we travel. I’m happy to call the Hayes Family Farm home.”

Nodding, she took a bite of her sandwich, and pushed her foot against the porch, sending the swing into a gentle motion. “I’m glad we can travel. But I wouldn’t trade this farm for any place on earth.”

Millie had been right. Rockford was a small town, but the world was a big place, and Valerie’s life had expanded just enough.

She rested her head on Derek’s shoulder, grateful that they had both found their way home.

The End

Lesley Ann McDaniel

I hope you enjoyed *Deadly Focus*, book 3 in the MONTANA PERIL series.

Please consider posting a review on Amazon or Goodreads. Honest reviews are an encouragement to authors, and help other readers find books to enjoy.

I love hearing from readers! You can find links to my books and contact information at my website:

lesleyannmcdaniel.com

Newsletter Invitation

My Thank You Gift to You . . .

High and Dry

CRESCENT COVE series Prequel

Available only to my newsletter subscribers. Get your copy for FREE!

Do you love Inspirational Fiction? Join my newsletter family and receive all the latest news about my books, plus contests, giveaways, and insider info.

www.lesleyannmcdaniel.com

ABOUT THE AUTHOR

Between working as a home-schooling mom and a professional theatre costumer, Lesley has completed several novels and screenplays. She would have done more by now if she didn't occasionally stop to clean the house. Fortunately, she loves to cook, so no one in her family has starved yet.

Lesley now resides in the Seattle area with her family, including three cats and a big loud dog. She is a member of the Northwest Christian Writers Association.

Her first movie, *Home Sweet Home*, was released in 2020.

In her spare time (ha!), she chips away at her goal of reading every book ever written.

Please visit her website at:
lesleyannmcdaniel.com

ABOUT THE AUTHOR

Between working as a home-schooling mom and a professional theatre costumer, Lesley has completed several novels and screenplays. She would have done more by now if she didn't occasionally stop to clean the house. Fortunately, she loves to cook, so no one in her family has starved yet.

Lesley now resides in the Seattle area with her family, including three cats and a big loud dog. She is a member of the Northwest Christian Writers Association.

Her first movie, *Home Sweet Home*, was released in 2020.

In her spare time (ha!), she chips away at her goal of reading every book ever written.

Please visit her website at:
lesleyannmcdaniel.com